DEATH
in
Heels

DEATH
in
Heels

KITTY MURPHY

THOMAS & MERCER

Text copyright © 2023 by Kitty Murphy
All rights reserved.

Published by Thomas & Mercer, Seattle

www.apub.com

Amazon, the Amazon logo, and Thomas & Mercer are trademarks of Amazon.com, Inc., or its affiliates.

ISBN-13: 9781542037235
ISBN-10: 1542037239

Cover design by Andrew Davis

Printed in the United States of America

DEATH
in
Heels

Prologue

Backstage, the mirrors were cracked and chipped, the lighting cruel. Bags littered the table and coats lay over the chairs, and on the other side of the long room, rail upon rail of dresses and costumes hung in a wild mix: lime green with orange, silver with black, candy-pink stripes with gold leopard print – every hanger a splendid migraine of fabric. All manner of feathers clung to necklines and hemlines, with rhinestones and glitter and sequins – fairy dust for the gods, tassels fighting over straps, and hooped skirts pegged with plastic flowers. Make-up covered every spare surface: blocks and shades, brushes and sponges, coconut oil, vodka and an overspilling tub of body glitter. On one peg, skinny jeans and a fitted shirt; over another, sweat pants, thick socks and an old grey hoodie. Under the table, a size-twelve stiletto shoe lay unmatched, forgotten.

The music blared and rumbled. Group numbers were the audience favourites, all four queens onstage at once. The song wasn't new, but it wasn't that kind of a club, and no one was looking for faults. The regulars smiled with the sweet comfort of routine, the newcomers found a fresh wonder in the night's end, and on the stage, the four queens sparkled in the lights. They moved perfectly in sync, every word in place, the choreography spotless. At the last chorus they laughed as a pyrotechnic blast went off too soon with a bang and a hiss, and golden lights misted over the curtain behind them.

They would be back in the dressing room any minute, their heels scuffing the dusty floor as they reached for the wipes, for the vodka. They'd work quickly and gather possessions from across the room and then they'd carefully hang up the dresses and take off their necklaces. Within such a short time, they'd be no one.

The wigs stood in a line, nine perfectly coiffed heads on sticks. Four more stands waited, empty. Behind them were extra wigs, old wigs, cast away from the others and kept as spares, as pieces – black, white, grey, pink – cheap nylon hair no one wanted, bought for one number and replaced for the next.

The music finished and the applause rang through the club.

It was almost too easy.

The roads were sodden, rain pooling in the gutters, the night heavy. The door opened.

She staggered, bright red heels picking up the shine from the single streetlight, red dress clinging to luscious curves.

She was beautiful. She was alone.

Then she was dead.

Chapter One

I leaned back, resting my head against the bench.

St Stephen's Green was busy, but Dublin was always busy. The gentle May sun was a sweet relief from the endless grey skies of the Irish winter. On the ground, and high above us, gulls called out their gossip, screeching the midday news, and the light breeze rustled in the trees, tempering the sounds of the passers-by.

Somewhere, a church clock rang the hour.

'I should go.' I stretched out my arm until my shoulder clicked.

Robyn groaned. 'Ten more minutes?' he said.

I brushed my hair from my eyes. The sun had warmed my skin. By the end of the day my freckles would appear loud and proud, splattered over my nose, awake from their pale winter hibernation.

All around us, people echoed the birds, children weaving and darting like tiny sparrows, men striding forward with their chests puffed out and their legs straight, their eyes intent on a single line through the crowd. At the bridge, two women stood hand in hand, watching the water below. By their feet, pigeons pecked and huddled and cooed, while ducks drew long ripples in the lake before disappearing under the delicate willow strands on the other side, in hope of food and of sanctity from the thuggish gulls that peppered the grass.

I breathed out a long, contented sigh.

'I wish we could stay here all afternoon,' said Robyn, echoing my thoughts.

I pushed up from the bench. That was the problem with lunch hours: they never quite lasted long enough. I gathered our things, peeling off his sweater, taking back my sunglasses. Robyn broke up the last sandwich and threw a chunk of bread toward a crumpled-looking crow by the path. The bird stabbed at the bread, edging closer.

By the look of the sky we'd had the best of the day. I was just turning when the birds shot up from the grass with a ruffle of wings, the ducks yelling their anger, as a small wet dog shot through the crowd. His mouth was open and tongue hanging out in delight as he ran past the people, his lead trailing behind in a wet streak. Somewhere in the distance a man called out, but the dog was having too much fun. He bounced as he chased another gull.

'Hey, pup?' I called. 'Come here!'

I opened my arms and the little dog ran up the bank and sprang on to the bench, jumping to lick my face, his stumpy tail wagging back and forth in delight as he set his two front paws on my chest to sniff my hair. 'Oh, you're just gorgeous,' I said. 'Soaking wet, but—'

Catching his lead, I gently eased him from standing on me and set him back down. I smoothed the top of his damp head as his owner came up, panting hard, and I handed over the lead.

'Sorry, miss,' said the man.

'He's lovely,' I said, truthfully.

The man led away the soggy troublemaker and the air settled around us, the birds returning to their lunch. It would have been great to run through the pond like that – to bark without a care in the world and then to laugh at the birds as they flew away – but dogs could get away with that stuff. Tired shop workers less so. I picked up my bag and brushed the dog hair from my jeans.

Robyn hadn't moved.

'You ok, hon?' I said.

He broke the crust of the end of his sandwich and shrugged.

'It's just work,' I said. 'You sell phones – you bring joy to the phoneless. There will be someone out there needing a phone and you're the guy to . . .'

But even as I nudged him, Robyn didn't smile.

Catching his hand, I pulled my friend up from the bench. The breeze cut through the willows. Robyn shivered. His long face and wide eyes were set in worry, the warmth of the day already gone, and there were shadows in his gaze as grey and parched as the Georgian square that framed the park. We started to walk back along the path, picking and choosing our way through the crowds. I knew what was bothering him – what had been bothering him every day that week.

We filed through the thin gate. 'You're ready,' I said gently. 'Your look is stunning. You know the words. You'll be amazing,' I told him. 'Everyone says it, even Del.'

Robyn smiled, but as he pulled on his sweater the smile slipped down his face like cheap mascara.

We stood back, waiting for the Luas to pass.

I kissed his cheek and skipped over the tramlines.

'Hey, Fi?' he called.

'Yeah?'

'Let's go out tonight.'

'That sounds good. There's a new photography exhibition on th—' I stopped. 'You meant go out-out?'

'Just out,' he said. 'Get a drink, watch cute guys flirting with the other cute guys – if you, you know, don't mind.' He bit down on his lower lip.

'Sure, OK,' I said. 'Where do you want to go?'

5

Like any decent drag club, TRASH was heard well before it was seen. We dipped down a side road and cut around the back of the main street, Robyn's pace already keeping the beat. Well away from the wide glamour of Grafton Street, the tall grey lanes huddled close together. The building itself was nothing special, another forgotten bordello of the gay-gone age. There were rumours that back in the golden-olden days it had housed a brothel but there were rumours of that nature about many of the establishments in the area, plenty created to add a little blush to the history of a business.

We stepped up to the door and in through the plain wooden arch. With shrieks and cries of 'Hey, honey' and 'Hi, baby', they surrounded Robyn, and he hung back on the stairs, greeting and meeting his friends. Smiling, I handed over my entry fee. On the wall was a framed poster: a drag queen, sparkling with unarguable majesty, with a huge wig and glittering earrings, and a silver wrap dress that wound tightly around her curves and her waist.

I was trying to remember who was onstage on Tuesdays when a cloud of tulle and sequins scurried down the stairs, and Del burst into the foyer.

'Fi!' He threw up his arms in delight, knocking back one of the young men on the stairs.

'Del . . . you look amazing!' I said.

'I *am* amazing,' he told me with a wink.

Del's hair was even bigger than usual, a giant green and orange swirl of twists and sparkles, each coil a shining example of the powers of backcombing and hairspray. Fake diamonds dripped from his ears and dotted his thick eyelashes; his brows shimmered with a sunrise of earthy golds and greens. His shoulders were bare, green satin gloves pulled up over his elbows. His skirt was a puffball of sparkling green tulle and his new green-and-gold satin corset pulled in his waist so far I found myself staring at the enormous boobs sticking out from the top.

Del caught my fingers, spun me to him and kissed the space two inches from my cheek, touching his finger to my chin, just for a second. He pulled open the interior door in a shimmer of glitter and hurried into the main body of the club, kicking his gold high heels as he went.

I grinned after him, the lights still twinkling in my vision.

'Del Peen's arms are too manly for that corset,' said a voice behind me. 'Someone should tell her.'

'His tits look fab,' retorted Robyn.

I shot him a look.

'What? He uses the male pronoun,' said Robyn. 'And anyway, they do look fab.'

The club was full, the bar thick, the lights flickering over the stage. Most of the regulars were men. Some women, like me, were out with their friends, some with one another. We headed for a gap in the crowd. At the back, in a bundle of synthetic shine, Del was talking to another queen. I felt Robyn lean forward and I gestured toward them, but he shook his head. He bumped me with his elbow and we tucked in, finding a spot with our backs to one of the columns where we could both see the stage.

The heat of the audience buzzed around me, anticipation bright even for a weekday. I scanned the crowd. There were plenty of tourists dotted among us; the shrewd eyes of the locals marked the good-looking ones, the edging of the wolves moving closer. I nudged Robyn to point out a handsome man near him with dark eyes and thick black hair and a clear Italian accent but as the house lights dulled, Robyn's gaze was entirely focussed on the spot between the curtains, his pupils already reflecting the stage lights.

The queens' intro music started, a burst of classics mashed together, fanfares and trumpets, the big boom of the drums. As one, the crowd woke, faces alight, bright with the promise of what was to come. The spotlights spun and flared, dancing from every surface, teasing us – the spiral staircase, then the steps, then the gap at the side of the stage. The curtains twitched, their uneven pleats bulged, then the music changed and the first low beats of Tina Turner's song, 'Proud Mary', boomed from the huge black speakers. I grinned – I couldn't help it. My shoulders started to move with the beat.

As the curtains finally parted, an older queen came running on to the stage, her stance perfect Tina, her cheap wig made classic by her faultless make-up and deep-red lipstick, her skin-tight rubber dress and high, high, high heels as exact as anyone could ask, from the thigh splits to her pronounced fake nipples to the way her skirt clung over her well-padded behind.

As the song rolled from the intro into the main beat, no one cared if there were no backup dancers behind her and no one cared if the lights were a simple cheesy set up or if the speakers buzzed. The crowd roared and cheered and lifted their arms in time, singing along. The queen's confidence and raw, untempered performance took control of the room and set us apart from the rain outside. The dull May weekday night was forgotten, and, for that moment at least, the only thing that mattered was the show.

The final chord rang through the club and the queen threw up her hands, dropping back her head, her lips stretched wide over mismatched teeth.

'All my trash and all my treasures,' said Del's voice over the speakers. 'Please put your hands together for our Miss Merkin!'

Merkin strutted back through the curtains. Robyn stared at the stage, his eyes filled with wonder.

Another song started, a Beyoncé special. Behind us, a woman shrieked, recognising it, and three other women screamed with her. The queen stepping through the curtains was one I'd met before, a bitchy young thing called Eve who was more interested in finding the spotlight than in entertaining the audience. I edged back to the bar.

I held up my fingers in a V to the bar manager, who nodded and tipped ice into a glass.

From the stage, Eve yelled back at a heckler.

I handed over my money. As the music dulled, the manager muttered, 'Oh, to be a woman in a man's world.'

I chuckled, and stopped for a minute to watch the end of Eve's set. Robyn was talking to one of his friends but his eyes kept flickering to the stage. He'd be amazing, up there, I thought. He was born for it. Robyn had a way about him; a natural sass and a wiggle in his hips, a turn of his head.

As Eve's number finished I clapped with the others, but then cheered loudly as Del came bursting on to the stage in a cloud of sparkle, throwing his arms up into the air, sending more glitter into the lights.

'Darlings, darlings.' He licked his full lips as he held the mic. 'Oh, what fun! And so many of you – just like I said last night when I popped over to Merkin's after hours. So much trash and so much treasure, who'd have thought such a crowd would be with us on a paltry Tuesday? Hey, chick!' He blew a kiss to Robyn. 'Well, my lovelies, you'll be delighted to know that Thora is finally on her way. I opened her coffin myself and with any luck they will have her reanimated fully by the time I'm done here and—'

Behind the curtain, someone shouted.

'Oh, come on,' said Del. He turned back to the crowd. 'You should see her before she's ironed out her face . . .'

Robyn tugged my arm. 'Hey,' he said.

'Del looks incredible,' I whispered.

'Ben said Thora has just thrown a hissy fit backstage. There's a right scene going on.'

All around us, the audience roared with laughter at something Del said. I looked up. Robyn took my drink, sipped and winced.

I nodded to the bar. 'Can I get y—?'

He shook his head. 'I'll go in a minute,' he said. More laughter rumbled through the crowd. 'Ben said they're doing . . . Oh, look—'

The stage curtain was pulled back with a hard jerk, rattling the rail. The spotlight split and we cheered and clapped with the others as the ruling queen of the club, Thora Point, stepped on to the stage. She wore a tight orange tube of a dress – tighter about her middle than it might have been when it was made – with a band of shining plastic flowers that ran around her neck like a slipped ruff, a noose of hideous tackiness only shown up by her yellow high-heeled shoes. On her head perched a fully puffed-out wig – a bouffant of silvery white magic, wider even than her shoulders.

Thora's eyes settled on the crowd. Still grinning, I shivered.

She lowered her heavy lashes. 'Such shade, Del, such shade. And no respect for your elders!'

'I never said you were old, darling,' said Del. 'But now you're here, do tell the class, what it was like when the Vikings ruled Dublin?'

'Hairy,' said Thora. She gave a long smile and put her fingers to her teeth, picking out an invisible hair, considering it.

The music started, old style, something I vaguely recognised but couldn't place.

'Nice,' said Del. 'But you know, Thora, I've come to think of you not so much as a friend but a sister . . .'

Moving smoothly, Thora took both mics. She handed them back into the space behind the curtains and brought out two enormous fans, each a giant semi-circle of cerulean feathers. Del took his and Thora held hers. Robyn nudged me, excitement buzzing through him.

'Please,' Merkin's voice roared out of the speakers, 'feast your eyes on the Shady Sisters!'

As Irving Berlin's 'Sisters' started to play, a knowing chuckle ran through the older members of the club. The queens stood together, the fans in their right hands, their heads set to the same angle. With a dip and a twist, they launched into the number, sweeping their fans in time to the words, gesturing and grinning and overacting every line. Del lip-synched perfectly to Rosemary Clooney's words but beside her, Thora was having too much fun with her fan, and by the end of the first bit she'd bashed at least two members of the audience on the head with the blue feathers.

'Class,' said Robyn, laughing.

Del and Thora stepped in time to the old song and when the instrumental swelled they both came forward in perfect, ridiculous harmony, rocking the fans over one another in wheels of glitter, twisting around, laughing and jibing and gesturing and dancing, and moving through each well-choreographed sweep until the curtains jolted and they both twirled away through the gap and into the darkness behind, the crowd roaring their love for the two drag queens.

'Ah, it's an old one,' said Merkin as she climbed back up, a mic in her hand. 'I won't say it's a good one because we've all just seen it . . .'

Another of Robyn's friends came over to talk to him. On the stage, Merkin was herding the audience into a song, threatening to come down to us and pluck someone to join her. Nervous tickles of laughter ran through the club as people backed away from her grip. Rihanna's track, 'Skin', cut the vintage feels of the previous number, pulling everyone back into real time.

A flash of green distracted me. Seeing Del slip around to the spiral staircase, I left the column and darted across the room.

Waving, Del led me into the hall.

'You look stunning,' I said.

'This corset is killing me.' He tugged it from his skin. Sweat glistened over his make-up and long red rub lines marked where the top had cut into his chest. 'Did you like the fans?' he said.

'I loved them!'

'An old classic for the children. Merkin found them in some shifty warehouse. I swear mine still smelled of c—'

A tall man looked down from the coatroom. 'Del? You're up next.'

'It's Eve on next,' said Del. 'I need a drink.'

'Eve's not here,' said the tall man.

'Well, where is she?'

'How the hell should I know?'

'Great.' Del started up the stairs, already pulling off his gloves. 'Bloody great. I'll do Britney,' he said. 'Tell Merkin to stall. Give me two minutes.'

'Are you Fi?' said the man, leaning around Del. 'Robyn's mate?'

I nodded.

'Tell him, would you, I have a free spot on Saturday.'

'Saturday?'

The man looked down at me. Built like an army boy, he wore a tight black t-shirt and black combat pants. His hair was cut short, a long scar on his neck unhidden.

'Saturday,' he said again. 'Tell him Mark said Saturday.'

'Right.' I nodded. 'Thanks. Saturday,' I repeated. 'Sa—'

Mark had gone.

I stood in the foyer, my unfinished word hanging in the air. Saturday.

Chapter Two

Saturday came whether we were ready or not. I left work ten minutes early. Dublin's streets were messy with tourists, a fresh batch at every turn, their chatter a constant hum behind the traffic. I pulled my coat closer around my neck. The first spots of rain had started to clear the evening dust, fat drops that would soon be falling thick and wet, soaking everything in sight. Skipping over the cobbles I hurried through Temple Bar and up a thin, paved alley to the last building, the door at the end of the row. I slid my key into the lock, pushed open the door and started on the stairs. I could already hear the music.

On the second floor, Mrs Harper's door was cracked, ready.

'Is that you, Fi?'

'It's me.'

The door opened and our landlady peered into the stairwell. Small and frail, wrapped in layers of grey flannel, Mrs Harper met me with a steely glare.

'He's doing it again, dear,' she said.

The melody rang through the floor. She was right.

'I'm really sorry, Mrs Harper.' I cringed as the beat doubled. 'I'm sure he doesn't realise.'

'You have to say something to him, Fi. I don't want to keep on about the noise, but . . .'

'I'll have a word,' I promised. 'I'm sure he's sorry too, and I'm sorry, and—'

'I know you are, dear.' Mrs Harper nodded. She looked up to our landing. 'Is he nervous?' she whispered.

'A bit,' I said.

'You tell him I said good things, yes? Break a leg!'

At our landing, I plucked a bright pink feather from the carpet. I unlocked the apartment door and dipped my head as I climbed into the little attic flat. Every light was on. Pink feathers floated in the air. Clothes covered all the surfaces, lost sequins dotting the sofa, the chairs, the pale carpet. There, in the middle of the fabric, Robyn turned, mid-pirouette, his arms wide, a bright pink feather boa stretched over his shoulders.

'Fi!' he yelled.

'Can you turn it down?' I said.

'What?'

I reached to the stereo. The music died.

'You're going to get us evicted,' I told him.

Tossing the boa over his shoulder, Robyn fell back into the arms of the dress-covered chair.

'Half of these are mine.' I pushed a long robe from the sofa. I rubbed my hand over my eyes as I walked, soothing the ache from the day.

'Not so. Your clothes are all . . . dull.'

'I like dull.' I picked up one of the bags, gently nudging aside a small pile of bras, wondering if the red one was his or mine. In the kitchen, I opened a cheap Merlot. Robyn looked in, and I handed him a glass.

'It's heaven sent,' he said, lifting it to his mouth.

'It was reduced,' I told him. 'Consider that a warning.'

I tipped a packet of also-reduced vegetables into the wok and took a sip of my drink. We grimaced in duet as the wine coated the inside of our mouths with a dull metallic twang.

'Reduced,' I said again.

'Well.' Robyn sat up on the table. 'Don't make anything for me, I can't eat,' he said. 'I'm too nervous.'

'You'll be fine,' I told him.

'But what if I'm awful?'

'You won't be.' I stopped, took his hand in mine. 'Really,' I said. 'You've got this.'

'I have nothing to wear for the group number.'

I stirred in the spice packet and then the noodles, and finally took off my coat as the veg popped and hissed in the wok.

'Wear the silver,' I said.

'Eve told me I'd look like a fork in the cutlery drawer.'

'She's just jealous,' I said. 'Don't let Eve get to you, you know what she's like. You've done your face every night this week and you've got the choreography.'

I kept my voice strong but nerves rippled through my belly for him. I set two bowls on the counter. Feed him, his mother had texted me. Make sure he eats early or he'll be even more jittery.

I sat at the table and plucked chopsticks from the pot. Robyn couldn't stay still. He stalked out to the mess of clothes in the other room, then back in. He moved a hairpiece, picked up a lipstick, and with every jerking movement I found my own nerves spinning and twisting my gut on his behalf. He'd be great – he'd be so great, I knew it, but I also knew how much it meant to him.

'Try some noodles?' I suggested.

'The Julie London number,' he said. 'Is it too predictable, though? The slit is so far up my thigh it catches on my tights . . .'

'You have great legs,' I told him.

'Maybe I should have gone more modern – I mean, who even gets these references – and what do you think of—'

I stuffed in a mouthful of noodles. As Robyn rounded the doorway I shrugged an apology and gestured, again, to his dinner.

He waited.

'You like noodles,' I said firmly. 'Noodles make you happy.'

'They used to.'

Robyn picked up a piece of courgette. He looked at me across the table and sighed, then drew chopsticks from the pot. Up on the wall, the clock ticked away the minutes. The kitchen was warm. I leaned to open the window, to listen to the sounds of the rain. Down in the street someone called for a friend and their voices lifted happily against the downpour.

Robyn muttered on and on about the songs.

'I'll wear the red for the first, and then silver for the group number,' he said. 'Fork Eve.'

'Absolutely,' I agreed. 'Fork her.'

Robyn darted back out and then reappeared at the doorway holding a long, skinny red dress to his body. Even in our damp little kitchen, the fabric shimmered.

'Wear the red,' I said.

'I'll wear the red, so.'

He soothed the dress over his body.

'You'll be great,' I told him, as I gathered my empty plate. I picked up my wine and stood, moving to kiss his cheek. 'You can do this, yeah?' I said. I looked into his eyes. 'It's going to be amazing.'

Robyn nodded, nerves bright.

'And anyway,' I said, 'what's the worst that can happen?'

I closed my bedroom door behind me, sealing myself in the calm of my uncluttered shelves, my silver rug, the cream bedspread and

16

the single armchair by the window, the view looking down at the wet, cobbled street – and there, just beyond the corner, the Liffey.

My Liffey.

I leaned against the window frame, watching the water. In the rain, the evening light picked up the river's shine. A woman walked toward the bridge. Her grey hair shone like strands of plastic, mirroring the light on the water. I picked up my camera and took a photo. I took ten, maybe twelve, making sure her face was turned away each time, focussing on her hair and the contrast between her leather boots and the rain-soaked pavement, picking up the detail from the lantern-style lights. Sitting back, I checked the shots. The last one was good. I uploaded the image to my blog and wrote a few lines. I figured I'd take some more pictures later on if I wasn't too tired. If Robyn was still on good form when we got back from the club, maybe I'd finally persuade him to pose on the bridge for me in full, beautiful, wigged-up, sparkling drag for my blog. I hugged my camera. I'd been longing to ask, to see him right at the top of the bridge, his succulent foam curves and giant wig giving life to the cast iron curls and swirls.

I picked up my wineglass and gently swilled the bitter red against the sides while I looked over the preview. I liked writing my blog. I posted pictures of bridges – Dublin bridges mostly – and strangers crossing from one side of the river to the other. Not exactly photographic greatness, and blogging was so old-fashioned it was almost vintage, but I liked how it connected me with the world, and with my own quiet little corner of Dublin.

It wasn't even that varied: hurried moments, romantic moments, lonely moments. Each picture I put up was a stolen snippet from a stranger's day as they crossed the little bridge there. All kinds of people but never their faces, that was my blog rule. Not just humans, either – birds, dogs, once even a fox in the early hours of a spring morning, carrying its heavy, red tail low to the ground.

I hoped Robyn would wear the red dress. It was so perfect. The silver one was OK for the group number – we'd found it in the second-hand shop in Lower Camden Street – but the red was made to fit his body like a glove. Not many had a waist as small as his and his new padding was wild – hips to die for, carved from the seat of an old sofa his mum was sending to the tip.

I chuckled, remembering his sister Karen's face as we'd sat at the family kitchen table, Robyn in his tight Lycra shorts, their mother, Edna, cutting and shaping the big foam panels with the electric carving knife.

I had no idea, before living with Robyn, how easy it was to become a different person – at least on the outside.

The stereo came on, the music set low. Sonique made way for Kylie. In the other room, Robyn sang as he got ready and worked through his routine. By now – by Kylie – I figured he'd have had a shower and shaved his face and chest, have on his grey jogging bottoms and the wide sweatband that held back his hair. By the third or fourth song in the album he'd be sitting crossed-legged on the floor in front of the big mirror by the main light, with each of his highlighters and his base sticks laid out in order on a towel, and his big palette of eye colours right in the middle of his lap: the silvers on the left, the reds and pinks in the middle, and the blues and yellows and greens on the right.

His voice lifted. The base would be done. After a while, Kylie was cut short and replaced by a dance mix I didn't know. I watched the other people on the bridge, the steady line drifting across the river, merging, twisting, some hurrying up to the Luas at Jervis, some pacing their daily grind from work to home, some on holiday, some already heading out for the night into Temple Bar, some just passing time watching the rain fall.

In the other room, a box clattered to the floor and Robyn's muttered curses followed it as he scrabbled to retrieve whatever it was that had done him wrong.

Del said I'd been crazy for letting Robyn take the big bedroom and not keeping the larger space as my own, and in fairness most people thought I was loopy for taking in a flatmate at all, considering how tiny the flat was, but in truth that view outside of my window was the best bit about the little apartment – and to me, the best bit about the city. I loved the Liffey nearly as much as I loved my friends. It was part of me.

The rain was getting heavier. I lifted my camera back from its cosy case. Sliding the window up fully I waited for the light to dip, for the last speck of the day to cast over the muddy ripples. Men walking alone, men together, a woman and a man hand in hand, a tall woman with long hair and nice shoes, I took their photographs, their moments. I played with contrast and I picked up on the rain – the constant, relentless Irish rain. I took more pictures of the wet night.

I opened the window as wide as it would go and tried to lean out, but the rain was already too heavy, soaking the edge of the sill.

The stereo stopped.

Then, as I listened, the final track came on, the same track he'd been playing over and over and over again since Tuesday: the slow, husky tones of Julie London. The words soothed the damp air.

I pulled on my jacket and checked my pockets for money. I longed to bring my camera with me to the club but I'd promised him that, this time, I'd be there – just me, without a lens between us. I'd promised no pictures.

The song finished.

'Fi?' he said.

I gripped my hands together, excitement burning through me. The door opened slowly. Robyn's face and his hair and his manner were gone and in their place was his drag persona, Mae B, so alive, so real, from her huge scarlet wig, her high brows and her thick lashes, to the tight, tight dress, and right down to her pinky-purple gloves. Her lips curled into a sensuous, wicked smile.

'Well?' she said. 'Tell me I'm gorgeous, darling.' She dipped her knees.

'You look incredible,' I said happily. 'Very definitely gorgeous, and . . .'

I stared at her, trying to find Robyn in Mae B, or Mae B in Robyn. She was stunning. The red dress split to the top of her thigh, the shine, the sparkle – the sequins glittered in the dull burn from my reading lamp, and her gloves – the way she moved her hands . . .

She was flawless.

'And the shoes?' she said. 'Are the shoes OK?'

I looked down her long legs to the sky-high red stilettos. I lifted my phone, waiting for the nod before I took the picture.

'I don't look like my mum, do I?' she said. 'Or . . . or like Karen?'

I laughed. The very idea of Mae B looking like Edna, with her sweet, rounded face, or Karen, with her flannel shirts and shapeless cardigans.

'Not one scrap,' I said truthfully.

'But are the shoes too much?'

'Yes,' I said. 'They're perfect.'

Chapter Three

In the taxi, I stared out of the window. The rain was mean, the sky hanging low. Mae B dipped her head to make room for her wig, filling the space with bright, sparkling colour. She kept still and breathed slowly, confined by the cincher that bound her waist. In my own grey jeans and t-shirt, I blended with the car seats. My jacket was blue, I figured. Or it had been once, before it faded to grey.

Mae B blinked, staring at the lights on the turn. I put my hand on hers and squeezed her fingers. As we pulled up in front of the club, she waved and a young man in black shorts and a black t-shirt ran to open the door, holding an umbrella over Mae B and her enormous wig. She stepped to his hand and was led quickly up the steps.

With a scurry of clicking and splashing heels, Miss Merkin came rushing down the street and in through the door. She held one coat over her wig like a headscarf and wore another over her costume, belted tight against the rain. She stopped just long enough to kiss Mae B and to welcome her, and even nodded vaguely in my direction.

I waited for our change and watched through the taxi window as Merkin turned back to beam at Mae B again, and then reached in to hug her, before hurrying away through the double doors to the bar.

I climbed out into the rain. In the foyer, the welcoming party was already in place. I waited on the mat as Thora Point, the club owner, entered the hall. She stretched out her hands to Mae B. Behind her, the young man with the umbrella found himself pushed against the door, squashed into the wet folds. He rolled his eyes behind Thora's back.

'Mae B, honey.' Thora flickered her fingers, beckoning her new baby queen. 'Let me take a look at you!'

With both hands in Thora's, Mae B bobbed a low curtsey. Her huge scarlet wig didn't waver an inch and if she reddened, the colour didn't show under the smooth make-up, but I knew that dimple in her chin and my heart exploded with bubbles of pride.

'You look stunning,' said Thora. 'Legs – those legs! Legs for miles. And those heels! Can you dance in them?'

Mae B laughed. 'Oh, umm, yeah, I—'

'Do I need extra insurance?' Thora chuckled. 'I won't be carting off my baby queens to accident and emergency with broken ankles! Is that a fake tattoo? Mark, look see here . . . she's even got the tattoo!'

From the stairs, Mark nodded down to Mae B. 'You're on time,' he said. 'I imagine that'll never happen again.'

He looked even taller up close. His eyes were dark and unreadable and he took in each one of us, a hawk watching over the sheep and lambs.

The interior door swung open. On the stage, Eve was running through the same Beyoncé number from the Tuesday night. Sure, she was good. She knew the words and she moved in time, and she could twist her body into shapes I'd never seen in real life, but the crowd were paying grace and she just didn't seem to have the same connection with the audience as the older queens.

Behind me, I felt Mae B shaking. I leaned, just a little, until my arm was touching hers. I looked up, and up, suddenly realising how much taller she was in her shoes and how tiny I felt in comparison, dwarfed by her and by Thora and by the huge Mark on the stairs.

'Oh, I see you brought the little straight girl,' said Thora.

I smiled as was expected of me, but inside I cringed at the snarky taunt. Thora leaned over me like an inflated cartoon head-mistress. I kept my spine strong under her powerful glare.

'How marvellous,' she said, after a moment. 'We can never have enough.' She winked, beckoned me to her. 'So, Fi, how are you? You've come to cheer on our baby queen and steal all our men?'

'Not all of them,' I said.

'Good to know, pet.'

I blushed. 'It's been so long, I wouldn't have a clue what to do with one if I got him,' I said.

Thora took my fingers in hers. She smelled of lavender and whiskey. Her skin was thick with make-up, foundation clogging the pores. 'Now, enough tittle tattle,' she said. 'Let me look again at my Mae B.' She stood back. 'Ah,' she sighed. 'Such perfection, such youth!'

Two men waited on the step. The curtain of rain was only just behind them.

'Honey,' said Thora, still gazing at Mae B. 'Oh, honey, honey.' She dabbed at her eyes with the back of her hand. 'And of course you wore the red, it's so—'

'Predictable?' said a young voice from the door. Eve stepped into the light. 'I mean, no one wants to say it.'

'It seems someone wants to say it,' I muttered.

'I'm just thinking of the club's reputation,' said Eve. 'After all, it's Mae B's first night—'

'Claws in, please, pet,' said Thora. 'Everyone had a first time, even you, my dear.'

'And Mae B will be awesome,' I said.

'Sure, she'll kill it.' Eve leered, like a cat at its dinner. 'It's just that no one wants to look cheap and nasty.'

Eve posed, mid-step. She touched a hand to her wig, lifting the bob of blond curls at her neck. She turned for the stairs. The interior door clanged behind her. As she moved, she put a hand to Mark's chest, drawing a line over his pecs, lifting until she was tracing a single finger up to his shoulder. I watched her. We all watched her. She walked up the stairs, one hand on Mark and the other set slightly ahead, her middle finger dipped, her nails pink and pretty.

Mae B raised one perfect arched brow, but underneath the mask the needle had hit home. Her eyes flickered and waned under the thick lashes.

Mark stood back. Eve turned on the middle stair. The hall light cast her pixie face into shadow, marking her cheekbones.

I braced myself.

'Ladies,' said Thora. 'Don't fight. Tonight is for family. We welcome my new daughter.' She held out her hands to Mae B again, pulling her gently, starting for the stairs. 'And, Eve, my poisonous, precious little Eve,' she said. 'Is there some reason you're still here after I fired you?'

Eve drew her mouth into a mope. 'Because I'm cute?' she said. 'Because you love me and you didn't really mean th—'

'You're not cute. You're surplus to requirement,' said Thora.

I watched as Thora led Mae B up the stairs to the dressing rooms, forcing Eve out of the way as they passed her.

'You'll miss me!' Eve shouted after them.

'Like I'd miss a verruca,' retorted Thora.

24

The bar was filling up. A woman pushed past me, heading out into the night. Left in the foyer with just Mark and Eve, I scuttled through the interior door into the safe anonymity of the club.

I was so nervous for Mae B I didn't know where to put myself. She'd be fine. I knew she'd be fine. However mean Thora was with me, she'd take care of one of her own. Thora was all right really, she was just stuck in one mode, as Del would say. She didn't mean badly. Like an elderly grandparent you loved very much but you wish they read the room as often as they read the news. And anyway, Del would fight a dragon for Mae B every day of the week, even if that dragon were wearing pearls.

I pulled out my phone and flicked through the few photos I'd taken in the apartment.

I messaged Edna and Karen. I attached the picture.

As promised, I wrote. Mae B lives and breathes – and she's gorgeous! All looking good for the performance.

Seconds later, my phone buzzed in return.

Oh, MY BABY!! Edna wrote. I can't believe how beautiful she is – she doesn't get that from my side, that's for sure – and Grandpa Joe really actually doesn't believe it – haha! Blow kisses to her from us all here, and take LOTS OF PHOTOS. Edna x

I was too excited to drink any more alcohol. I didn't want to miss a second, but I was too nervous not to have something to do with my hands; I bought a lemonade, filled to the top with ice, and I swilled it around and around, letting the ice clunk against the glass, catching the light.

I longed for my camera. It wasn't that I didn't mix with other people, it was just that most of my friends were usually a bit louder than me. With my camera, I became invisible. Even at big events like Pride. Faced with a lens, most people smiled and turned and posed, and I knew I could make them happy. Years of evening classes and online tutorials had me confident with my ability; there was nothing better than how someone's face lit up as they saw themselves how others did.

Seeing Del by the stage I sent Edna another picture. I knew she would get a kick out of his striped tights and bright yellow baby-doll nightie. I thought about sending more but I'd made the promise to Robyn. Just see with our eyes, he'd said. One night, he had pleaded to me, one night with no cameras. Everything is on our phones now, he said. Everything we do is recorded and shared and liked and considered before we've even had a chance to consider it ourselves, and this was the first time – and with luck, as Edna had told him, simply the first of many, many other times – but this was the very first time he would step out on to the stage in drag and he needed this to be gentle, he said. He needed to have other firsts. He wanted his sister and his mum to see him then, later, when he'd got over his nerves, and when he was sure of himself. He wanted them to be proud of him.

I hugged my phone in my hands. A lump rose in my throat. We were so proud of him already.

The music changed.

I pictured Mae B backstage in her red dress and red heels. The air was hot in the little space behind the curtain, years of grime still clinging to the fabric walls. The floor was covered in ridges, wires taped down with gaffer tape, crossing at weird angles, running from mics to speakers to the sound box, to whichever technical magic Mark was using. They had smoke machines one year and weird spikey lights, and at the New Year's Eve party they had a queen from Scotland who did fire eating and she swung her flames a bit too high, and now the bar over the curtains was tinged with burn marks around the back.

And even then, Robyn had longed to be up on the stage with the others. Any excuse, he'd put on Del's wig or his heels.

I wanted to creep back there and do the overeager thumbs-up sign that Edna would have done, but Thora was right: it was Mae B's time now. This was all about what she needed, and Thora would protect her against Eve. Spoilt little Eve – whatever it was Eve did to get fired this time, she'd be back again the next week. Del was always saying that the only reason Thora hadn't thrown the little witch out on her heels was because she was so cute – cute as a queen, and cuter as a boy, he said. Eve wasn't worth it. That was what I'd told Del, back when his eyes were red from crying and he pressed his fingernails into his palms.

No one was that cute.

The club was packed. Perfect bodies writhed together, tight t-shirts, skinny jeans. Somewhere below, there would be expensive runners and bare ankles. The DJ was tucked up behind her barricade of machines. Beside her bunker, two women leaned against the wall together, one with her hand on the other's waist. I sipped my drink and stood alone.

Mark came down the thin spiral staircase. After a moment, Thora came around from the interior door and stood beside him. Both were watching the crowd and watching the stage. The curtains twitched.

'Lovely people,' Merkin's voice boomed over the speaker. 'Please put your hands together and give a very special, trashy welcome – let's hear it for Miss . . . DEL . . . PEEN!'

Under the spiral staircase, Thora leaned over to Mark to say something. I watched her lips move. I started to make my way toward them but then the spotlight held on the curtains and I hesitated, not wanting to miss even a second.

Del stepped on to the stage and the crowd roared with delight. I cheered with them, barely noticing that I'd spilled my drink over my jacket. Del had changed outfits and he twirled, his pink-and-white ruffled skirt lifting to a perfect circle as he spun around, showing matching ruffled knickers. He raised his arms and huge puffed sleeves billowed out like glittery clouds. I kept looking behind him. All I could see was the occasional flash of sparkling red that passed behind the gap in the curtains. I barely saw Del move across the little stage, barely noticed the high kicks and flicks. The number finally finished and he took up the mic. It was nearly time – I felt the lump in my throat drop down into my stomach, curdling with the noodles.

I clutched my empty glass. Del lifted the mic to his lips.

'Well, aren't you just lovely?' he said. 'Tonight, darlings, my trash and my treasure, we have something special.'

I peered past Del, trying to see through the gap in the curtains. Again, a flash of red glittered between the dark folds – then just for a second she was there. Mae B stood in the dark.

She was beautiful. She was alone. The red dress was to die for.

So many months of Robyn trying on corsets and cinchers, ordering cheap wig after cheap wig and all kinds of dresses and costumes, every colour of sequins and silks, every type of fabric hanging on the rail in his room – and then finding the right drag name and the right shoes . . . And then the endless, endless collection of wrong shoes, the make-up spread on our towels, lipsticks everywhere – in the kitchen, in the bathroom – his mother sending us packages of yet more lipsticks to try and more shoes. And all the time, the stereo blaring the same songs, over and over again as he learned the steps and the words.

I held my breath. By the staircase, Mark leaned against the post. He was nearly as tall as Thora, his wide shoulders tight under his clothes. They talked together, gesturing to the stage. I moved quickly, darting behind people until I could hear them.

Mark nodded, his attention on the stage.

'Eve's done this time,' said Thora. 'We can't afford to lose any more.'

'We can't afford to keep her,' said Mark.

The club lights dimmed. The stage was empty. With the crowd, I leaned forward.

'Now,' said Del's voice. 'A cherry for the plucking,' he crooned. 'Something a little bit special, and . . . untainted . . .'

The music started, the dark sexuality of a Parisian jazz bar – the slow bass, then the sultry, sexy brass – the spotlight shrank to a circle over the curtain folds and Del's voice dripped with all the delight of a French showgirl.

'Introducing, for her very first time to the stage – so be gentle, boys – it's Mae B!'

The curtain twitched.

First her foot, pointed in the high heels, then her ankle.

The music rose. The long, low trombone.

The audience was still, Julie London's voice like silk.

My heart hammered in my chest.

I watched, unblinking, as Mae B's leg appeared between the curtains. The song was so slow but the reveal was slower, and as Julie London's vocals filled the room, the crowd were swept into the moment. When Mae B finally stepped out, she wobbled – only a fraction, just the tiniest little shake – and for that second I saw Robyn's worry in her eyes. Then it was gone. Mae stood fine, her back strong, her body incredible – tiny waist, those long, long legs, and huge, sweeping curves – her plump, bright pink lips perfectly lip-synching as she slunk across the boards to the front of the stage.

She was amazing. I looked around, desperately hoping.

They all adored her. Everyone adored her.

Mae B was everything they loved. Not just sexy but also funny. And, as the song went on, it turned out she could really dance. I'd had no idea how well she could move.

The crowd were in love. She connected with everyone in the room. She remembered all the words and as the song ended, we roared and cheered and clapped and whistled, and Del joined her on the stage, taking her hand, giving us one last look at the new queen before he led her away behind the curtains.

And it was done.

I grinned so hard my mouth hurt. I couldn't stop grinning. I was so happy for her I could explode.

Mae B had slayed it.

The music changed and other queens came on and off, and after a while, I settled back to enjoy the rest of the show. Finally able to relax, I watched as Del ripped into the front row, teasing the regulars within an inch of their comfort, leaving the club buzzing with laughter.

When Mae B and Merkin came back for the group number, even I had to admit that Mae looked wobbly on her feet, and she definitely missed some of the lyrics in the middle bit, but with the first song over it no longer seemed to matter, and as she turned, right at the end, she peered out into the crowd and I waved and beamed in delight, so damn proud I could have squeezed her tighter than her cincher.

The last song faded, and the applause rumbled away. The other queens climbed down and took the seats in the big square chairs under the spiral staircase. The lighting changed and people broke away from the stage. Some danced, and some clustered in groups. Del and Mark had their heads bowed, deep in discussion. I watched for a while, tucked back from the queens. Ben, Del's husband, waved to me to say hello, and I was just about to speak to him when Robyn finally reappeared, his face scrubbed clean, wearing his jeans and t-shirt, his hair wet. Smiling so hard my face hurt, I ran to hug him. I'd barely let go when the dance music cut short.

The house lights died to nothing – not gradually, but in a stutter – then the spot grew again, in that same place on the stage curtains, and from nowhere the first notes of Mae B's song started again.

Mark looked up.

'What's this?' said Del. 'Robyn, are you—?'

'Not me.' Robyn frowned.

Thora waved to Mark, flapping her hand. 'Helen must have made a mistake, would you—?'

But the song didn't stop. The spotlight shuddered and as we watched, a thin leg with a red shoe struck out of the gap between the curtains and wiggled. Eve's face appeared above it. She winked, checking the crowd were watching, then darted back. Then her leg again.

People started to move back toward the stage. Nausea rippled through me as I realised what was happening. All around us, people were laughing.

'She's not . . .' said Mark.

'She couldn't . . .'

It was Mae B's red shoe. It was Mae B's song and Mae B's red shoe.

'She is,' said Thora. 'She bloody is.'

Eve burst through the curtains, tripping on to the stage, Mae B's red wig planted askew on her head. The expensive, fabulous red dress clung to her skinny frame and she had two giant beach balls stuffed into her chest. Playing for laughs, Eve blinked into the headlights, feeling forward as if blind – she took each step, taking the comic timing right to the hilt as she wobbled and fell.

Robyn had his hand over his mouth.

'Stop her,' said Del. 'Thora!'

The song, once soft and sensual, seemed to grow mean with its sleazy brass. Sensing the takedown, the audience cheered for blood. A man called out, and Eve staggered toward the front row, lapping at their hands as she pretended she might fall on top of

31

them. Loving the obvious joke at the new queen's expense and the growing horror by the stairs, the crowd whooped and cheered her on, calling their sides.

Robyn shrank. He shook, his body curving in on itself.

'Don't watch,' I said. 'Don't let her win . . .'

I put my hand on his shoulder but neither of us could turn away. Eve was good at winning. The more the audience gave to her, the more she played to them.

Mark swore. Miss Merkin stared, open-mouthed.

'You have to stop this,' Del said to them again. 'You can't let Eve do this.'

'I can't exactly stop her,' said Thora.

'Yes, you can – you can pull her off the bloody stage!' Del hissed. 'Stop the track – stop her!'

'Leave it,' said Robyn, his voice thin. 'If you stop her, you make her a legend. Let her have her little moment.'

The song was nearly halfway through, but already people had clambered forward, their phones turned to the stage.

'You want more?' Eve called to their cheers. 'You want more?'

'To hell with this!' Del started forward but Mark was already moving. Right behind him, Ben pulled aside someone in the front row. He reached the stage first and grabbed for Eve, tugging on her leg. Eve extended her hand, pulling Ben to her as if to kiss him. But Mark was there. Catching Eve's tiny waist with his big hands, his eyes burned with hate as he pulled her, tripping, off the stage. With Ben's help, Mark swept Eve over his shoulder and carried her, kicking and screaming through the delighted crowd, to the door.

The track stopped dead. The house lights came up on full, highlighting the dirt on the floor, the abandoned glasses and bottles. Some people laughed, some jeered in disappointment, awkwardness mixing with the alcohol already deep in their blood. Upstairs, Del was arguing with the DJ, the volume of their words growing with each jab, but when the music showed no signs of coming back in any form, people grew bored of standing under the bright lights for nothing. Drinks were finished, coats found. There were other bars to go to.

I looked around but even Robyn and Thora had both disappeared. The evening was ruined. Mae B's first night had been stolen. On the emptying dance floor with my jacket in my hands, I never hated anyone so much as I hated Eve Harrington.

Slowly, the last of the stragglers spilled from the club. The hook-ups separated from the herd and the singles went on or went home. I wondered how many of the photographs taken of Eve fighting and kicking, pinned on Mark's shoulder, would end up all over Instagram and Twitter before the poster had even made it through the front doors. And I wondered, with an ache in my heart for him, how many of those pictures had captured the look on Robyn's face as Eve destroyed Mae B's performance in front of all their friends.

I stood at the stage. I ran my fingers over a scrape on the bare wood from Eve's shoe . . . from Mae B's shoe. It would have been funny if it hadn't been so mean, but that was Eve through and through.

I picked up a pint glass from the floor, taking it to the bar. My footsteps echoed in the empty space.

As I moved, Del leaned down from the top of the spiral staircase.

'Fi?'

'Hey,' I said. 'Is everything OK? Is Robyn with you?'

Del's puffball skirt creased against the handrail. 'He's not up here,' he said. 'I thought he was with you.'

Del disappeared and I walked out into the foyer. On the landing, Mark was going through the last coats. His hair was wet. He ran his hand over the back of his neck, then slipped behind the desk and straightened the hangers, each one moving, just a bit, knocking into the next.

Del stepped on to the landing. 'Eve's nothing but trouble. It's what she does,' he said. 'She takes good things and she poisons them.'

Mark didn't answer.

Robyn stumbled in from outside, visibly shaken.

'Fi?' he said.

I reached for him.

'I was looking for you,' he said. 'I, um—'

'You were amazing, girl,' said Del, with a point. 'That's the important bit. You know you were good, right? You were better than good. Didn't Thora say you were good?'

Robyn didn't answer.

'You got your stuff?' I said gently.

'Oh, um, actually Thora said I could leave my drag here, if . . .'

'This is your home now,' said Del. 'Whether you like it or not,' he added with a bitter laugh.

Robyn tried to smile in return but even as he opened his mouth, he had nothing. In all the years of knowing him, everything we'd been through together, I'd never seen him so broken.

'Thanks,' he said quietly. 'You've all been great. I, um . . .' He stopped.

'Shall we?' I started toward the door. The others looked at one another. Del opened his mouth to speak.

'First night drinkies tradition,' said Mark, interrupting. 'Merkin has gone home, she's working early in the morning. Thora's just putting her in a taxi. She'll be—'

The front door clanged back, the night's storm brushing in ahead of Thora.

'Mama, dearest,' said Del from the top of the stairs. He lifted his hand, his fingers beautifully turned.

'Oh, the rain, the rain, the interminable rain,' Thora groaned. 'Now, where is my baby? How are you, pet?' said Thora, taking Robyn's hand. 'But what is wrong? You're in pain?'

'It's drag,' said Del. 'Of course she's in pain.'

'They were all watching me,' Robyn whispered.

'That's the idea,' said Mark. 'The giant wig and big fake boobs . . .'

'Not onstage. That was great. I mean . . . when . . .'

'You'll find it easier next time,' Del said. 'Eve won't be here for a start.'

'There won't be a next time,' said Robyn.

'Hush now, honey.' Thora brushed the rain from her outfit, shuddering like a ginger cat. 'The matter is dealt with, darlings, and little Eve Harrington is no longer our problem.'

Del lifted his hand.

'Gone.' Thora swept the air and shook out the word.

'She's never gone,' said Del. 'She's like a disease.'

Thora turned to him. 'You have more reason to hate Eve than many,' she said. 'But just as many reasons to let go.'

Del drew in a breath.

'Ben has shown you his true colours,' said Thora. 'You know what they say, pet: if someone shows you who they are, you believe them. Well, it wasn't just Eve there, that night. Ben—'

But behind her, Ben stepped up to the door. Soaked to the skin, his hair dripping, his t-shirt stuck wet to his chest. He took a step back into the dark, and he stood in the rain without moving.

He turned and disappeared into the wet night.

Del hurried down the stairs, his heels scraping the carpet as he stood on the lip, peering into the dark. 'Ben?'

Sighing, Thora touched her fingers to Robyn's face, wiping away his tears. 'What's done is done,' she said. 'You did good, little one, and now we will put the ugliness out of our minds. Tonight

35

we celebrate your first. It's TRASH tradition and, God only knows, Mama needs a drink.'

Leading them into the belly of the club, Thora put one hand behind Del and one behind Robyn. Del turned to me, reaching out. I went to follow but Mark stepped into the gap, an immovable force.

'Sorry,' he said. 'Family only after hours.'

My heart sank. I was, as Thora would say, surplus to requirement.

The club door closed behind me. The night was cold as well as wet. I did up my jacket and set out into the heavy rain. The streets were sodden, water pooling around the drains, the gutters deep, overspilling. On the other side of the road, trees hung heavy against their railings and the lights of a car in the distance picked out the shine of their wet leaves.

I frowned.

I should be with Robyn.

I had been there for all of it – I was there when he tried on heels for the first time, and there when he got his first wig, and when he tried out Del's make-up, and—

I stomped through the puddles.

It was tradition, they said. And that was just bloody fine.

Up ahead, three men walked in the middle of the road, their legs clumsy with drink. One of them shouted, another laughed. I moved into the shadows. I didn't need any trouble. The rain was so heavy they hadn't seen me but if I carried on down the road there would be no avoiding them. Gritting my teeth, I ducked into an alley. I was only a block away from the club but the thin, dark street was a different place. High buildings, grey concrete walls and boarded windows. No one lived there; not even the whiny gulls from the river would hang out on these roofs. Footsteps disappeared at the far end – someone hurrying to get away.

I walked down the alley. I could barely see where I was going. The rain blurred my sight. It couldn't be . . .

I started forward.

The body lay face down in the gutter. Her legs were skewed, her red sequin dress rucked up over her hips. Her shoes were lifeless, one barely on her foot, one cast to the side. Her bright red wig spread like blood in water.

Robyn!

I ran, falling, stumbling forward. I didn't think— I couldn't think—

Behind me I heard a shout but I couldn't stop. All I could see was Robyn – my best friend, Robyn – lying broken, lying dead. I screamed out his name, over and over again.

I dropped down beside the body—

It wasn't Robyn.

She was pale. So young, so thin. My fingers slipped on her wet skin as if the rain was fighting against me. I turned her, pulling her to me, freeing her face . . .

Eve was dead.

Chapter Four

I pulled out my phone but my fingers slipped and tipped it into the water. I knelt in the rain, staring at Eve's face. In the light from the distant streetlamp, her eyes looked at nothing, glazed, as if a layer of water still covered them. Somewhere behind me, a man shouted – a sharp call, not the voices of the three drunk guys in the road. Someone was running toward me.

The red-sequinned dress shone in the shady gloom.

'Fi?' Ben bent down beside me. 'Fi, is that . . . ?' His voice shook. 'Oh God.' He covered his hand with his mouth. 'No,' he said.

'Can you call the guards?' I said.

I held Eve's head on my lap, out of the water. I smoothed the wig from her face. She had a bruise on her forehead. I rubbed the mark on her cold skin as if I could wash it away. I looked up. Even in the rain, Ben's face was wet with tears, his lower lip wobbling as he tried to speak.

'Please can you call the guards?' I said.

He fumbled with his phone. 'My fingers are shaking,' he said. 'Oh God, Eve – I – I don't . . . H-hello – hello?' He stood as the line connected. 'I need, umm . . . I need an ambulance, quick – please, come quick, I think . . . Send the guards, please . . . My friend is . . . Hello?'

Ben ducked back into one of the doorways as he stuttered and stammered the directions. The rain dulled his words. He called out a question, repeating it, but I shook my head. I was no expert on anything, but Eve was really, really dead. There was no point in trying to resuscitate her, or even removing her wig. There was nothing left to wake.

Still holding his phone clutched to his chest, Ben came and put his hand over Eve's. He closed his eyes and cradled her fingers, covering her thumb with his. On and on the rain poured, pooling in the gutter, flooding the pavement. The evening's show and the little drag club around the corner were a world away.

Her head was heavy in my lap. I'd never seen anyone dead before. She was still beautiful but as the rain washed her face, underneath the make-up it became clear that Eve's charm had been in her mannerisms and movements, her quick mind and her poisonous tongue. She was beautiful in the way a marble statue had beauty, but the feeling was painted on. In the dark of the alleyway, nothing moved, just the rain, drenching everything it found, pulling the night closer.

The first car broke the dark with its headlights. Then the next. The ambulance was behind them, then another.

I blinked into the lights like a bruised rabbit. Ben called them over. He went and pointed down the thin lane at me as if there were three other dead queens to choose from, each with their heads on the laps of passing women.

A camera flashed over me. In my mind, I pictured Eve checking the angles and the lights to make sure she was centre of the frame, sniping at the photographer to go again and again until it was right. I tried to lean her head up so they could see her face, figuring that was the very least she deserved, and then I remembered how she'd snarled and sneered from the stage, and I turned her again so her chin doubled.

'Here,' said one of the guards.

I looked up at him. I wanted to say something canny. To at the very least explain why I was knelt in eight-inch-deep gutter water with a dead drag queen laid out over my lap, but they were talking – barking orders, stating the facts without me. Before I knew what was happening, two men reached down into the water, sliding their arms under Eve, and they carried her to the higher pavement.

I didn't move. At the wall, Ben stood alone. Eve was dead. It was insane, it was ridiculous. Eve was actually dead. The sentence circled in my mind.

Someone was told to lift me up. I put my hands on the guard's arms. Too late, I reminded myself it was absolutely not the time to notice his biceps. I was set to lean against the wall like some sopping umbrella. The pack moved around us, uniforms merging in the dark. Everyone seemed to know what to do except me. Was I meant to say something? What was the protocol for finding a dead drag queen in the rain?

I looked for Ben. He bent away from the headlights with his phone in his hand, jabbing at the screen.

One of the younger guards wound tape between the corner buildings, looping it around the drainpipes, separating us from the outside world in a pen of weirdness. I felt like holding out my hands to be taped into the scene, a human chalk print. I was soaked. I could have been no wetter if I had swum fully clothed in the Liffey. I tried my own phone, but the screen was dead. I rattled it as if the water would flow out of the headphone socket and my lock-screen picture would ripple back up. Even if I could have texted, some things needed way more than a bunch of emojis in a WhatsApp message.

I clung to the wall as they examined Eve's body. The guards crowded around her, leaning into her face, talking about her. If she was there in some ghostly dead form, she'd have liked that, six men and one woman peering at her, one of the men gently removing her wig and snaring it in an evidence bag.

Ben stepped out of the shadows.

From the main road, the TRASH family came together through the rain, striding feet first into the puddles, their already ruined heels still strong, their spines bolt straight, their shoulders back, their drag holding heavy like the sodden trees behind them. Lit by the headlights, Thora and Del walked centre stage, Mark and Robyn either side. They came quickly, Del holding his phone, his eyes on Ben, Robyn wringing his hands. Thora stepped forward. Mark swore, muttering under his breath as he looked beyond us to the muddle of guards and the body between them.

'Fi?' said Robyn.

I lifted my hand in a wave.

One of Del's puffed sleeves gave up its hem and slid from his arm into the water at his feet.

As the guard with the tape came forward, Thora pushed herself up, muscling against the line. The guard struck out his hand, but his feet moved back a step.

'Take me to Miss Eve Harrington,' said Thora.

'I'm sorry, err, ma'am, but—'

'Did I ask for your apology?'

'No, but—'

Thora looked down at the stammering guard, piercing him with her glare. A piece of her wig slipped over her eye and without losing focus she lifted her hand, pulled the hairpiece free, and stuffed it into her bra.

'Young man. Take me,' she said, 'to our Fallen Queen.'

'Oh, um, that is . . .' The guard blushed. 'I'm not really allowed t—'

'Young man!' Thora snapped.

41

Del put his hand on her wrist. 'Please,' he said softly to the guard.

From the other side of the lane, Ben was being questioned. He pointed at me, and he gestured to the gutter. I squeezed my eyes closed but in the dark I could still see Eve's face under the water with her make-up glassy and smeared and the highlights in her cheeks and her forehead too bright against the night gloom. I scrubbed my hands over my face, but my fingers smelled creepy, turning my stomach.

'Take the names,' a tall man called to the guard binding the tape.

The young one got out his notepad. He started writing, marking the date. The rain soaked the paper straight away, but he kept going with his pencil.

'Umm . . .' he said.

'My name is Thora Point.' Thora stabbed her finger at his paper. 'Thora. Point. This here is Del Peen,' she said. 'And this here is my daughter, Miss Mae B. And this is Mark.'

'Mark?' said the guard. 'And are there any other . . . um . . . ?'

'We're drag queens, honey,' said Thora. 'It's not like you could mistake us for a team of damp archaeologists now, is it? We work at TRASH. Just there? You probably have an uncle who knows us. Drag queens, boy – say it.'

'Um, drag queens,' the guard repeated. 'But—'

'The only queen missing here is Miss Merkin,' said Mark.

The young man giggled. 'Isn't th—?'

'Does Merkin have a boy name?' said Del. 'I don't think I've ever heard it.'

'Of course she does,' said Thora. 'Just because we're given something doesn't mean we have to use it. Take your brain—'

'Fi McKinnery?' The tall man waded through the water toward me. He wore a long raincoat over a brown suit, and wellington

42

boots, though he stood like someone used to very expensive shoes and to the pacing of a carpet in a corner office looking over the park. He towered over me. 'You're Fi McKinnery?' he said.

A detective, I figured. The only one who had come in wellies.

'I am?' I said.

'Fi?' Robyn called. 'You OK, hon?'

'If you'll stand back, please, sir,' said another guard.

'Fi!' shouted Del. 'We—'

'I'm fine,' I said.

Like some nodding eejit, I smiled and bobbed my head as if everything was perfectly normal and we weren't standing ankle-deep in gutter water with Eve's dead body on the pavement and Thora bearing down on a stumbling young guard, and a detective glaring at me.

'Right, so, Miss McKinnery,' said the detective. 'You were the one who discovered Liam's body?'

'Who?'

'Liam Flanagan, ma'am.' The detective gestured toward Eve. 'We have the deceased identified by this gentleman here' – he waved vaguely toward Ben – 'as a Mr Liam Flanagan?'

'Oh, yeah – you mean Eve?' I said.

'That's his stage name?'

'Her drag name.'

The detective frowned. I tried to remember if he'd told me his own name but my brain was muddled and strange and half of it was working out if I was about to be sick or not, and if I was going to be sick, then where I should lean to throw up, and if it would be contaminating a crime scene by throwing up on my shoes. Then I remembered Eve's comments earlier about Mae B looking cheap and nasty, and I had an undignified urge to storm over there and kick her.

I needed a hot shower and fresh clothes, and I needed for someone else to be talking and no one to be asking me questions. I needed to sink into a sterile sofa and to put on Netflix and to watch Disney movies and to close my eyes and for absolutely none of this to be happening.

Most of all, I longed for a drink. Tea or coffee, but preferably something much stronger. The club was right there, around the corner. I chewed on my lower lip. The detective frowned at me as if he'd just asked me a question and I'd said nothing. There'd be no chance of a quick drink from him. Nothing handy with the brandy about the man. He wasn't much older than me, but he looked like the type that didn't drink at all and would pass by a pub saying, 'Well now, that wouldn't really be my scene.'

'Maybe you'd tell me how you found him?' he said, obviously repeating himself.

'In the gutter.'

'Not where – how. How did you find him?'

'Well, she was face down, kind of spread-eagled a bit – I turned her around in case – well, you know – but she was dead. I mean, not just a bit dead,' I said. I was talking too quickly, gesturing as I went, spinning my hand around and around. I stopped moving. 'I mean, she was really dead,' I said. 'And her skin was kind of pale, and there was this water that came out of her mouth, and—'

I blanched. Then coughed, forcing the nausea back down.

'And where were you coming from?' said the detective. 'I take it you weren't just out for a stroll this time of night?' He leaned back on his boot heels.

I went through how I had left TRASH and how it was raining and how the three men were walking down the main road and they were clearly pissed – and then I apologised and changed that to drunk, as if pissed were too rude a word to say to a detective.

'So you chose an unlit street as a woman, alone, in the middle of the night?'

'Of course. If they can't see me, then they can't kill me,' I said with a laugh, repeating the same thing I'd said so many times before—

I stopped talking. I blinked, suddenly realising I was staring at the space where Eve had actually been murdered. In the dark. The detective raised his eyebrows. I'd managed to make a weird situation so much weirder.

'What time did you leave the club?' he said.

'What time?'

'The club,' he said again. He gestured behind me. 'TRASH?'

I shook my head. 'I'm sorry, I don't really know.'

'You didn't check?'

I was too busy being seen to the door by Mark, I thought, but that was another thing I was trying not to say, along with asking where Mark had gone, back then, and why his hair was so wet when he was in the coatroom, and why Robyn had been outside too, around then, and why his hair was wet, and why if Ben had been so close to where I was outside, why he hadn't been the one to find Eve and—

'You recognised Liam Flanagan right away, did you?' said the detective.

'Eve? Well, she—'

I glanced back at Robyn.

'Is something wrong?' said the guard.

Clearly there was a lot wrong. It was all very, very wrong indeed.

'So you were friends with Liam?' he said, speaking slowly. 'You knew him?'

'Everyone knew Eve,' I said. And everyone hated her.

I shivered. It was getting to the point where there were so many things I couldn't say out loud, my brain was aching with the effort of keeping them clamped inside.

'Drinking, was he? Experimenting with illegal drugs, maybe?'

I imagined Eve's days of experimentation were over a long time before and she had fully worked out what she liked and didn't like. I closed my mouth.

'Hmm. Out at night,' the detective went on. 'In this weather, with so much water on the paving slabs and those ridiculous shoes.'

He took a long sigh. Then he bent his head and clasped his hands together as if in prayer. I glanced to the side. No one else was praying. I wondered if he was just thinking, considering, or if it was a mark-of-respect thing. I bent my head a little, lowering my eyes. The rain ran from my nose and I lifted my hand to wipe my face but my fingers still smelled of gutter water or drain water or dead Eve.

'Fi, are you OK, child?' said Thora. She leaned over the tape and tapped the uniformed guard on his shoulder. 'Excuse me now,' she said. 'Would you look at her, there? She's wet through. Come here, Fi, child, come to Mama.'

Thora tipped her lopsided wet-wigged head to one side, kindness personified. In defending his line, the young guard had started winding another strip of tape from one side of the street to the other but there wasn't a drag queen alive who was afraid of a bit of sticky tape. Thora broke the line, pushing past him. She stepped toward me showing no sign that her heels were by then fully underwater, and she pulled me to her, and I breathed in the reassuring smells of whiskey and stale drag that surrounded her like a perfume. I leaned into her hold.

'This woman is done,' Thora said to the detective. She started back toward the club, steering me with her.

'What happened, sir?' Del moved into the middle of the lane, facing Eve's body. 'What happened to her? Was she – was she attacked?'

Each of the queens stopped moving. Thora's fingernails dug into my arm.

'There's no sign of any sexual attack,' said a woman at the body. 'As far as we can see, anyway. I'll have to get her back to the lab but it seems clear enough.' She glanced at the detective.

'Tripped and fell, by the look of it,' he said. 'There's nothing malicious here.'

'But—'

'Probably knocked himself out and drowned in the water. Silly boy. The autopsy will confirm it, but in the interest of keeping calm I don't see any need to make a mountain out of a molehill, as it were.'

'Eve tripped?' said Del.

'Those shoes, the rough road – a tragic case of accidental death,' said the detective. He nodded, as if confirming his decision to himself. 'Such a waste of a young man's life.'

I looked from the queens to the body, wondering exactly which one the detective meant.

◆　◆　◆

Mark opened the club door. The bar staff had gone home. In the empty space, the bright lights and the debris of dirt and spilled alcohol seemed to echo against the strange, busy scene outside. The space was deathly quiet, our footsteps echoing on the empty floor. I stood, dripping, on the mat.

It was barely two hours since Mark had pulled Eve, screaming and kicking, from the stage. If I blinked I could see her pouting on the stairs or up on the stage, under the lights.

Del kicked off his shoes and took off his wig. His dress hung from his body in sodden sheets. He unzipped the skirt and slid it to the floor, leaving it there in the foyer and stepping out in just his tights and corset. Moving to the bar, Mark took out six small glasses. He sloshed whiskey into five and turned the sixth over, on to the bar.

'To Eve,' said Thora, taking hers in one deep swallow.

'To Eve,' the others repeated.

Robyn set down his empty glass and looked away, holding the bar as if it were the only thing keeping him upright.

'I don't care,' said Del. 'I don't even care who killed her.'

'No one killed her,' said Thora.

'She hardly fell!'

'It was an accident. Accidents happen.'

Sickness rolled through me. I swallowed, hard. My wet clothes rubbed on my skin. My feet sloshed, too loud in the big hall. I put my hand over my mouth.

'Time to go home, little straight girl,' said Thora.

The cruel jibe pierced through me. My shoulders fell.

'Will you back off calling her that?' said Del.

Thora crossed the floor. She smiled at me, sweet as a nightmare. 'Whatever terrible accident happened to Eve Harrington happened outside of those doors,' she said. 'It did not happen here, pet.'

I stared up into her painted eyes. *Little Eve Harrington is no longer our problem.*

She looked away. 'I will not have my club turned into some grisly murder scene,' she said.

Robyn lowered himself into one of the square chairs like a fallen leaf in a storm.

'Mae B will take the early slot tomorrow night,' Thora said to him. 'You can bring the rest of your make-up and stuff and we'll make room upstairs. Don't be late. I'll have th—'

The interior door swung shut, closing me into the foyer and muffling their voices. I stepped into the wet night. The rain was merciless. The alley was cut from the road by layers of crime-scene tape crisscrossing and binding the gap as if the young guard was determined to prove his point. The ambulance had gone and some of the cars, and three uniformed officers stood together in the downpour, their coats streaming with water.

Del came to the door.

'Hey,' I said. I smiled.

He was naked apart from his tights. His chest was marked with the red trace of his cincher, his base foundation stopped in a deep V over his sternum. As he leaned out, he turned his face to the sky and wiped the rain on his skin, smearing his make-up. 'Are you OK?' he said. 'Do you want me to walk you home?'

I looked at his tights, the feet torn, the knees laddered. His bare chest, his eye liner streaked down his cheeks.

'Give me two minutes,' he said. 'Or I can call a cab, or—'

Behind him, laughter filled the empty club.

'Robyn will be a while.' Del glanced back, fondness in his smile. 'It's his first night,' he said. 'It's a lot.'

I started to speak.

Del held up his hand. 'Thora is a bitch and I'm sorry,' he said. 'But there's something that happens. The first time. It's like, you always knew and never realised, and then there you are.' He scrunched up his lips. 'It's more than just a dress and a wig and a bit of face paint,' he said. 'It's not about the name or the shoes or even the audience in the end. You can walk your kitchen a hundred times in a dress and make-up and you will never be a drag queen. It isn't the same. But you put it together – you step out here into the world, and you take that breath, and, honey . . .'

He wiped the back of his hand over his cheek.

'Mae B brought us life tonight,' he said.

I took another step into the rain.

'You have to give Robyn time, Fi,' he said. 'It's too much.'

A Garda car slid into the night, the officers watching us as they passed. 'I'll walk you home,' said Del again. 'It's late. I just need t—'

Someone cheered from inside the club and Thora laughed, her low cackle rumbling behind the door. I pictured Robyn in the middle of them. I imagined them celebrating his debut night, reliving it there, in front of the stage, every moment of Mae B—

I waved as I walked away and Del blew me a kiss, sending it fluttering toward me with his fingers, into the dark night.

Chapter Five

I'd been asleep two hours and thirty-eight minutes when my alarm clock screamed at me from the shelf. I stumbled out of bed, rubbing my eyes, before remembering it was Sunday, it was a day of rest, and—

On the desk in big black capital letters was the note I'd written myself the morning before, knowing I'd forget:

MRS LANSBURY'S PEKINGESE!

Muttering curses, I pulled my camera bag from under the bed. I checked the time. Part of me hoped that Karen would forget but she was more reliable even than Del and relentlessly on time.

I showered, picking my way over the heap of wet clothes I'd left on the floor the night before. We were out of towels, the last two under another damp pile by the sink, but I was already late. I opened the door and peeked into the apartment. I could hear Robyn's snores from behind his door. I left clean, wet footprints running into my room. It was still raining. I cursed the gods of inconvenient weather. I dragged on clean clothes, hurrying as I went, pulling a brush through my hair, stuffing my feet into my old runners. Karen would have texted as she reached the city, but my phone was dead, its screen grey and unresponsive, and I had no way of telling her.

I crept into Robyn's room. He lay on his side, curled around the covers. His face still held a slight trace of make-up and, as he slept, his fingers dug into the cotton sheet. I took his phone from the side, punched in the password, and clicked on Karen's name. Fi here, I typed. Don't call me on this, Robyn is sleeping, I don't want to wake him. Long night, will explain when I see you, I'm—

I glanced at his clock.

—running a tiny bit late, I wrote. Don't reply.

Rereading what I'd put so far, I pictured Karen's disapproval.

I'll bring coffee, I put. I added an X and pressed 'Send', and then left his phone and crept back out of the room.

I was a full twenty minutes late when I finally made it to the taxi rank by the river, next to O'Connell Bridge, and Karen's face reflected the time. I fumbled with the car door, trying to balance the coffee. As I slid my knee into the gap, I handed one of the cups over to Karen.

'Star,' she said as she inhaled the steam.

'Sorry,' I told her. 'Sorry, sorry, I—'

'Fine. Not a bother. I've done the loop twice,' she said, nodding to a taxi driver who was gesturing furiously. She swung into the traffic. She looked as tired as I felt but I didn't think the day would be improved by mentioning that; she was a farmer, she was always tired.

I waited until we were through the next set of traffic lights.

'So, how's it going?' I said instead.

'Shattered.' She scowled. 'Lambing. It's mental.'

She spoke in a clipped Dublin accent and drove with the ferocious strength of someone used to pulling baby cows out of mummy cows, whether or not they wanted to be born. She shot out in front of a bus and blasted her horn at a pedestrian considering the crossing. At the next corner she took her coffee and drank deep, peering over the top as she steered around a truck. I clung to my cardboard cup. As soon as we were past the Convention Centre, I risked a slurp, instantly burning my tongue.

I muttered a curse; she gave me a look and I smiled, hoping my eyes didn't look too manic.

I tried to remember the details of the photoshoot. I'd taken notes when Karen had rung the day before. She'd apologised for the late ask but begged me to do the pet portrait, telling me how Edna and she would love to see me anyway, how they would be after hearing all about the club and how Robyn did – and how, sure, didn't this old lady want a pet portrait of her dog, and they were neighbours, Karen said. There was something else she'd mentioned about the dog, but I couldn't place it.

I patted my pocket for the notes I'd made before remembering seeing them on my shelves, next to the alarm clock. Still, the owner was an elderly lady from their village and it was only one dog so it wouldn't be that hard – the jobs that took the most time were the multiples, trying to get three or four dogs to look up together and be cute, and not to lick their bottoms or bite one another. Even worse were the cats. Any breed of dog was easier to photograph than a cat. One little dog would be fine, I told myself, stifling a yawn. And it was nice to do the O'Neils a favour. Nice that Karen and her mum wanted to give the old lady a birthday present and Karen had suggested one of my pet portraits.

She'd come and get me, no big trouble, she'd said, and the dog in question was a treasured Pekingese, a tiny little thing, hardly a bother, she said. Karen made no bones that she didn't approve of any dog smaller than a springer spaniel, but this was a little sweetie, she told me, and she and Edna were just sure I'd do a great job.

I sat back in the car and read the posters on the endless wooden boards by the docks, the gigs I often thought about going to but never quite had the money. At the big roundabout, I dug in my bag, checking I'd brought all my gear. At least it was digital, it was cheap enough. And I knew what I was doing, unlike when I first started taking pet portraits with my old camera at university. Not that I would have charged Robyn's family anyway. We did the dance, of course – I'd insisted I would do the work for free and then Karen had argued for nearly ten minutes without naming any numbers at all before I gave in and finally quoted them a tiny percentage of my usual price and promised to throw in a free frame and second choice of print if they wanted. It was Sunday, after all, I'd told her. What else was I doing? I would be delighted to help, I said. Sure, I couldn't be happier. It was the very least I could do.

I lowered myself in my seat as I remembered how Del had been at me for being more assertive about my Sundays, but it wasn't like it was a stranger, it was Robyn's family. Even when we were teenagers, and she and Robyn fought like beasts, Karen had never complained about me being there at the farm with them every weekend, however much she bit at her brother.

We swung past the docks. I put a hand over my mouth, trying to cover another yawn.

'So, any news?' she said.

'Me? Oh not really. I mean, it was Robyn's big night last night—'

'Every night is Rob's big night,' she said, rolling her eyes.

'Well . . .'

'Will you look at that – they think nothing of closing off half the bloody road for a march about something or other and they still can't sort out the mess around Capel Street.'

Karen glared as she took the thin side road, dipping into the cycle lane before popping back out into the traffic.

'But you said Rob is still sleeping?' said Karen. 'So he's OK then? He's at home? I mean, Mam was worried.'

Too late, I realised Eve's death must have been on the early morning news and how concerned she must have been.

'He's totally fine,' I said. 'Sorry. We didn't get in until late – I mean, I was late, and he was even later, but – yeah, there was this . . .'

I tried to frame the word.

'That is, after the show, there was a . . .'

Accident? Murder? I glanced at Karen as she tore through the traffic. She had never really fitted in with the city life. She was uncomfortable in crowds, always more suited to a field of cows than a bar filled with people. She and Robyn were completely different, like a lamb and a bullock born to a mare, as Grandpa Joe had once said to Edna's uncharitable chuckle.

'It was a thing that happened to someone else. Robyn is fine,' I said firmly. 'Really.' I smiled, trying not to look too terrified as she overtook a bus. 'Fast asleep but safe as houses,' I said. 'It was this thing, this attack, just down the road from—'

'Rob is OK, though?' said Karen. 'He wasn't hurt?'

'He's fine,' I told her. 'He was all done and dusted with the show and then there was this other queen, and—'

A car pulled out in front of us and Karen slammed on the brakes. She leaned out of the window and shouted at the driver. My coffee spilled over my fingers.

'Anyway, Rob is fine,' she snapped. 'Sure, that's grand then.'

She pulled into the right-hand lane and swung out around a cyclist, tipping me toward her. Holding tight to my cardboard cup I gulped down the magic creamy latté, figuring it didn't matter how hot it was as long as it was inside me and not on me. Without it I had no chance of functioning at all.

She glanced over. 'So,' she said. 'What happened?'

'Oh, at the show? It was amazing. Robyn was—'

'The one who died,' she said. 'What happened?'

Slowly, recounting everything I could remember, I told her how I'd found Eve in the gutter and how she was dead, and then how Ben called the guards and—

'Who's Ben?' she said. 'Was this Ben there . . . at the scene?'

'Yeah, I think so – although, actually, I don't really know . . .'

My words were coming out all muddled. I was going to tell her how Eve was in Robyn's drag but I stopped. He was her brother. She didn't need to know that. She was already worried enough. It wasn't fair.

'Robyn's OK,' I said again. I touched her arm. 'He's fine. Really.'

It took just under an hour to get there but as soon as we were past Swords, Karen breathed a little easier. She opened the window. I picked through my bag, hoping the little Peek would behave better than the last one. Not that I minded – I'd take photographing a hundred bitey little dogs over some of the customers we got at the shop. The money was better in photography too, and dog people were good people in the most – give or take the odd older gentleman with grabby hands, and that was exactly why I didn't go up to single men's apartments any more without either Del or Robyn. After all, as Del said, no cute little puppy pictures made up for hurting your hand by punching some bloke on the nose.

We rumbled down the village main street past the farm and up a long boreen. The white cottage at the end had settled into the land around it. Three hundred years of spiders cluttered the outside windowsills, binding their webs over the old wood, but inside, the house was spotless.

The old lady had a signed picture of Gay Byrne in the front room. We drank tea and I left Karen talking to her as I set up my equipment. The little dog was a real sweetie. At least as old as her owner in dog years and twice as canny, she watched me drape a cream cashmere blanket over one of the chairs. She leaned up and set her head to one side, questioning me. I wasn't ready but I reached for my camera. As I focussed the lens on her pretty face, she stuck out her tongue, licking her tiny nose as much to say, *Yes, I'm here, I'm bloody gorgeous, so I am, take my picture.*

I grinned. Gotcha, I thought. I knew a princess when I saw one.

I went through the other poses with her as I'd planned but by the second round, the dog was tired and her eyes dull. I pleaded and petted and dug out more packets of treats from my bag but she lay down with her head on her paws and closed her pretty eyes. I was done in every sense and in the kitchen Karen was also beginning to sound as tired as she looked. She nodded as she spoke, dipping her chin, and each time her posture was lower. They went from local gossip to the government to the GAA and back to the news. Inevitably, the death of the young drag queen was next.

'Sad business,' said the old lady. 'Not your Robyn now?'

I bent to my camera bag.

'No, not Rob,' said Karen.

'There, then.' Mrs Lansbury leaned over and patted Karen's hand. 'It's not so bad with him being a bit gay, you know, now he's a superstar drag queen,' she said.

I hid my face in my bag, smothering my giggles.

'Fi said he's fine, anyway,' said Karen. 'Sure, Rob's always fine, isn't he?' She looked at me. 'Are we done?'

I woke as Karen pulled up in front of the apartment, my stomach rolling from the scones and tea Edna had given us at the farm.

'You slept like a baby the whole way,' Karen teased me.

'I'm sorry,' I said, yet again. 'Just, you know, the late night and— Do you want to come up and—?'

'Lambing.' She sighed, her eyes already on the road ahead, and I imagined a line of sheep waiting for her at the farm gate, their legs crossed, their tummies swollen. 'Nothing doing, I'm afraid, Fi,' she said. 'Nothing doing.'

My bag had fallen open in the car while I was asleep and my equipment and kit spread itself into the footwell. I stuffed everything back without looking, the spare lenses in with my portfolio, my business cards into the little slot where I put my phone.

Finally finding my keys in my jeans pocket, I thanked Karen again, and promised to have the framed photograph ready by the following weekend. I opened the door and tripped on to the pavement. I trudged back up the three flights of stairs, cursing the weight of my bags.

If I were Robyn's family, I thought, I'd be a bit miffed that he hadn't invited them for the show. Edna was just as excited as I'd been, after all, and Karen had clearly only arranged the photography session so she could quiz me. He was all she really talked about and I didn't blame her an inch, even if an uncharitable part of me did wonder if she just wanted him to fail, to mess up so she could rib him about it, but I'd never had a sister so what did I know? I'd only ever had a best friend: a Robyn.

The apartment was empty. In the kitchen, the washing machine was already taking care of our wet clothes, the towels in the drier. Finding a Twix on my pillow, I smiled as I opened my laptop. I flicked through the news and stumbled sleepily from one story about the government to another story about the government . . . to Eve.

The picture they used was old.

An accident, it said. A tragic accident.

I set down the rest of the Twix.

They were wrong. It wasn't an accident. Someone else had been there – I'd heard heavy boots running away, I didn't imagine that

– and then there was Ben. Ben had appeared only seconds after I found her . . .

I curled deeper into my pillows.

All of us came and went from that little club without a thought as to who was hiding in the shadows, and if they were saying it was some accident . . .

I huffed.

It wasn't my business. I pulled my old Aran cardigan from the back of the chair, my last Christmas present from Edna. I slid the card from the camera into my laptop and started going through the pictures of the Pekingese. They were nice, some of them, but none were as good as the very first one with her tongue touching her nose. I played with them for a while and then drifted to Twitter, to Facebook, and to my blog.

My fingers hovered over the keyboard.

Thora had said, *Whatever terrible accident happened to Eve Harrington . . . it did not happen here.* But it did. What happened to Eve had to be connected to TRASH, one way or another. She had died only just down the road – and she was one of them. Sure, Thora had fired her, but she would have been back. Like Del said, Eve was always coming back.

And it wasn't an accident.

I'd never been very good at being hushed. I was too nosy, that was my problem. It wasn't that I wanted to be in the middle of stuff, I just liked things to make sense. A dead drag queen made no sense to me. Eve had no gunshot wounds, no abrasions around her neck, no frothing blood streaked over her lips – she wasn't run over or punched out. Her tights weren't even torn or scuffed, and her hands had been milky smooth when Ben held her fingers in his, so she hadn't fallen hard because she would have put out her hands.

She hadn't tripped and fallen at all. The only bruise was on her forehead.

The rain was insanely heavy but was it so bad no one would hear a scream? The alley where she died could not have been more than a couple of minutes' walk from the club door and people came and went down the main street all the time.

I stared out of the window into the wet street.

If it wasn't an accident then it was murder, and if the guards weren't going to do anything then maybe someone else should start asking questions. It was Dublin. It was one of the safest cities in the world – and people didn't die face down the gutter. Not in Dublin.

Chapter Six

I woke slumped in my chair with the pattern of my Aran cardigan imprinted in my cheek. It had stopped raining at last but the air was damp and the sky grey and my legs were stiff, my hips aching.

I scrubbed my hands over my face. Monday. As my vision finally swam into focus, I saw the time. I was late for work again.

I dragged myself up, grabbing at clothes, anything I could find – it didn't matter what I was wearing but it did matter if I lost my job and couldn't pay the rent. I glanced into the mirror. I looked like a feral hamster in a hot sweat. I pulled a cotton hat over my head in the vain hope that it would shield the very last remaining scrap of my pride. Two minutes later, I was running down the stairs, out into the street. I turned the corner and broke into a sprint. As I burst through the open door of Jenkins and Holster, home of Artisan Foods and Speciality Coffees, my hat finally gave up the fight and drifted to the floor, just in time for me to stand on it.

'You're late,' said Mr Jenkins.

I held my hand to my chest, panting hard. I tried to scoop the hat from the floor and smooth down my hair at the same time, but my brain still hadn't woken up and I got my fingers stuck in my tangled hair.

'Why are you late this time?' said my boss.

'I'm really sorry,' I said, still gasping for breath. 'It was the weirdest weekend and—'

Mr Jenkins eyed me with suspicion.

'It won't happen again,' I said, as I hurried through to the back room to straighten myself up.

'It will,' he muttered.

Without coffee, the first four hours at the tills passed like a thousand years, the endless ping of each item travelling over the scanner, the smell of the customers' food and of their perfume and – worse, so much worse – of their beautiful, richly made, smooth takeaway coffee. The constant noise and chatter hammered at my head.

At my lunch break, I finally made myself an enormous latté and sat outside on the wall, eating one of the reduced wraps from the day before. I was just pondering how life would ever work without caffeine when Robyn passed by on the other side of the road. I gestured for him to join me, but he shook his head, pointing in the other direction. I beckoned again – he'd been out when I got back and I was longing to tell him all about Karen and the Pekingese, and to hear what the queens had said about Eve – but he mouthed something about his mam and waved as he walked away.

I brooded, deep into my coffee.

Usually when he met Edna in town for lunch, she would pop into the shop on the way past and say hello. Sometimes she'd text me and invite me to join them, and if Edna and Karen were in town and Robyn wasn't coming, then the lunch might mean a bar and the sandwiches might end up a stiff gin and tonic all around, and Edna's face would take on the same rosy shine as Robyn's did when he drank one too many vodkas, and I'd spend the entire afternoon talking rot to the customers in Jenkins and Holster.

I still didn't have a phone, though, so no one could text me anything, and I had seen them the day before. And anyway, Robyn was hurrying away so I clearly wasn't invited.

I pulled my hat lower over my eyes. Was I looking so unkempt? No one usually minded out at the farm – working with the cows, Karen spent her life in old jeans and baggy grey fleeces, and Edna was a woman who believed in dressing for warmth and comfort.

I retreated back to the till. How anyone could go out for lunch like nothing had happened and Eve hadn't been murdered was beyond me, I decided – knowing full well that I'd have happily joined them if I'd been invited.

'Lovely day out there,' said the next customer.

'Brightening up nicely,' I replied.

I slid his cream cakes past the pinger.

I wondered if the guards had gone from house to house near the alleyway like they did on TV programmes, but there weren't really any houses there to go to and even if someone lived on the next corner, or the following one, it was dark and the rain was heavy. And anyway, the detective in charge had obviously decided it was an accident, for all the time he'd taken in figuring that out.

Mr Jenkins scurried past with his order book. I counted out the next customer's change. I smiled and I agreed, again, how it was a grand day out there and how the weather was awful at the weekend and how it was nice to treat oneself with something tasty – and had they tried our coffee, I asked them, in case Mr Jenkins was listening; the same questions, the same routine.

I watched each one of them, trying to imagine if they had been the one to kill Eve. If she was still running through their guilty dreams in Robyn's shiny red heels. If they were watching themselves killing her, over and over again. I looked at their hands as they counted out money, at their eyes as they gathered their goods.

At the very least, I thought I should pop in on the guards. Have a chat. See if they knew anything more. They might want me to sign a statement or something, since I'd been the one to find Eve.

Or to go over the details again in case they missed the glaringly obvious fact the first time around that she'd clearly been killed.

I greeted the next lady, sliding her pork tenderloin over my scales as I asked her how she was doing. In my mind, I measured the space from the club to the gutter where Eve had died.

I should definitely go back to the guards, I decided. I had nothing to hide, after all. Of everyone at TRASH that night, I was the least likely to have killed Eve. I wanted to know what had happened – I wanted to know if the coroner or the pathologist or whomever it was that dealt with these things had finally figured out how she died and if, for instance, they were officially opening a murder investigation, and if it was going to be on the news. I mean, if they wanted to interview me and therefore I was going to be on the telly as having found her – then surely it was only fair that I ask them why her shoes had fallen away like they did, and why, if she was just walking when she fell, her knees weren't scuffed and her tights weren't torn and her hands were still soft . . .

'Everything OK?' said the customer.

'Lovely day,' I told her, with another work-smile. She had a bruise on her knuckle.

'Better than yesterday,' she said.

I narrowed my eyes as I tried to imagine if she was strong enough to kill a young queen. If she were the type.

'Did you try our new blend of coffee?' I said sweetly.

I sorted the change but in my head I pictured myself on the television screen, my hair tied back neatly and my best black jeans on, and some kind of white shirt that said I didn't just dress for warmth and for comfort, and then the reporter would ask me all kinds of questions as to how I felt when I saw Eve in the water . . .

I pinged a freshly roasted bag of Columbian coffee and leaned close to inhale the smell of something other than the gutter water in my memory.

'Grand day out there,' said Mr Jenkins, as he waddled past.

'It is, so.'

'Some rain we had, yesterday. You'd never know it was nearly summer.'

Rain. Rain pooled in the gutter. Rain washing over Eve's dead face—

The silence around me prickled at my skin. Stuck behind the till, I was frozen in some kind of weird normality while the rest of the world went to pieces. I pinged cakes and coffee and dog food and mushrooms, but all I could see was Eve's face in the rain, Eve's body, lifeless, and the look on the detective's face as the TRASH family entered the dark street.

It was ten minutes before closing when the news finally reached the nice, respectable shop.

'It was a young boy,' said the first man.

'A gay kid,' said another. 'Really young, though.'

'Twenty-two.'

'It was drugs.'

'Face down in the rain, they said.'

'Sure, you can't be too careful, that time of night.'

'Evil is everywhere,' said a woman. 'Even after the vote and everything.'

I pinged three boxes of artisan muesli and a tin of handmade dark chocolates and two pears and a big box of dog biscuits and I swept my hand over the red light as if it would ping me too, and the words would come up on the screen, 'Anxious Cashier, €27.99'.

Someone else heard the victim was stabbed, another that they'd been shot.

'It was a young drag queen, they said on the news,' said Mickey, our barista.

I looked up from another box of cheese crackers.

'On the radio just now,' he said. 'Awaiting a coroner's report or something, but my mate, Henry, his brother is a guard down in Wicklow and he said—'

'I'm sure we don't need to hear what your brother's friend's something or other once said about something else or other, Mickey,' said Mr Jenkins. 'Gossip is never healthy, lad.' Mr Jenkins shuffled to the side of the doors to the last customer.

Mickey opened his mouth to respond again, but the clock had finally hit the hour and Mr Jenkins eased the lady to the door, rattling his keys. 'Thank you,' he said loudly. 'Good night, then, madam. Have a good evening now, won't you?'

'It's—' Mickey started.

Jenkins glared past me, cutting Mickey's words, ending the conversation. I waited for another lecture on how we didn't need blabbermouth conversation and how gossip ruined lives and I turned to the till, busying myself at tidying the notebook with the barcodes.

Jenkins tapped on my pinger.

'Your friend is here.' He rolled his eyes comically and then winked through the glass at Robyn. 'Shall I lock him out, so?'

I glanced at Mickey but he'd obviously given up trying to tell us whatever the thing was about his brother the guard, or his friend's brother, or the story that now burned in my brain like an unfinished chapter. Nodding to me, Mickey drew two lattés in takeaway cups and placed them by the till.

Robyn knocked politely at the door.

'Fi?' said Mr Jenkins.

'Go on with him,' I said, grinning. I put the money in the till for my coffees. 'Toss him from the step.'

'Ah, she's a bold one,' Jenkins said to Robyn.

'I'm led by my peers,' I told him.

'No one's tossing anyone anywhere,' said Robyn. 'I'll have you know this is a place of good repute.'

He bowed. Mr Jenkins passed him a spare cream slice wrapped in a plastic container.

'Last one, sonny.'

'You spoil me,' said Robyn.

'Well, someone has to. You're terrible skinny again, boy.'

'I spoil him all the time,' I complained. 'No one gives me cream slices.'

'Don't listen to her,' said Robyn. 'It's lies! All lies. I'm withering away.'

Mickey let out a short huff, covering it with a squirt of the steamer.

'Come and work for me, lad. You can job share with Fi, here,' said Mr Jenkins. 'Your time keeping is better than hers – you can work the morning shift.'

'Our Fi thrives on the pressure of having a reason to get out of bed,' said Robyn.

I left the two of them messing with one another as I cashed up the till, but when Mickey went back to get his coat, I scuttled in behind him.

'What did your man from Wicklow say?'

I plucked my coat from the peg as if I hadn't been watching him for the ask.

'Shocking business,' he said. 'Your little friend is here for you again, though?'

His choice of adjective rubbed against my spine, but Mr Jenkins burst into the back space and stared at us as if we'd be planning on sneaking out of the tiny window and over the ten-foot-tall wire gate there, with cream cakes stuffed into our pockets. Jenkins planted himself between us and started on about Mickey's hours for the following week, and about needing to run a stock check and how he'd really like us to take a proper clean of the end shelves there, right underneath them—

Once Jenkins had an idea, he was unmovable. I could wait, I decided. After all, there was nothing I could do anyway.

I shivered as I walked back through the store. I straightened a line of postcards.

Maybe Eve'd had a heart attack. Maybe a stroke. Maybe she'd taken something and her brain was messy, or she'd drunk more than we thought, or she'd turned to see someone and she'd twisted her ankle or she'd been running away from a man in the dark or—

Or any number of questions that no one was asking.

It was the messiness that bothered me the most. The lack of resolution. Folks didn't just die like that, tucked away in the shadows. It wasn't right.

I'd ask Mickey again in the morning, I decided, and make him tell me what his man from Wicklow knew about Eve's death. I'd find the time and the right space. I'd ask him outright if I had to, over the counter, when Jenkins went out for his mid-morning stroll along the pavement to check the storefront was all it should be. After all, even if it was just gossip, at least it would be something, and it couldn't hurt if I knocked on a few doors, maybe asked a few of the locals.

'You OK, girl?'

Robyn took the coffee cup from me and held out a bag from his fancy shop, a new phone inside. I leaned up and kissed him, and smiled.

'Thank you. I'll blip the money over to your bank. So, how's Edna today?' I said.

'Ma? Oh, um . . .' He stared at his feet.

'Did you not meet her for lunch?'

We walked on together but something was different. Something had shifted in the air between us. I could see his face working as

I knew mine was, but neither of us spoke. He didn't apologise for not coming home with me, after Eve, and I didn't apologise for using his phone and not waking him the day after, and going out with his sister.

'You want to get takeout tonight?' he said.

'I'm not hungry.'

'You are, so. You're always hungry.'

I sipped on my coffee, feeling sicker than ever.

'Come on.' Robyn nudged my arm. 'Let's eat at the Mongolian.'

I hummed and haaed as we walked, and I changed the subject and thanked him for picking up the phone – and he cut across me.

'Wait . . . you're sulking because I went out for lunch without you?' he said.

'I'm not, so.'

'I met Thora, actually, if you want to know.'

Of course he did.

'Don't be mad,' he said. 'It's different now. Thora is my drag mother.'

The muscles around my jaw clamped down. We crossed the road in sync. Robyn had longed to be in this world. For years we'd heard Del talk about his drag family just as a real family. And Del had a loving, caring birth family too, as much as Robyn did. And I'd encouraged Robyn right from the beginning. I knew how much he loved drag. From the clothes to the wigs to the sheer glittering fabulousness of it all. I saw how he'd yearned for the spotlight. He was happy now, and I was happy for him, of course I was, even if that meant I couldn't follow him on to the stage.

We crossed the road, our steps matching perfectly in time.

'We haven't been to the Mongolian for ages,' said Robyn.

'Because you said you were over it.'

'Yeah, but there's this cute guy working there. And they have noodles. Noodles are our happy food,' he said.

'I live my life pandering to you, Robyn O'Neil.'

'Then you should be better at it by now.'

We crossed again, toward Temple Bar. He tucked his hand into mine.

'I know you, Fi. You're obsessing,' he said.

'I am not.'

'Eve's death has nothing to do with us – let it go.'

I shrugged.

'You're too far inside your own head, Fiona McKinnery,' said Robyn, full-naming me in return. 'We're having noodles, and that's that.'

He grinned and gently shook my hand, rattling me out of my sulk, and I followed him into the little restaurant, but even as we queued up to fill our bowls, as we tried to talk about everything under the sun that wasn't Eve or the rain or the guards or murder, by the time we reached the table our conversation had ground to a halt and we both stared at the food on our plates.

Even in death, Eve Harrington was a nightmare.

Chapter Seven

Three days passed and still the guards seemed to think that Eve had dropped dead of her own accord. None of the others at the club would talk to me about it. Robyn kept teasing that if I didn't let it go, he'd get me a magnifying glass and a deerstalker hat, but after a while even he simply changed the subject or walked away. The press let it drop, the customers in the shop stopped talking about her, and it seemed to me as though Eve's death had been washed away down the gutter with the rain.

I tried to let go of it – I really did – but it was always there, a tickertape of fear through my mind. The idea that there was someone here, someone who had taken Eve's life.

Thursday night, I left the shop late after an unbearable eight hours stuck on the till, with Mickey on the coffee and Jenkins constantly drifting between us, chiding me for not being smiley enough and snapping at Mickey that he should get on with his work if he knew what was good for him, and nearly exploding every time I brought up the topic of Eve's death. When Jenkins finally sent Mickey out the back after his lunch hour, demanding he use the time to sort through all the old boxes and tubs and things that had been there for many months – a job that could certainly have waited another year – I realised this was no normal grumble for our boss. The more Jenkins tried to keep us apart, the more I wanted to know what it was that Mickey had to say.

Finally heading out, I pulled on the belt of my coat, tightening it against the grey drizzle that hung over the city. Jenkins had kept me late to go through my following week's shifts – not that they ever changed – and Mickey was away twenty minutes before and would be long gone. I looked around the street anyway, watching for his lanky frame and dark hair.

Mr Jenkins hurried out alongside me, peering from the door like a mole.

'Something wrong, Fi?' he said. 'No friend?'

No, I thought. Robyn hadn't met me after work since the Monday. Not that it mattered – hell, he didn't have to – but we always met at the shop at closing. Sometimes I got coffee, sometimes he did – sometimes we went out for dinner and sometimes he rushed home for a date, or out to the farm to see his mum – but we always met there.

Now, everything was wrong. The world was upside down.

'Maybe he's late,' said Jenkins.

I smiled, forcing up the corners of my mouth. 'Working, I expect,' I said, although I knew full well the phone shop would be closed.

I hitched my bag a little higher on my shoulder and started off down the street. I was hungry and tetchy but I couldn't face the apartment the way it had been for the past three nights, with Robyn twitching and biting his nails and constantly changing the subject away from Eve's death whenever I raised it, and then dashing out at eight thirty with his face bare and his drag-bag stuffed full, scarcely even saying goodnight as he ran out to the club without me, only creeping back in at gone two.

Which was fine, I reminded myself. It was all just absolutely bloody fine.

I sloshed through the streets. I'd been down there before but this time I looked at every stone on the ground, every mark on the wall. I turned left. I frowned as I worked through the latest interview I'd had with the gardaí, that lunchtime. If I could even have called it an interview. I was barely sure they'd wanted to see me at all. I told them that I'd assumed there would be a formal process at the very least, and that someone would be looking for Eve's killer, but as the guard on the front desk took my details, yet again, I could see by her face that she was merely running through the paperwork. Tidying the edges, that was all. She had no note even that I'd contacted them since it had happened, and no notion to make one, as Edna would have said. They had no intention of investigating how Eve had died.

I had told them I thought I should pop in. I answered the basic questions again, and I confirmed how I had found the body, where I'd been and where I lived, and my new phone number. I spoke and the guard nodded. Her auburn curls were frozen in place by a thick layer of hairspray. Then she typed and I said some more. I could have said a whole bunch, but she clearly didn't need anything else, and I could tell by the tone of her voice that she was pandering to me just as I pandered to Robyn when he worried about a dress or about a pair of shoes, or about any number of unimportant things.

'Do you have any suspects?' I'd asked.

'Sorry?'

'For the murder.' I pulled myself up, still picturing that white shirt.

'Murder?' The garda barely hid her smile. 'We don't believe this death was suspicious,' she said, speaking slowly and clearly.

'How much more suspicious does it need to be? She died for no reason, face down in a puddle six inches deep.'

'According to the file here, there was considerable bruising on his forehead, and considering the circumstances . . .'

'Eve's sexuality, or her job as a drag queen?' I said.

The woman pursed her lips. I was right. I saw it in her eyes. She sat back in her chair.

'We can only really discuss the matter with family,' she told me.

'So you think she just happened to die there?'

'Are you related to Mr Flanagan?'

She'd just taken my details. She knew full well that I was no more Eve's cousin than she was. She crossed her arms.

I'd made it weird.

'Look,' I said. 'I didn't know Eve's family but—'

'Liam's,' she corrected me.

I paused. Then I smiled, with no humour at all. 'Eve's,' I said again.

'Liam's. His. He was a man.'

True, I thought, but we'd gone way beyond truth. We'd reached petty, and I may not be able to walk in heels, but I am Queen of Petty.

'She was a man who preferred the female pronoun when she was in drag,' I said sweetly. 'If a queen is in drag, she is her drag name and her chosen pronoun.' I slowed until I matched the speed she'd used for me earlier. 'Most go with the female pronoun. Although there are some, like Del Peen, who use the male pronoun.' I was being pedantic but the woman was annoying me. 'If he was in his boy clothes, he would be Liam. She died in drag. She is Eve.'

The woman pursed her lips. 'He's not in drag now,' she said.

We were getting on so well.

The clock ticked behind her.

With a long sigh, the garda pushed back from the desk and disappeared through the interior door. I stood, leaning against the counter. Behind me, two other women came in, their hair ruffled by the weather, their countenance no less pointed than mine. They saw me in the way and tutted.

The interior door opened with a waft of cheap, instant coffee. The detective from the alley pushed out his chest as he came up to the counter.

'Thanks for coming in,' he said. 'Fi? Is that right? Fiona McKinnery?'

'Hi.'

'And you were there when Liam Flanagan died?'

'I was there after,' I said. From petty to pertinacious. 'I found Eve already dead.'

'Liam.'

'Eve.'

This was also going well.

I ran my hands through my hair but my fingers stuck on a small piece of jam sandwich from my lunch. I tried to slide my hand back down to my side. The jam dislodged and plopped on the floor.

'So you are here to . . . ?'

'To enquire about Eve's death,' I said. 'And to answer any questions you might have had about it, of course – about what I might have seen, you know? Detective, I was thinking about it, and—'

'Where do you work? Oh, I have it here.' He ran his thumb down the computer screen. 'Jenkins and Holster? They do a good meringue pie.'

'They do. And good coffee.'

'My mother shops there when she wants to impress the neighbours,' he said. 'And what was it, exactly, that you were thinking about Liam Flanagan, Miss McKinnery?'

White shirt. White shirt. White shirt. 'I think Eve was murdered,' I said.

'Ah.' He sounded weary. He was only a little older than me, but his suit was creased and he smelled slightly fusty. His eyes were dull, as if he hadn't slept and he held himself just a little too high in his esteem, for me. If I'd been photographing him, I'd have set him against a grey background and focussed on the slight lines around his eyes where the softness came unwilling to his face. He had a good jaw. He could have been good-looking, I thought, if he hadn't been such a dick.

'He was wearing fancy dress and ridiculous shoes on a rough-cut road,' he said. 'End of story.'

How could the detective not see that Eve could never have tripped and knocked herself out, like that – she wore heels all the time: sky high, spindly little heels.

I'd told him that. How could he not listen to me?

'We'll let you know if there's anything else we need from you,' he said, with the same half smile as his co-worker.

'Did you question them at all?' I said.

'Question whom?'

'The other queens.'

I tugged my hair back from my eyes, then gripped the counter as I realised what I was saying.

In for a penny . . .

'Did you ask them where they were?' I said. 'Did you contact all the people who were at TRASH, and do that thing where you map out everyone's positions and then make a list of everyone who had a grievance with Eve? Because believe me, Detective, I have, and that list is pretty long.'

'Is there a reason you think we should question your friends?'

'Well, no,' I said. 'No, of course not. But—'

The detective reached over and patted my hand.

'Liam died in a tragic accident. Now, I won't keep you,' he said. 'I imagine those meringue pies won't sell themselves.' He smiled, as

76

if I were one of Karen's small bleating sheep, waiting to be pacified. 'Sometimes,' he told me, 'things just happen. We look to blame when we are grieving. It's natural. But that doesn't mean we are right.'

I was herded from the building. I waited until I was around the corner and then said a very bad word indeed.

All afternoon my irritation festered and boiled and by the time I'd finished work and was walking down the long road past the church, I was no less riled up thinking about it all. Not that I wanted my friends to be in trouble with the guards, but when someone dies – and that person was dressed up as someone I really care about – I want to know why.

I ground my teeth as I walked.

Each one of the queens at TRASH loathed Eve, both as her drag self and as her boy self, and if they pretended otherwise then they were lying – not just to me, but to one another. There was something shady going on. Even Robyn was being weird. And while I could not believe Robyn would kill anyone, the way he refused to talk about Eve's death, it felt like even he was hiding something.

Walking away from the throng of Dame Street, I tried to centre my mind. I rounded the corner by the church.

The tape was gone.

The street was just a normal street, with no imagined white outline on the rain-soaked road and no cones, no security guarding the running gutter. Behind me, traffic curled along the thin road and in the darkening sky a single gull screamed as it played in the soft, rolling clouds. People moved along the main street but no one walked down the lane there, almost as if they knew, as if the ghostly presence of murder had stained the air.

I tucked in to one of the doorways and pressed my back against the old black door. I set my head to one side and focussed on the spot where I had found her. I noticed a small bouquet of flowers and a little cross tied to the drainpipe.

Was it worse to die in such a miserable, dour little street? Or did the mere act of death supersede any indignity of the manner and circumstance? If Eve could have chosen, I'd think she'd have fallen from some great height in front of a huge crowd, her body turning and twisting gracefully in the air. She'd have preferred something dramatic, not a forgettable space in the shade where no one would see her flowers.

I had pictures of her on my laptop. Photos I'd taken over the years. Eve in the background with the classic blond wig. Eve behind Del with her open-mouthed grin, the sweetie-pink lipstick and the sparkling, richly painted eyes. And then all of us together from a night at Del's – the only shots I had of Eve as her boy self, his peach-coloured shirt done up to the collar, his hair controlled and careful, his face poised as he looked up and smiled at some-one just out of shot.

I'd never seen Eve looking kindly at anyone. I wondered who the person was.

I stepped out from the door. Robyn was right. I was obsess-ing. It had been so wet – so crazy, insanely wet – that night. My jeans had been pure soaked from kneeling in the road, right up to mid-thigh. She'd fallen, they said – but if she'd tripped on her own and she'd knocked herself out, surely there would have been more bruising on her face, not just that tiny mark? She'd been drinking, but not so much she couldn't perform onstage.

The way she'd faked her wobbles and twists – and the way she'd leaned right back on her heels without falling – was a bitchy, nasty little performance, but it was also clever, as much as it pained me to think that. The way she stole each of Robyn's insecurities as Mae B and displayed them up for the crowd with her cartoonish ghoul, that was something someone could only do if they were both relatively sober and also fairly physically stable.

If it was down to me in those heels, I'd have staggered into a wall and knocked the speakers flying, but Eve knew full well what she was doing.

I turned back toward the club and then came around, as I had that night. I walked the pace of the street from where Eve would have turned into the shadows, to where she last lay. No cobbles. Not even any troughs. True, there were doorsteps on the side and some of the paving slabs were uneven, and it had been dark enough to hide any number of villains in the inset doorways. I clapped my hands and shrieked, looking up and around at the high windows, but every glass was faded and dusty, many painted over, many boarded, and there were no faces looking down through the remaining windows. In an experiment, I screamed an ear-splitting cry.

Nothing happened.

No one came running.

It wasn't the rain or the night. If Eve had had time to cry out, no one would have heard.

I knocked on each door, calling up a greeting. The air was still.

I took my spare camera from my bag, my little point-and-shoot. I didn't really consider what I was doing or why, but taking pictures of things helped me think. I took long shots, close shots. I focussed on the gutter.

I tried to remember exactly how she had looked: her legs sprawled, slightly too wide, her dress rucked up but not pulled over her hips. Her body flat to the ground. I tried to remember how her arms had been and how her hands were floating slightly in the water.

I'd stopped where I first saw the flash of red. Was it then that I'd heard the footsteps? I'd turned her body, and I remembered the rush of relief that it wasn't Robyn.

One of her shoes had fallen from her foot. The red sky-high heels that I'd finally found online in Robyn's size and that he had saved for, for months, only buying them when his mum offered him half the money – the heels he'd treasured, kicking together like Dorothy, knowing they were real drag shoes and strong enough for him to dance in and high enough, bright enough, insane enough for the look he'd so wanted as his debut.

I pictured them as they had fallen, with Eve, into the water.

It was before I saw her, that I'd heard the footsteps. Heavy, clunking, catching in the rain. Footsteps that could only mean one thing. Someone else had been there that night. Whether they were there to kill, or whether they had seen the killer, someone knew what had happened.

Chapter Eight

The weekends were the busiest time of the week for TRASH, so I figured I'd be less likely spotted in the Sunday night crowd. I didn't tell Robyn I was going, but then he didn't ask, either. I read through my list of notes I'd made so far about Eve's death.

I filed in with the others, standing far away from the square seats, and away from Mark and from Mae B and the other queens. There was no reason why I shouldn't be there, I told myself firmly. None whatsoever. It was a public bar after all and if I asked a few people whether they'd been at the club that night, and if I took a look around, then I was no different to anyone else. Half the customers were talking about Eve's death anyway, even if they were convinced she'd simply fallen over and knocked herself out, drowning in the rain. And sure, as one of the pretty young men said with a roll of his eyes, it couldn't have happened to a nicer person.

As Del walked through the crowd in his Marie Antoinette wig and giant frock, I ducked back behind a column. You always know when you're doing something you shouldn't be doing, my dad used to tell me, even if you don't want to admit it. I downed my drink and turned back to the bar for another.

The house lights dropped as the show began. Miss Merkin started. Stuck behind all the tall people as I was, I couldn't really see her. As soon as the other queens had gone backstage, I crept up the spiral stairs. I slipped into the balcony usually used by Mark on the follow spot and by the DJs, and one time, the summer before, by me, when Del arranged for me to take a heap of promotional shots for TRASH's social media.

Sliding unseen on to one of the benches, I watched as Merkin danced on the stage in her white PVC boots and sparkling rainbow tinsel dress. The song was ridiculous and very funny, and she moved with surprising agility considering how much she complained about her aches and pains. Switching and walking like a duck in a toilet roll, she pushed her knees forward and nudged her huge, round boobs into place. I laughed with the others, and a braver woman than me called out from the crowd. In her sharp Cork accent, Merkin bit back, setting off a torrent of stupid from the woman. Miss Merkin stopped the music to rip into the heckler, leaving the crowd roaring and the woman speechless, before the show picked right up and Merkin slid seamlessly back into her routine.

A movement to my right caught my eye. Thora was standing on the platform, looking not at the stage but at me.

'Our little straight girl.' She looked me up and down but there was nothing malicious in her glance. 'You're here alone? On our balcony.'

I sat bolt upright, refusing to flinch in front of her.

Thora lowered herself on to the bench beside me. Another roar of laughter filled the hall as Merkin took to the mic again, and ripped into the crowd. She was born funny and she took no prisoners, a guaranteed gift for the rest of an audience even if it brought out the gladiators. She went into the next song – an old musical number I knew but couldn't place.

'Watch this bit,' said Thora.

Midway through the first verse the track changed, splitting seamlessly between a Katherine Hepburn sketch and a *Golden Girls* snippet, and then back to the song. Merkin lip-synched perfectly in time to both the spoken words and the music, and the crowd drank it in.

'It's not fair. She made her dress there for three quid in nineteen eighty-nine,' said Thora. 'And her make-up took her ten minutes, applied using the back of a spoon.'

I giggled. Thora and Merkin had been friends for many years and rarely missed the opportunity to snipe at one another, however exaggerated the claims.

'She doesn't give a rat's arse, see?' Thora nodded to the stage. 'She has complete confidence. She knows who she is. Ah now,' she said, as the number finished. 'Now I think this is more what you came for?'

Merkin left the stage to more thunderous applause and Mark climbed in behind us, up to the spotlight. The house lights dimmed, and the follow spot wobbled. I glanced back, and Mark waved.

'I don't think you've seen this number,' said Thora.

The curtains opened a crack and Mae B peeped out, her mouth open wide. I grinned. I couldn't help it, she looked so funny, and she was clearly trying to amuse as much as to entertain. The music started, the old stripper music by Joe Loss – long, comic trombones, high trumpets, big bass swelling loud into the club. As Mae B stumbled on to the stage, she wobbled in and out of the circle of light, feeling her way to the edge before screwing up her face and falling back. But this time, unlike the first night, her wobbles were wildly overdone and really very funny. She teetered on a new pair of shiny black high heels like a sexy baby deer. She wore satin gloves and fishnet stockings and black suspenders, and a black cincher and black bra, and a loose red robe, fastened at the waist, barely covering anything, and as the song grew, she pulled at the tie of her robe as if to start stripping, but the tie stuck. She tugged and squirmed, and then turned around so the audience could see her yank at the cord, finally ripping it from her gown and sending it flying into the crowd. She started to pull at one of her gloves but that stuck as well, and she tugged and ripped it back, stumbling, falling forward. Screwing up her big mouth, she caught the joke with the crowd – she flung the glove toward them, then nearly toppled forward after it, fake-teetering right on the edge of the stage. Over and over again, she stripped and fell, and stripped and fell, and the audience laughed with her, cheering and clapping as each piece finally came off.

It was funny, but . . .

I looked at Thora. She was watching me.

'You don't get it,' she said.

Then it clicked.

'She's taking back her act?' I said. 'She's . . . she's taking it back from Eve?'

Behind us, Mark chuckled, not at the act but at me. Thora's mouth stretched into a wide, Cheshire Cat smile, her fat lipstick framing her teeth. Her breath smelled of whiskey. There was a faint spattering of stubble on her upper lip.

'You don't approve, Fi,' she said.

I didn't. It was too soon. I was the queen of making things weird but this made things very weird indeed. It was just over a week since Eve stole Mae B's routine and then died in her outfit.

Was Mae B laughing at Eve, as well as at herself? Was that even OK?

Thora's steely eyes bored into mine. 'She said you wouldn't approve.'

'I don't think it's up to me,' I said.

She leaned closer. 'Drag was never meant to be nice,' she whispered.

The song slid into the middle hook. Thora stood and brushed out her skirts. She climbed quickly down the stairs and as Mae B whipped off her bra, wildly overplaying the comic wince as tape flew from her nipple, Thora stepped up on to the stage, clapping and cheering with everyone else.

Mark slipped in beside me.

'So, you came back to TRASH,' he said.

I'd been before, I wanted to tell him. Tons of times.

Still, I wasn't Robyn. I was Background. Audience.

I wondered if that was how it felt for Karen, growing up alongside such a beautiful boy. Not that I minded one scrap. I'd never been one for the spotlight, steady or otherwise. And Karen and Robyn had figured out their differences in the end. Mostly. Or else they'd buried them deep enough that they only spilled out when one or both of them were drinking something other than Edna's legendary strong tea.

Karen had the farm, anyway. I couldn't picture a time when she wasn't calf-deep in mud, mucking out horses or cows, or whatever it was she did there. That was hardly the moment for a shiny dress and high heels. She was like me. She was born to stand behind the pretty ones, even if they never saw us in the shade.

Nancy Sinatra blared from the speakers and Thora chased Mae B along the stage, the baby queen laughing as she ran from Thora's big silver boots, ably tripping and dancing across the boards, still playing the character.

'You think it's strange?' said Mark.

'Not strange.'

Different, I thought. *Wrong*.

'She's good,' he went on. 'See . . . look at how she moved across the stage there, even as she's wobbling around. Total confidence. It's like Thora was saying about Merkin. And there's not many that can stand alongside Thora Point and still keep their eye. See the way she looks at the crowd? She holds their gaze, she plays with each one of them. She knows, and they know that she knows. It's a game, that's the secret. Knowing – really knowing – who you are.'

Mae B crouched behind Thora with her face turned to the light, the shadows caught from her cheekbones. I lifted my phone and took a quick shot. I wished I had my camera. I longed to take picture after picture of her, to frame her beautiful face, and her lush, padded curves.

She was tremendous.

'That can't be taught,' said Mark. 'It can be faked, like Eve faked it—'

'But everyone said how good Eve was,' I said.

'She was, but it wasn't real. You can't tell, down there – this is my nest you've wandered into, baby girl. Up here, they can't hide,' he said. 'You see the light in their eyes. Underneath Eve's cocky arrogance there was a frightened little boy desperate for his father's attention in any way, shape or form he could get it.'

I raised my eyebrows. Del always said that Eve's drag was more like a mask that enabled her to be beautifully unpleasant.

'Oh, come on, no one turns that nasty for no reason,' said Mark.

'Was she nasty to you?'

'Eve was nasty to everyone. And don't you start that.' Mark waggled his finger. 'Robyn's told us all about you, Fi. You've been sniffing and sniping and asking questions all over the place.'

I opened my mouth and then closed it again, realising that of all the millions of things I wanted to say, everyone one of them was a question.

Mark shrugged. 'I knew Liam when he was nothing more than a twink with an expensive taste for older men,' he said. 'And trust me, Eve didn't bring out the best in him.'

The crowd let up a cheer at something onstage.

'Thora's not faking,' I said.

'That old cow is terrifying,' Mark laughed. 'In or out of drag, there's nothing about her that isn't real. Merkin is the same and Del is just adorable, whatever he wears. But Mae B, there? I've been up here ten years now, in one shape or another,' he said. 'And over that time, we've seen a fair few young ones wash through the club scene. Half of them give up when they realise how hard it is or how expensive the kit can be, and a handful more just get bored, lose interest in the long haul. They don't want to put in the work – they think it should be easy. Mae B has a gift. The audience are like Plasticine to her. She tells them with every flick of those pretty pink nails that she knows what they want even if they don't know it yet themselves. They're desperate to follow her and love her.'

'She's really that good?' I said, squinting at the two queens onstage.

'Well, not quite,' said Mark. 'But she will be. Give her time. If the club can stay open long enough for her to grow into her heels – and let her ease into the bigger wigs that Del has lent her, the new dresses Merkin is making . . . Mae B will outstrip every queen here in this ratty, tatty little castle. I'd put money on it if I had any.'

'Is the business really going that badly?'

I watched as Thora finished her act. The crowd were happy, but from the balcony I could see the bar staff were barely stretched. Mark fixed his eyes on mine. The music was too loud, the lights flickering, but he didn't blink. I looked down at his big feet.

'Were you there?' I said. 'Was it you that I heard, running away in the alley?'

'I thought you were going to ask me if she really stole from us,' he said.

'Did she?'

'Every penny she could,' he said.

Ben looked in from the door. He held two drinks, his own gin and tonic – a single ice cube bobbing in the mix – and an open bottle of beer. He started toward Mark, then saw me.

On the stage, Del took Thora's place.

'You're here to watch?' I said.

'Sorry?' said Ben.

'To watch Del?'

'Oh.' He smiled. 'Sure. Are you here to . . . ?'

To ask questions? To figure out what happened to Eve?

I smiled. 'I should probably go,' I said.

'Don't leave on my account,' said Ben.

As I slid past him, I breathed in his warm, spicy aftershave. 'Del looks amazing tonight,' I told him, gesturing toward the stage.

Ben nodded. 'Who doesn't love latex?' he said, but he hadn't looked at the stage once.

I crept back down the stairs. I stood behind a group of women, but alone in the crowd just wasn't the same as a night out with Robyn. After Del, there was a group number I'd seen before, and as the first notes of the Little Mix classic came roaring from the speakers, this time it was Mae B and not Eve who ran up onstage with Merkin, Thora and Del. She was wearing the silver dress and a wig I didn't recognise, darker than the scarlet waves that Eve had stolen. It flowed over her shoulders like silk. Her dress glittered and shone, the sequins catching every light, and she had on a chin choker at her neck, but there was something more than just her outfit that had changed in the few days since I saw her debut. Mark was right. A new confidence and pride ran through her performance like a thread of steel.

The group worked the number to its core and as it finished, I clapped and cheered with the others until my palms were red raw, and I grinned. Forgetting myself, I called out.

Mae B saw me.

She hesitated – not for long, not even much more than a second – but I knew her too well. I knew the look in her eyes. It was the look she gave when she didn't want to see someone.

Chapter Nine

A shadow of doubt, a worry I'd been trying so hard to ignore, sunk into my belly.

In a panic, I hurried back to the bar and eagerly over-ordered. I bought a double whiskey on the rocks for Thora, and vodka and oranges for Mae B and Del, and a gin and tonic with a single ice cube for Ben, and another beer, and a double shot of vodka for me, because by that point I might as well soften the blow – and I handed over my credit card and mentally said goodbye to the purple fluffy cushion in Dunnes' sale.

I made my way through the crowd, excusing myself and apologising and holding out the glasses. Drinks for the drag queens, I told them, coming through with drinks for the drag queens.

'Fi,' said Thora, as I made it through the throng. 'Ah, I knew we kept you for a reason.'

Del took his with a kiss. We chatted for a minute, but I could not stay focussed. Mae B hung back, just far enough away so I couldn't hear what she was saying, talking to a good-looking guy in a tight white t-shirt and black jeans.

I found myself standing alone, beside her, the last drink in my hand. The good-looking man glared at me. Mae B moved, just a fraction, until she had her back to me. I tapped her arm. It was warm, her skin sticky with sweat.

She took the drink and smiled, but then started to turn again.

'It's busy tonight,' I said.

'Why wouldn't it be?'

She didn't look at me when she spoke. The sheer ice wall that I'd felt between us became a mountain, a world, a bloody universe.

'You're up, Mama,' said Del, calling from the steps.

Thora bustled past me, her glass already empty. The next part of the show was due to start, and I'd barely even said hello to Mae B.

Mark was watching me.

I blinked.

He was tall – well over six foot and built to last – and he'd proved that he could overpower Eve when he carried her, kicking and screaming from the stage. He hated her just as much as the others did, and he had been outside that night. His hair had been wet . . .

He brushed past Mae B, resting his hand on her shoulder.

'We need you up for the last again,' he said.

'Sure thing.' She smiled prettily as she spoke, lowering her lashes, flashing her teeth.

Behind us, Ben came down the stairs. Del stepped to the side. Mark moved back – they were shadowing one another like a play, like a dance.

'Did you watch me?' Del said to Ben.

'I missed it,' he said. 'I'm sorry, love – I was just fixing one of the rails in the coatroom for Thora. I didn't realise you were on.'

'Did you watch?' Mae B said to me, echoing Ben's question.

'You were great,' I told her quickly. 'And I loved the silver – and the group number was really good, and—'

And I know it was the same number that Eve used to do with the others, I wanted to say. You were standing in the same place that Eve used to stand.

'Del gave me these shoes,' she said.

'They're fab.'

Del grimaced. 'Too big for me. Shame. They're pretty.'

'No shame for me,' said Mae B.

She lowered her lashes again, long black whips curled up to high brows. She stood with her hands down by her sides, but I could see the flinch where she wanted to set them on her hips. I could see the muscle twitch in her cheek where she wanted to snarl and bite.

Gone were the nervous twitches and the delicate lowering of her eyes, and gone was the torturous humiliation and the embarrassment that had hung so heavily over her after Eve's mocking performance. In fact, Mae B seemed almost a different person to the one who had stood in her first heels in our cramped little apartment by the river.

'What?' she said.

Pain lodged in my throat.

Mae had moved on. She was happy. She was in her element. The last thing she wanted – I could see it written all over her pretty, painted face – was someone to remind her what had happened before, what had happened to Eve. Her predecessor. If the floor had opened up, I would have stepped willingly into its mouth.

I should not have come to TRASH.

I started to back away. 'I'll catch you later,' I muttered.

'But you have a full drink?'

'You can have it.'

'Fi, was there something you wanted?' she said.

Not this, I thought.

Maybe it was just a weird night. Everyone had weird nights. Only a few days before, there had been nothing in the world that would come between us. Now, it was a million miles from my hold to hers. Maybe we were all a bit tense and a bit scarred. Del was bitching with Merkin. Beside me, Mark now watched Thora, worry etched all over his face. No one was settled. Not even Thora on the stage. Was it just that – a cruel shadowy night – or had Eve, even in her death, managed to mess with us all?

I pulled on my jacket. I should have spoken to Mae B again but there was nothing I could think of saying that would help.

Mark had followed me to the door.

'Mae B needs to move on from what happened,' he said with a grunt.

'Here we are again,' I told him. 'Family only, eh?'

'She felt that certain . . . events . . . clouded her debut.' Mark put his heavy hand on the door frame. 'Thora explained how we all need to move on,' he said. 'It's done. There's nothing anyone could do to bring Eve back so it's best to leave the whole messy business well alone.'

'Of course.'

'You say that as if you almost meant it, Fi.'

'I do,' I said.

Behind him, Del came bustling through the main door. Mark relaxed his hold on the wall, checked his stance.

'Did you see where Ben was while I was onstage?' said Del.

'No, why?' said Mark.

'I . . . No, OK, it doesn't matter.' Del started up the stairs. The backs of his ankles looked raw even through three pairs of tights.

As I looked back, Mark was gone.

Again, it was past two when Robyn came home.

'Christ, my feet,' he hissed to himself as he closed the door. I looked out of the kitchen. He saw me, lifted one hand in a wave, and I did the same, my scrubbing sponge in my hand. He came into the room. I started to speak when he brushed his t-shirt and a tiny cloud of sequins flittered into the air and drifted, sticking to anything they found, clinging to the cooker and the kettle and the table legs and the dust on the floor. Both of us watched them, and then I carried on cleaning the kitchen sink, scrubbing at the aluminium like I hated it.

'What?' he said. He put his hands on his hips. 'What's the problem?'

'Nothing.'

I pulled open the press and started wiping the shelves, jostling the cans and jars to the side. Robyn peeled off his t-shirt and shoved it into the washing machine. His skin was sore where the bra straps and the cincher had cut into him, and there was a light pink flush on his chest, maybe a rash, maybe a reaction to the make-up or to Del's spare silicone boobs.

Mr Jenkins was right. Robyn had lost weight.

I brushed more glitter from the counter. 'It gets everywhere,' I snapped.

'You didn't like the silver?' he said.

'I always liked the silver.'

I scrubbed at the taps.

I didn't like touching dead queens in the gutter, that was all, I thought. And I wanted to go back to when I just slept without dreams. And when we ate pasta packets, and toast, and when we could both be in the flat at the same time. And when I knew what he was thinking. What he'd done.

I spun around, tugging my hair out of my eyes, leaning in to scrub at the back of the cupboard.

'Ah, come on, Fi,' he started.

'Come on yourself, Robyn.'

'Why are you being like this?' he said.

I closed the cupboard door and started on the front. 'I'm being like nothing,' I told him, fully aware I was being like everything with every swipe of my cloth, but incapable of stopping.

'You're cleaning,' he said. 'You hate cleaning.'

'I like things to be clean.'

'No, you don't, you like them tidy, which is a completely different thing. And it's the middle of the bloody night.' He opened the fridge, stared at the contents, and then closed it again. 'You're pointedly cleaning,' he said. 'You stayed up for a reason – you came into the club for a reason—'

'I came to support you.' I turned to the shelf so he couldn't see the lie. 'But . . .'

'What?' he said. 'You have something to say, say it to my face.'

'I didn't say a single thing.'

'You did, you huffed.'

'I don't huff.' I slammed the cupboard door closed and it bounced back, catching me on my cheek.

'Oh, girl, you huff,' said Robyn. 'You're all het up about Eve. You're convinced we're in some kind of Who-Dunnit.'

'I am not, so.'

'You are, so. You think you know better than anyone what happened, just because you found her.'

'You were there too.'

'And I hope that bitch rots in hell but it doesn't mean anyone killed her,' he said. 'She fell over. Those shoes were agony, and they were too big for her anyway.' He ran a finger along the shelf. 'If I couldn't walk on them—'

'Eve could walk on a thimble.'

Robyn's face darkened. I started to take it back, to tell him I didn't mean it. To bite off my tongue, to tell him I was sorry.

'It's good to know what you really think,' he said.

'Oh, come on, Robyn, you know I think you're amazing, that's not the point. The shoes aren't the point. The water was six, eight inches deep, and you think she slipped and drowned? Really?'

'Everyone knows you can drown in a bowl of ice cream if you knock yourself out. You have to let this go. You think you know more about Eve's death than the professionals?' he snapped.

'I'm not saying I do.' I swiped my cloth over the kettle, started rubbing it manically, smearing glitter into the handle.

'Yes, but you're not saying it, like, you're yelling it into the room,' he said. 'You're making yourself well and truly heard, Fi.'

'Let's leave the topic.'

'I already have,' said Robyn. 'But it's the middle of the night and you're cleaning like the kitchen's got a bloody virus. What is it, the poor little straight girl sh—'

'Don't call me that! You know I hate that,' I said. 'How would you like it in reverse? Or doesn't any of that count now you're one of Thora's girls?'

'What do you mean?' Robyn's voice was cold.

The world stopped.

Everything stopped.

I should have known I was about to mess up because the world always seemed to stop right when I said the worst things, the things I needed to take back a second later.

'Is this it?' I said, blindly pushing on. 'You're going to be at TRASH every night of the week? Work all day and party all night?'

'Why? Is that a problem for you?'

'I just want to know who I'm dealing with, that's all,' I said. 'Is this Robyn – is this my best friend, Robyn, or—'

'Don't,' he warned.

'Or . . .' Tears welled in my eyes. I couldn't stop them. 'Is it just Mae B now?'

'I never thought you'd have a problem with that,' he said.

'That was before Mae B turned out to be such a stupid bitch. Before she put herself before her friends. Before she refused to see what was right in front of her thick lashes and—'

I'd gone too far.

The words had fallen out of my mouth.

'Robyn,' I said quickly. 'Look, I'm sorry, OK? I didn't mean it.'

He swept from the room. A minute later, the apartment door slammed closed. His jacket was gone. All that was left were the sequins on the floor.

I flung my cloth into the sink. In the belly of the kettle, my reflection was judging me.

'Fine,' I said out loud. 'But I'm right.'

I was so, so wrong.

In my room, I sat on my bed.

I was worse than wrong. I was mean. I was a giant jerk, and I deserved that door slammed in my face. And . . .

I stared out of the window. Cars still rumbled along the road. On the other side of the river a woman walked quickly, and in the shadows a man crept away so as not to worry her. Not for the first time, I longed to have a roof garden, to watch Dublin's night sky.

The moon was clear. If I'd been closer to the window, I'd have seen the reflection in the river. Instead, I opened my laptop. I found myself looking at the pictures of the empty street where Eve had died.

My heart hammered at my chest, regret mixing deep with my self-righteous arrogance. I had been a jerk to Robyn, but I was right about Eve. I didn't care what Mark said or what Robyn thought – or what the detective had said, for that matter. I was the one who found her and that had to count for something. She just didn't drown by some freak misfortune. Someone killed Eve. Someone out there had taken the life of a young drag queen, and no one was lifting a finger to stop them from doing it again.

I started typing.

My dear old uncool, unmodern blog had been running for ages, but I had always stuck to the same thing: to an arty, sweet little bridge picture, maybe in the daylight, maybe in the dark – maybe a man hurrying to meet a lover or a woman staring into the water – and just the same few words about the mood or the night or the weather or the water. It was harmless, Edna once said. That's why people liked it, she told me. There was enough pain and misery and news and drama in the world, and at the end of the day sometimes people just wanted a quiet picture and a few words, and something to stare at that didn't leave them running screaming to the hills.

I started typing, and this time both the words and the title came easily.

WHO WOULD KILL A DRAG QUEEN?

Chapter Ten

The doorbell rang. I opened my eyes. It was nearly dawn, the sky just touched by the first light. The bell rang again, and then again, over and over. Bleary-eyed, I leaned out of the window, half expecting Robyn to have forgotten his keys. A tall, stout man stood beneath me, his finger pressed to the bell.

'Hey!' I shouted. 'Cut it out.'

'You get down here, Fi!'

He knew my name.

I slammed the window closed. My heart hammered in my chest. His voice seemed familiar, but I couldn't place him.

I inched the window open and looked out.

'Fiona McKinnery, you get down here, right n—'

He rang the bell again. Then he slammed the heel of his hand against the door, knocking and thumping, banging and shouting.

'Fi? You hear me?'

'We all bloody hear you, mate,' someone shouted from down the road.

Pulling on my fleece, I tapped at Robyn's door.

'Hey?' I whispered. 'You awake?'

I tried the handle. The door was locked.

We never locked our doors.

'Robyn?' I called. 'Rob, are you there?'

Outside, the man's voice was way too loud. His shouts filled the street. I could hear him even from the middle room.

'You get down here, little straight girl! You get here—'

Little straight girl . . .

It was Thora.

I flung open the apartment door, tripping on to the landing in my nightshirt and fleece. On the second floor, Mrs Harper looked out of her door. Her hair was in a net, her face deathly pale, her long robe and nightie swept around her like a gown. She shot me a look of a thousand cannons.

'Well, really,' she said. 'A gentleman, on the doorbell. Now, Fi, this isn't acceptable.'

'I'm sorry, Mrs Harper,' I said as I ran down the stairs. 'I don't know wh—'

The door rattled and shook as Thora hammered against it. I tore down the next flight. By the first floor I had already imagined every possible terror happening to everyone I knew and loved, my brain in overdrive as it invented more and more unreasonable deaths.

The bell rang again. A fist knocked hard against the wood, pushing it back against its hinges. I jumped the last few steps, tripping and falling.

'Fi, I'm going to bloody kill you, girl!'

Fury laced through the words.

I put the chain on the door. I opened it, just a crack. Suddenly aware I was only wearing a thin nightshirt under my fleece.

The man thrust his foot into the door gap.

'What the hell are you thinking?' he hissed.

'Sorry, I—' I stared into the strange face. I knew her eyes, but I did not know his mouth.

'Girl, did I not tell you to leave it alone? Did I not say to walk away?' Thora's voice rang through the little hall.

'I'm calling the guards, dear,' said Mrs Harper.

'I—'

'*WHO WOULD KILL A DRAG QUEEN?*' he snapped. 'What kind of blog title is that?'

I blinked. 'I'm sorry?'

'Your blog?' he said. 'You couldn't help yourself, could you? You whip yourself up—'

'I didn't whip anything.' I rubbed my eyes. 'Sorry, wh—'

'You think you have the right to tell people that Eve was murdered?'

'I'm getting my phone right now,' said Mrs Harper.

'It's just a blog,' I said. 'No one even reads blogs any more. I just wrote what I think. How do y—?'

'It's nothing to do with drag. You write about bridges, Fi. You take pictures of people you don't know on bridges, and you write some shit about them, and for some strange reason, people follow you for that.'

'No one really follows me.'

'I bloody follow you, you stupid girl.'

As his eyes flashed, I saw the queen in him, the Thora I knew.

'People like your photos,' he said. 'I like them. Why do you think I follow you? Why do you think you have two thousand people clicking on your pictures in the middle of the damn night?'

'Two thousand?' I said. 'I never have t—'

The man down the road leaned further out of his window. 'Christ, will you reel it in over there? If you repeat everything he says each time he says it this will go on so much bloody longer!'

The man who was Thora and also not Thora jammed further into the door gap.

'Well?' he said. 'You want to say something about my family, then say it to my face. You weren't afraid to speak out on your laptop, you little gobshite.'

'I'll call the guards,' said Mrs Harper. 'You wait right there, Fi, don't let that man in, I'll—'

'No,' I said. 'No, it's OK, thank you, Mrs Harper.'

It was way beyond OK. It had bypassed OK and Weird, and gone straight into Uncomfortable.

'What's the problem, Fi? Not so brave now?' he said.

'I don't know what happened to Eve,' I said quietly. 'But something did happen – someone did . . . and it doesn't matter that I didn't like her, that none of you liked her. She deserves more. I just wanted to say it out loud, that's all. That someone killed Eve and—'

The man who was Thora leaned right up into my face. Along down the thin street I could see the lights of a car peeling toward the river, and the flash of a cigarette lighter, and a woman walking in the half-dark, her cleaning scrubs under a cardigan.

'Did it ever occur to you,' he said, 'that maybe the reason the guards didn't declare her to be murdered is because she wasn't?'

'No,' I said. I stared right back at him.

'You're a typical w—'

'Typical what?' I said, pushing back. 'Typical what?'

'You just can't let it go and be told that someone else would know better than you. The detectives, the guards—'

'They don't care,' I said. 'You think they'd come to the same conclusion if Eve was a straight athletic boy, studying economics at Trinity?'

'Yes,' he said. 'I do. If they so declare that she tripped and fell and drowned, then that is what happened, baby. They are the experts, and not some jumped up, nosy biddy-body little straight g—'

'Back off with that.'

Down the street, another door opened. 'Hey, you!' shouted a woman. 'You wanna lay off her?'

'Let me in, Fi,' Thora snarled.

'Why?' I said. 'So you can shout at me some more?'

On the next landing, Mrs Harper clung to the handrail.

'Don't you dare let that man in,' she said. 'I am calling the guards right now. Don't you budge, Fi.'

'I'm not opening the door any further,' I said. 'Look . . .'

I didn't know what to call him. Was he like Del, using his drag name as his boy self, or was he like Robyn, switching between them, between pronouns? It was hardly the time to ask and definitely not the time to get it wrong.

'Look,' I said plainly. 'You don't get to come here like this and yell at me.'

'You came to my house!'

'I came to your club,' I said. 'I paid the entrance fee and came to your club, and I bought you a drink, and—'

And I had paid the damn entrance price every single time, I wanted to add, and took photographs of your shows for you, and individual pictures for your posters every time you asked. I'd stood for hours and hours on that dusty stage one cold day in January waiting for Miss Merkin to finally finish her make-up so I could get the group shot done as you wanted it. Because orange was overdone, or not in vogue, or whatever crap it was that she pulled.

I found your precious Eve too, I wanted to say. I stayed with her and I talked to the guards and I went home and I dealt with it, without your family. Even Del, who had been known to call me in the middle of *Line Of Duty* so we could watch together and both repeat 'Mother of God' with Superintendent Ted Hastings – even Del hadn't called me to see how I was about Eve. And to top it all off – by this time, I was breathing hard – I wanted to say to him, even my best friend Robyn is now being weird, and it's all thanks to that Tool in Heels, and your family, your bloody family, not a single one of them has come over and said, Hey, Fi, how are ye, and –

I clamped my mouth closed. I scowled, setting my inner retorts into my deeply furrowed eyebrows.

'I trusted you,' said the man-Thora.

'No, you didn't,' I retorted. 'I saw her th—'

'You saw a man in a dress who drowned in the gutter, in heavy rain. It was an accident, Fi, but you chose to see treachery and drama where there was none. You think that you care about her more than the rest of us? You who barely knew her? What gives you the right to talk about my family?'

'I d—'

'You wanna think how Eve's mum would feel, after she read that? You think how her cousins would feel? Did you think about anyone, while you were hammering out those words?'

He pushed back from the door.

'You told them someone killed her,' he shouted. 'You wrote that as far as you could see, no one slips and drowns in a puddle. A puddle?' He threw his hands in the air. 'The rain was nearly a foot deep, and you made it sound like . . .' Breathing hard, he put his hand to his chest. He winced.

'Look,' I said. 'Please . . .'

'The gathering is tomorrow,' he said. 'The club is closed to anyone who isn't family. Don't come, Fi. You won't get in.'

I watched as he walked up to the end of the street and got into an old Skoda and drove away, and then I took off the door chain and stepped out. Down the road, the man who'd been hanging out of his window went back inside, and the woman at the door nodded to me and did the same, and behind me, the first light touched the Liffey, waking the blanket dark, and the bridge stood elegant in the soft mist over the water, and high up in the sky, a plane slowly banked over the city, circling to the airport.

It was just a stupid blog. No one read blogs any more. No one cared. It was just a bunch of photographs of an empty street.

I walked slowly back up the stairs.

Mrs Harper harrumphed.

'I'm really sorry to wake you,' I said.

'Too much drama will give you ulcers, my girl,' she told me.

'It's not my drama.' I set my foot on the next step. 'It's not even my business.'

'It sounds like you wrote it, so?' Outside her door, the air smelled of lily of the valley and burned toast. 'Was it an unkindness you wrote?' she said.

'No. Not particularly.'

'Did you write disrespectful things about the boy who died, now?'

'Not at all,' I said quickly. 'I could have done – she was awful.' I climbed the stairs step by step.

'So you simply told those old bollixes how you didn't believe them?'

'Someone killed her, Mrs Harper. I'm sure of it.'

'Well dear, you have to do you. Isn't that what they say now?' Mrs Harper patted me on the arm.

'Thora didn't think so, there.'

'So he was another one of those . . . you-know-people?'

'A drag queen? Yes,' I said. 'She's actually really nice.'

'But not when you cross her?' said Mrs Harper. 'I had a sister like that,' she told me. She gripped my arm, squeezing it like I was the banister rail. Her skin was dry, so pale it had become an ill-fitting glove, each finger wrinkled.

'That camera of yours,' she said. 'It might make it easier to keep it between you and the world, but don't forget that the world can see you perfectly without a lens, dear.'

◆　◆　◆

I sat in the kitchen, my laptop open on our little table. The scent of the lemon cleaner still clung to the air, a reminder of our row. I made tea.

I re-read the blog but there was nothing there that I regretted.

Why did Thora feel so strongly that I shouldn't ask the question? Why did she care what I wrote?

More and more, people were reading and responding and sharing. It was weird. I don't know what I'd expected but it certainly wasn't this kind of number. Even Robyn would tease me about my silly bridge blog.

I browsed the comments.

> So sad. This is outrageous that the cops aren't investigating.

> Poor kid, she's so young, so beautiful.

> Well said – someone has to tell them if the law isn't listening.

> (What, no bridge?)

I waited for the bigots, for the hate-criers, but as I refreshed my tea and made toast, the little words that dropped into my screen were nothing but love and support and thoughts for Eve's family. If this was how people were reacting then surely Robyn would see the support for the city's queens. He'd see what I was trying to do.

His work jumper was there on the peg. His work trousers were there too. He had to come back before eight forty-five.

The clock ticked slower and slower. I was already late for Jenkins and Holster but I didn't care – I would have sat there all day if I'd needed to. I edited the Pekingese pictures and I confirmed for a Pug the following month, and I replied to an enquiry about photographing children. I never, never photographed children; they were much harder work than even cats and more likely to pee on my props.

Finally, the apartment door opened.

'Robyn!' I jumped to my feet. 'You're back! It's been crazy. Thora came over here, all angry and shouty, and—'

His face was like stone. 'I thought you'd be at work by now,' he said.

'Oh come on, babe, not you, too?'

Pushing past me, he took out his key – the room key I had insisted on giving him the day he moved in, that he hadn't ever used. He'd said we'd never need to lock our doors.

'Robyn?' I said. 'Honey, please, I—'

'You had no right,' he snapped. 'You have no idea what you're doing, interfering like that. It's not your world, Fi.'

'I live here. It's my city too and—'

'So? You go to TRASH but you're the audience. It's different for me. They're not your family.' Robyn stood with his feet planted, one hand on his hip. 'It's not about you,' he said. 'Eve's death is nothing to do with you.'

'It's just a blog,' I said. 'No one cares, Robyn, no one that matters, anyway—'

'Don't I matter?'

I blinked.

He raised his eyebrows nearly to his hairline. 'I care,' he said. 'I care a great bloody deal. Don't I matter?'

I stared at him. He mattered more than anything else in the world to me – how could he not see that?

Robyn held my gaze. 'So you're going to take down that blog post, are you?' he said.

I felt tears sting in my eyes.

'It's just words,' I told him. 'That's all.'

'So? You barely met her. You didn't know her,' he hissed. 'And more is the point, Fi, you're not up on the stage five nights a week in her place. You're not the one they're going to blame.'

'Why would anyone blame you?' I bit down on my lip, tasting blood.

'Who else do you think they'll blame?'

A grey shadow showed his face wracked with pain.

But of course they'd blame him. Anyone who saw Mae B onstage with the new routine would blame him. They'd blame him for taking Eve's shine too, and they'd be right.

'So?' he said.

It was a tiny, ineffectual blog. It was nothing. It wasn't flashy or important, it wasn't the Instagram-ed words of anyone who had a following, but it was my voice. It was mine.

'Someone killed Eve and no one else will say it out loud,' I said. 'Doesn't she deserve that?'

'If no one else is saying it, maybe ask yourself why.'

'You hated her,' I pleaded. 'Come on, Robyn. She ridiculed you, up there on the stage, that night. She made fun of you in your debut clothes and—'

'I know, OK?' Robyn slammed his hand against the doorframe. He swore under his breath. 'Do you not think that's in my head, all the time? And do you not realise, Fi, that your little Hagatha Christie act here leaves me right in the firing line? I'm the first one they're going to look at.'

Shaking, Robyn lowered his head against the doorframe.

'But you were with me,' I said. 'Robyn . . . look at me. Please. You were with me, weren't you, the whole time? You couldn't have—'

I begged with every part of my soul, already knowing the answer.

'But I wasn't with you, was I?' he said. 'I had time and I had motive. And thanks to your post there, now everyone else will be asking if it was me. The guards will be asking. And with no alibi, Fi, I have nothing I can tell them, so if that was your aim then thanks very bloody much.'

I reached out but Robyn shook his head. He fitted the key in the lock and closed the bedroom door behind him.

I put my hands on the latch.

'I thought it was you that died,' I said quietly. 'When I found her. Just for a second. I thought you were dead, Robyn. I thought it was your body in the gutter.'

I heard the bed creak as Robyn sat down.

'I know,' he said.

Chapter Eleven

After two nights of staring at the ceiling without sleep, I still managed to be late to work on Wednesday. The walls of Jenkins and Holster seemed to wobble and fade.

I smiled to a woman as she placed her groceries on the conveyor belt.

'That's twelve eighty, please,' I said.

'I'm Marianne. You're Fi,' said the woman quietly. She spoke in certain sentences, stating facts. 'You know my son, Tommy.'

'Hi, umm . . .'

Tommy. I didn't know a Tommy. Marianne rustled through her bag for the money, and I tried to picture a younger manly version of her face. I knew a few men called Tom. There was Farmer Tom, the O'Neils' ancient neighbour whose land Karen had taken over the running of along with their farm, but he had twenty years on this woman, and she would never see sixty again. I was pretty sure I'd been to college with a Tom or two but I couldn't remember any of them particularly clearly. The only one I could think of was my gynaecologist, Dr Tomas Muto and—

'Del,' said Marianne, with a wink. 'My boy, Tommy. Del? He works with Thora.'

'Del Peen!' I laughed. 'How funny, I had never considered he had a different boy name, but of course!'

Marianne rolled her eyes. 'Honestly, of all the names he could have chosen,' she said. 'I didn't know what it meant. Naughty boy.' She grinned. 'Why would you call yourself after a Thing? So many lovely names out there for a drag queen – I wanted him to be something like a flower, Lobelia or Daisy. Katricia, I suggested, after our tabby cat, she was very particular. Anything he liked, he could have picked. Not a Thing!'

I gave her the change and she squeezed my hand. She held on. 'You were the one who found little Eve,' she said.

In the back of the shop, Mr Jenkins coughed behind the overpriced biscuits.

'Fi?' he said. 'Would you—'

'You stayed with her, Tommy told me,' said Marianne quietly. 'That night. You didn't leave her there in the rain.'

I closed the till drawer, keeping my eyes down.

'Fi?' said Jenkins. He circled closer like a giant bear in an old suit. 'Is there a problem?'

I wondered if there would ever be a time when I didn't see Robyn in Eve's place. When I didn't relive the moment over and over again.

'I'm going on my break now,' I called to him. 'I'll help this lady with her shopping. This way please, ma'am, let me take that for you?'

Outside, cars and people and bikes jostled for room on the crammed pavement. Marianne gestured to the corner on our left and I followed her around a parked Nissan, squeezing between the car and the wall where I ate my lunch.

'Is your boss a bit of a twat?' she said.

'Sorry?'

'Is he homophobic?'

'Just chatter-phobic.' I handed her the bags.

'Ah. It wasn't really anything I wanted,' she said. 'I was just going to say that I never liked her. Eve, that is,' she explained.

110

'She damn near broke my Tommy, when all that happened. That's all.'

It clearly wasn't all. She leaned against the wall and I found myself stepping back against the Nissan.

'I'll say this though,' she went on. 'I wasn't impressed with Ben, neither. If he hadn't gone with Eve, then none of this would have happened.'

'I dare say Eve would still be dead,' I said, without thinking.

'I don't know . . .'

I started to reply, then stopped.

'I saw your blog.' Marianne stuck out her chin like her son. 'Nice bridges, of course. We do a good bridge in Dublin, and that's one of our best. Nice piece on Eve too, now.'

Again, the same sad smile.

'You did good there,' she said. 'Just because that bitch is better off dead doesn't mean that someone had to go and kill her. About time someone said it. Still, that's all.' She turned as if she'd just had a thought. 'You should pop in to see Tommy today,' she said. 'You know where they live, don't you? You should go there this evening.'

'I'm not sure I'd be that welcome,' I said. 'Thora asked me not to go to the gathering and . . .'

'My Tommy told me he'd be home straight after the do, in case I wanted to pop over, and I know for a fact that Ben is working late at the restaurant.'

She gathered her bags to her.

'Lovely to meet you, Fi,' she said. 'Here.' She fished out a net of our organic Irish apples from her bag and gave it to me.

I blinked; a rabbit frozen in the headlights of the woman's determination.

'You give Tommy those from me. Tell him every time he thinks he'd like an entire packet of tortilla chips he's to have an apple instead, otherwise he'll never be fitting his new frock.'

111

'Oh, um . . .'

'You give him my love now,' she said.

Stammering and apologising, I tried to thank her but also somehow to explain how it might be weird if I went over there, and I was really trying not to make things weird, see, and how after what Thora had told me—

'Those stairs are a bother for my knees, if I'm honest,' she said. 'Still, I'm sure you won't mind.'

Planting a wet kiss on my cheek, Marianne ploughed off into the busy pavement and I stood with the bag of apples in my hand, wondering how I just got spun over by an old lady steamroller.

Del, at the grand old age of thirty-five, was one of life's true romantics. Like Thora, he knew his own mind, but his heart was a different matter. In the years I had known him, he'd fallen in love only once, but he'd given everything he had in his soul. He used to be so serious before Ben. When they met, Del changed. He smiled and he giggled and his eyes softened. Slowly, not everything that came out of his mouth was an acerbic cut against society or a snipe, a dig against the Dáil. He'd come over on his own for the evening and he'd say Ben's name in every sentence. Swooning and blushing, he declared Ben to be the only perfect man he'd ever met.

He'd grinned, his eyes sparkling.

Ben liked to swim, Del said. He went to the pool nearly every day, strange boy. We laughed at how Ben did the work but Del got to reap the rewards.

Then one night, Ben was at the pool again and Del stayed for dinner, which was a kindness in itself considering the harsh comparison between his own cooking and my one-shot-stir-fry skills, or Robyn's inability to boil an egg. No one commented on how

Ben was gone for four hours to the pool. None of us said anything about the shadows under Del's eyes. It became a bit of a habit, not saying it. Ben and Del's dinner parties, in turn, were magnificent – the tables laid with gold candlesticks and red candles and glistening tablecloths and four, five, six courses, exotic foods piled high – and all of us crammed in together around the one table – ten, or even twelve of us.

And Eve.

I don't remember when Robyn first noticed the difference in Ben, but it was before I did. I didn't want it to be true. Del was so happy – it was so, so nice to see him happy – but I caught Robyn frowning the nights when Ben was late, or when he left early, or when he didn't show at all.

Then I saw it. I stopped Ben outside a restaurant, and I asked him outright, because Del was my friend, I said, and—

Never ask a question if you're not prepared to hear the truth, that's what my dad would have told me.

And then it was too late to stop it. And worse, when they'd healed the cut in the relationship and they'd already got over that first bump, and Ben had confessed and apologised and said how it was only the one time, anyway . . .

Then Eve made her play.

And I still believe in justice, but Marianne was right: there really were some people who were just better off dead.

I went straight to Del's after work, carrying the apples like a newborn baby.

It was different when you love someone, Del had insisted. You make allowances, he told me. You love them more than you hate what they did, that was the secret. You move on. It was just Eve. And he and Ben got married, and it was beautiful, and I took fourteen hundred photographs of the ceremony.

But it wasn't just Eve, it was Ben too, I said to Robyn, when we were alone. And then later, it was Ben who brought Eve to the flat Del had inherited from his grandmother, after the honeymoon. It was Ben who brought back those shadows to Del's eyes, who made him quiet and serious again.

Ben took away Del's Happy.

Their apartment looked out on to one of Dublin's more beautiful nineteenth-century squares, the iron railings and the original sash windows a sign of a time that was once rich and poor in the same breath, and was now juggling payments between multiple credit cards. Divided only at the corners of the square, the terraced houses stood three flights tall, some with perfectly kept balconies and freshly scrubbed steps, some with boards covering their windows. In the middle, behind yet more iron railings, a landscaped garden filled with quiet herbaceous borders and elegant, stately trees gave the square's tenants a green space that none of them had time to enjoy if they were going to meet the mortgage payments.

My finger trembled as I rang the bell. I'd known Del for years. I scolded myself for being nervous just because Thora was having a tantrum. I'd never had a wide circle of friends, even at college, but excluding irate drag queens hanging on my doorbell in the early hours of the morning I usually got along with most people. And anyway, nothing had changed. Not really. I would not be made nervous, I decided, because Thora was having a hissy fit.

I pressed the bell. The speaker crackled and I stood back.

'Hi?' I said. 'It's Fi? I, umm, I have some apples from your mother?'

The lock clicked open. The stairs were lush, the round banister rail was painted a deep burnished bronze, the carpet olive green, the walls creamy white. On the ground floor, the post boxes were neatly sorted, each was labelled clearly with the owner's number. Up three flights of stairs at the very top, a high-corniced ceiling framed the curl of the banisters and under Ben and Del's number was a single brass knocker in the shape of a cupid holding an axe.

Del opened the door. He wore a neat grey suit with a pale pink shirt and a black tie. His shoes were the kind I knew Robyn hankered after but could never have afforded and even the handkerchief sticking out of his chest pocket cost more than my entire outfit, but his face was drawn, and the clear mascara did nothing to hide the deep-set sorrow in his eyes.

'Your mother sends love and apples.' I held out the net. 'She asked me to come over,' I added. 'Not that I didn't want to come over, of course, but she asked me to come over and—'

Del pulled me close for a hug, and then steered me inside as he closed the door.

'I would have called,' I said. 'Only I didn't have your number on my new phone, and . . . that is . . .'

And Robyn was being a git, I added, in my head, so I couldn't ask him.

'To paraphrase,' he said slowly. 'My mother read your blog, and then she came and found you at work and she bought me apples, which I clearly don't need, instead of buying me gin, which I might actually use. And then she asked you to deliver said apples in order to get you to come over here, so you can solve the crime of the death of the young drag queen that both she and I and you detest but whose passing is still, for heaven knows what reason, keeping us all awake?' He smiled. 'Did I miss anything?'

'She told me to save her the stairs?'

'She does an aerobics class three times a week and she's fitter than I am. Don't worry,' he said. 'My mother, as you probably realised, is as immovable as a tanker on a rock when she gets one of her ideas – which is why we now have a homicidal cupid on our door. She would have hounded you for days if you didn't do what she wants. She's no better than Robyn's mammy.'

'Edna's sweet,' I said.

'Yes,' he conceded. 'But a tyrant is still a tyrant, even in a gingham pinny. Anyway, now you get the good coffee, of which my mother doesn't approve because of the terrible expense, and we both get the cake I cajoled Ben into bringing from his work, because Ma said she was coming over.' He put the back of his hand to his temple. 'She'd say she'd only eat it, you understand, to save me from gaining any weight in case she has to let out my purple dress again. It was all of an inch I asked her, and it took her an hour, and I damn well paid her, you know – more than Merkin would have charged me and all. Looking back, it would have been less painful to break a rib. The trials! Now, let's pop on the coffee, and—'

Del held up his hand, interrupting himself. 'No,' he said. He leaned in and squeezed me. 'Let me look at you. You're a fresh breeze on a dull day, Fi, honey. We've stood on the mat for too long. Now. So. The coffee . . .'

The apartment was beautifully decorated. The kitchen was on the left, set with tightly hung wooden cupboards, a long oak table, and every open shelf on the back wall stacked with beautiful things. The middle hall space from the door stretched around to the front room on the right, with dark grey linen curtains hung from steel poles, the carpet luxuriously thick, the mismatched sofa and chairs arranged around a series of glass coffee tables. I took the chair by the window, a high-backed antique piece that was once Del's grandmother's and still fitted well into the bright corner of the room where she used to sit. On the sideboard next to me stood a framed photo of the wedding. I wondered if Ben had already been with Eve by then.

'So, Fi, my sweet,' said Del.

I smiled, breaking away from my bitter thoughts.

He set two mugs on the table – tall, frothy lattés – and two plates, each with a perfectly cut slice of chocolate gateau and cream on the side. Del smiled, but he'd been crying in the kitchen. His eyes were red, his cheeks flushed, his jawline pale and his eyelids tinged with pink.

'I hear you upset Robyn,' he said.

'I was out of line.' I hung my head.

Del nodded. 'You said a whole thing in your blog too, Missy.'

'Thora told me I had no right.'

'Since when did that stop any of us doing what needed to be done, let alone her? Oh, don't get me wrong,' said Del. 'Your little Hagatha Christie act—'

'Don't call me that.' I curled away from the table. 'Robyn said that. I'm not—'

'It suits you.' Del grinned, teasing. 'There, in your cardigan and lace-up shoes.'

'I like these shoes.'

'They look very comfortable, dear.'

I scowled.

'Why does it matter?' he said. 'And don't you ever let anyone tell you what to wear.'

'You tell me what to wear all the time,' I said.

'No one except me, then.'

'I live with Robyn.'

He raised one eyebrow. 'However brown those shoes are, there's such a fine line between vintage and garbage. Although I suppose if you like them then that should be the only thing that matters.'

'I do like them,' I said, determined to believe myself. 'I do. And I only wrote a blog post.' I picked at my cardigan. 'Who cares if I wrote a blog? No one reads blogs – they're as vintage as my shoes. Which *are* vintage, by the way, and not garbage.'

'Clearly some people care about the blog,' said Del. 'And just because those shoes are old that doesn't mean they're vintage. And I love you, darling, but blogs—'

'I know, it's hardly Instagram or Facebook. No one reads blogs any more.'

'But it's nice,' he said. 'Like a cup of tea and a bit of fruit-cake, when you've had too many fancy vegan dinners. Don't get me wrong, Fi, I'm not knocking what you do. In a time when the rest of the world sometimes seems like a swirling mess of unpleasantness and bile, a few stories set on bridges can be a blessed relief, blissfully unimportant. With Thora and Robyn, though, I suspect that the problem isn't so much your subject change – from bridges to young dead queens – it's more that you might, more than you realise, have it right on the nose. Hence' – he pointed his finger at my chest – 'Robyn's newly scalped pet name for you. Hagatha. Or should that be a pen name? How about Haggie? I like that . . .'

I grimaced. 'I don't,' I said. 'He's being mean.'

'He'll come around,' said Del.

'He's been weird with me for days. It's usually me who makes things weird.'

'He's confused. Did he never tell you he once had a thing for Eve? She wouldn't look at him, but oh he thought she was gorgeous.'

I looked up. 'But he hated her.'

'We all hated her, but she was cute.' Del's eyes were drawn to the photo of him and Ben. 'He used to watch her from the stairs, waiting, hoping she'd even look at him. I could see it in his eyes . . .'

And yet again I'd missed it, I thought. I missed so much when I hadn't been looking.

'So,' said Del with a sad smile. 'We know the rules, don't we? The last one to see the dead queen was the one who killed her? If it wasn't you, being the one who found the body, and statistically that makes you thirty-one percent likely to have been the killer—'

'Thirty-one?'

'I don't know, I made that bit up,' said Del. 'But if it wasn't you and it wasn't me, seeing as I was in the club the whole time, and I honestly couldn't bear to touch her . . . then who was it?'

'You think she was killed?'

'Of course,' he said.

'But Thora—'

'Mama Thora said what Mama Thora has to believe.' Del shrugged. 'She creates her own truth. It upsets her too much otherwise.'

I picked up my mug and frowned into my coffee. It should have felt good for Del to agree with me. I should have been relieved.

'You're wondering if Ben killed her, aren't you?' Del turned his mug in his hands. 'That's why dear Marianne sent you here,' he said. 'Not to bring me the apples, or to lecture me on my eating habits. She wants you to solve the mystery.'

'That's a big ask. What makes any of you think I can do that?'

'The shoes don't help, love.'

I picked off a piece of cake and threw it at him. Del laughed, then screwed up his face.

'She wants you to ask me if Ben killed Eve,' he said.

'Did he?'

'What difference would it make if he did?' said Del.

A great deal to Eve, I thought.

'Ben's a good man,' he said. 'He loves me. It was all her, when that happened. I know I said it before, and I said it a hundred times, but Eve really is poison. If you never saw her in action, you wouldn't believe it. She would get her teeth into someone and rip them apart, just for kicks. She tried it with me first, and then when I said no . . .' Del swept an imaginary hair from his face. 'No one turns her down, not as Eve and not as Liam. She was like this twisted, determined little weed.' He shivered. 'And honestly, I don't care if she's dead, and I don't care if he did it.'

The photo of them both mocked us from its silver frame.

'Hell, we should be celebrating! Ding-dong, the witch is so dead, girl.' Del's voice broke and he slumped back into his seat. 'Instead, we were all gathered at the club together to remember a life that, frankly, I didn't even recognise. And as soon as they're done at the autopsy there will be the mass, the great shebang, the priest swinging away with his stinky balls, the mother up there with Liam's this and Liam's that – she brought his stuffed bear today, can you believe it? She set it there, with its one mean eye looking down at us like it knew. And with Thora leading the gathering in full drag – just a quiet little number, bright lime green and grey stripes – the whole thing was a nightmare . . .'

'Did Ben go with you?' I said.

Del shook his head. 'He was working. He took the early shift, right through.'

I picked at my sleeve.

'Do you think . . .' I started. I looked at the window. The floor. 'Do you think Robyn—'

'Look, he's doing OK,' said Del. 'He stayed with us the other night, but all he did was talk about you.'

Did he mention Eve, though? I thought. Did he say where he was when she was killed? Did he say how much he detested her? How his life is so much better now without her?

'He hates me,' I said.

'He doesn't hate you,' said Del. 'He's angry because he thinks he should have said something like you said, to the guards, and now he's angry at you because he didn't, and you did. Unlike us, Robyn thinks the best of other people.' Del leaned over to nudge me. 'Eh, Haggie?'

'Should I take down the blog, then?' I said.

He took my hand. 'Why did you write it?'

'Because it matters,' I said quietly. 'It wasn't right that no one said it out loud – it wasn't fair. The detective won't hear me, he won't even consider that she might have been killed. It's like her life wasn't important just because she was wearing a dress and high heels.'

'It does matter,' said Del.

Silence settled between us without discomfort. I let go of him and picked up a fork. The cake was dark and rich and incredibly chocolatey; it was right on the very edge of Too Much.

'Ben wasn't there when she was killed,' said Del quietly. 'He was outside, but he wasn't with her, and I don't know where he was or what he was doing and I don't want to know. And this is off the record, you understand?' He waited until I put down the fork. 'But he might have noticed someone.'

'In the alley?'

Del nodded. 'Not one of us, though. He wouldn't tell me for sure, he wanted to check something, or . . . I don't know. And he says that if he's wrong . . .'

I leaned forward. 'If he knows who it was then he has to say.'

'And what if he says but he didn't know? What if he was wrong? Another life becomes ruined – more than one life. Ripples cast from here to nowhere . . .'

'Who was it?' I said.

Del shook his head. 'I couldn't tell you, even if I knew. I've been wracking my brains. Think back, little Fi. Think who might have been there. Who else saw Eve, as she ran?'

Del picked up the other fork and slid it straight down the guts of his slice of cake.

'I always preferred my tarts sweet rather than sour,' he said. 'Easier to swallow.'

'What if it wasn't any of us?' I said. 'What if it was a stranger? What if it was just some random guy?'

'There are one point two million people living in Dublin,' said Del. 'With good old Mr Detective Welly Boots not giving a toss about one of them, we just have to hope that you figure it out before it happens again.'

'You think it'll happen again?'

Del took his fork and cut another slice of the cake, then left it untouched on the plate.

Chapter Twelve

Strangers filled my thoughts, my dreams. Like the faceless characters from my blog, each leaning over Eve as they pushed her into the dark water. The figures became Ben, then Mark, then Merkin, twisting in my imagination as I searched to find the answer I was missing. Every day the line felt tighter.

By the following week, I had barely seen Robyn. In a desperate attempt to fix the ugly atmosphere between us, I decided the only thing I could try was going to the source of the anger. After three days of my begging, Del finally gave me the address, a quiet little property in a little street in the nice side of the city.

The front door was painted white. Either side, set in white planters, tall green box had been sculpted into perfect teardrops.

I knocked. The door opened, the chain holding fast.

I lifted the bouquet of white roses to the gap in the door.

'I don't want to see you,' said Thora's voice.

'I'm sorry,' I said.

'You brought me flowers, little straight girl?'

I did what Del told me, I thought.

'I'm sorry,' I said again. 'I get it. I messed up,' I said. 'And I really am sorry.'

The door opened.

Some drag queens looked very similar from their drag selves to their boy selves. Thora – or Daniel, I realised, when I saw his name on a letter in the mailbox – looked about as different as it seemed possible. Dressed in a Dunnes checked shirt and a navy-blue sweater, even the cut of his jeans seemed to emphasize a lack of attention to his appearance. Only a very faint mark on the back of his neck where he'd missed some foundation gave light to his work.

He took the flowers and breathed in the scent.

'I won't ask who gave you my address,' he said. 'Seeing as Del is the only one who knows it apart from Merkin. I see no cat scratches on your pretty little face, so you haven't been to her.'

The long hall split. To the left was a flight of stairs carpeted in white, with white walls and white banisters, and a single black-and-white picture, framed in black. Daniel steered me down the stairs to the right where wide steps led into a tiny kitchen with a huge window, looking out to a sun-drenched patio and back garden. Outside the glass, there was a world of passion and colour, plants crammed in with other plants, each one a gorgeous specimen of life.

'Sit, pet,' he said. 'I'll see to these first. They're more handsome than either of us.'

In my pocket, my phone pinged. I glanced at the clock. By now, Jenkins would have listened to my excuse voicemail, how I'd had to suddenly take the afternoon off work. For once, I'd told the truth, although I didn't imagine that he'd take 'lady business' as meaning bringing a big bunch of flowers to Thora Point.

Daniel rummaged in a long cupboard above the kitchen counter and drew out a glass vase. He took time to arrange the flowers. He set them on the windowsill and then moved just one, an inch to the right.

Reaching slowly, he took out two martini glasses. He stopped and smiled at a bird on a seed feeder outside.

'You've come to ask me if I killed young Eve,' he said.

I said nothing.

Daniel watched the birds on the feeder.

'No, you're right to ask,' he went on. 'Oh, don't get me wrong, I'm mad as hell at you for your silly blog, and for you ringing up the guards as you've been doing. Don't think I don't know about all that.'

A deep blush burned over my face.

'No, don't look away,' he said. 'We have to own our actions. I forget, sometimes, how it is when we are young. How important we think we are.'

'I don't think I'm important,' I said.

He put up his hand. 'But why would you not? The lesson here, I think— Do you take an olive?'

'Pardon?'

'The lesson here,' he said again, 'is when we should speak and when we should keep our thoughts to ourselves. Umbrella?'

'No, thank you. But—'

'I was wrong.' Daniel turned to me. 'Don't you tell a soul I said so, but I was, pet. And I'm sorry for it. I shouldn't have shouted at you like that. I'd finished at the club and got back here, and I was messing with my phone, and I read your blog and it felt like you were all up in my face – and I got angry. As I drove over, the anger got to being furious. I should at least have waited until the morning to tear a strip.'

By which time he'd have been using his teeth . . .

'I really am sorry,' I said again.

He took out a mixer and scooped ice from a small tabletop freezer.

He poured in gin and then vermouth. 'You know, of all the birds that come here, there is only one bluetit. They've been my favourite as long as I can remember, and yet there's only ever been one. I fill the tubes with nuts and seeds and worms and all sorts

125

of disgusting stuff that they're supposed to like, and I have entire families of sparrows and starlings and blackbirds and chaffinches. All the standards. And just the one, single bluetit.'

He added olive juice to the mix and I said goodbye to the rest of the day's shift at the shop.

'Eve was a good little performer onstage,' he said.

He selected a long silver stick and gently stirred, around and around and around.

'She took everything I had.' He smiled, his eyes filled with sadness. 'All the money. Until it was gone. Last week, I couldn't pay the staff. I can't pay anyone. The insurance is due again and I've used my savings but . . .'

Around and around and around . . .

'Why didn't you call the guards?' I said.

'You never met Eve's mammy, did you?' Daniel shook his head. 'Lovely woman, so she is. Quiet as a mouse. Adored Liam, of course. But then there are few of us who turn out to be so obnoxious, like little Liam Flanagan did, without some help along the way, don't you think?'

I closed my mouth. I decided it was probably best if I didn't think.

'He was just a young lad when he first tried coming to the club,' said Daniel. 'Horribly underage, of course. I had to mind him, make sure he was sent right back to his ma – and then later, well, you saw what he became. Everyone saw. His daddy was long gone and Liam was over twenty-one by then, and look, see . . . who could deny her the spotlight?' He turned to me. 'Some of us, Fi, we need that light like we need oxygen.'

Behind him, two sparrows were fighting on the bird feeder, each keeping the other from the seed.

'Did Eve steal from anyone else?' I said.

'Everyone, I imagine. Her ma included.'

I remembered the little flowers and the cross in the alley.

'Have you talked to Benjamina Yahoo about her?' Daniel poured the martinis. 'Stay out of that mess, girl. That twosome – if it can be called a twosome, at this stage, and not a three or four, a spaghetti of men – they're better off left to fester.'

'Del said he and Ben are trying again, though.'

'Are they?' he said. 'You're certain about that?'

'Del loves Ben.'

'Of that, you're right.'

The little birds pushed back against one another and as they fell to the side, one snuck in, taking the seed.

'What was Liam like?' I said.

'If work was a bed, he'd sleep on the floor.'

I smiled.

'What do you want to know for, Little Miss Christie?' he asked.

'I see her in my mind, in the alley,' I said. 'I see her dead, all the time.'

Daniel stuck a line of olives in each glass. 'Liam was just what the world needed, another Dublin twink.' He passed me a drink and swilled his, perfectly cradling the slender stem, his nails pale and dry. 'His ma is a dote.'

'And his dad was—'

'No,' he said, interrupting me. 'His dad wasn't kind at all. We can blame everything we do on our history, but it makes the past terribly crowded. Liam became what young, spoilt boys often become. He became a thistle.' Daniel smiled a still, sad smile. 'He liked to stand out for all the wrong reasons.'

'Did he have enemies?'

'Of course. So do I. So do you, my dear. Liam was surprisingly quiet out of drag,' he said. 'But you knew he was in the room. As Eve, it became hard to look past her when she wanted you to see.'

'And the other queens?'

'They loathed her.' He laughed, plucked an olive from the line. 'All except Merkin, who has a bit of a habit of collecting the treasures that fall through the cracks. Not a good habit. If I'm honest – and I rarely am, so I can't think what's got into me today, this is only my second martini – I only kept Eve on at TRASH because the antagonism helped spur the others into better work.'

'Did no one like her?'

'What was to like?'

I shrugged. It seemed so harsh, but I couldn't come up with a single thing.

He pushed away from the table again. 'This is making me sad. I don't want to talk about Eve any more.'

'Did she have a boyfriend?'

'Apart from everyone else's, you mean?' He shook his head. 'So, are you going to ask me?' he said.

'Ask you?'

'You've come all this way,' he said. 'You might as well, pet. After all, you think I killed her, don't you? Everyone thinks I killed her.' Daniel turned to the window.

'You didn't kill her,' I told him. 'But you don't believe it was an accident any more than I do. You want to think she slipped and fell but you know that someone murdered her, and now they crossed a line that cannot be undone, and there's every chance they will kill again.'

Daniel smiled, with Thora's sharp eyes. 'You're not as daft as you look, girl,' he said. 'You realise you've left your Robyn in the firing line, though?'

I held the drink to my lips, but I didn't take a sip. I stared at an olive.

'Think about it,' said Daniel. 'No one had a reason to kill Eve. Not really. She was poisonous and beautiful but if that were reason

128

enough to take someone's life, there'd be few of us left to grace the stage.'

'So did the killer just hate drag queens?'

'Then why go for Eve? Why take out the one who can run faster than any of the others, and can move slippery, like a damn eel.' Daniel pointed his long, elegant finger at me around his glass. 'Catching her must have been like skimming salmon from a stream.'

He picked up the line, dipped it into his drink.

'No one had a reason to kill Eve,' he said. 'And yet poor little Eve is dead. Your question – the question I don't think you have asked yourself yet – is not who killed Eve Harrington, but why?'

'Do you know why?' I said.

He popped an olive between his teeth. 'If I knew that, even you couldn't stand in my way. Eve was a nightmare, but she was mine.'

Chapter Thirteen

The train rumbled along the track in no hurry to leave Dublin, easing between the houses and the flats and the dark little streets, and then the wide stretches of industrial estates. Slowly, the buildings eased from one another. With each town further away from the city, gardens cut into the back of the tracks, then fields, gates by the railway line, cows barely acknowledging the chuntering carriages. A woman stood bent over her allotment, a plastic trug beside her filled with something muddy and rich, and in the next field, a child ran with a young horse as his parents watched from the wall.

However mad Robyn was with me, there was no way I was going to miss his mother's birthday tea. I clutched the paper bag to my chest, the framed photographs of the Pekingese, and on the tray table over my knee I kept tight hold of a gift bag.

Edna was a proper Irish mammy. Her stove was never without the stout little kettle, she had a tin of shortbread in the dresser, and she did a wash every fine day. Robyn often claimed that she ruled the rambling old farmhouse as a benign dictator, but the truth was she served love. As strong and as pure as anything, her love could hold you tighter than a swaddling blanket.

She'd loved me right from when she first met me, when I was a child. She believed in doing things as they should be done and she had no time for a silly argument, she said, not then and not now.

Back when we were young, she'd put up a stocking for me at Christmas, knowing my dad would be working right up to the holiday, and she'd let Robyn have bunk beds, with my name on the top pillow for the weekends I was allowed to stay over. Not that I was hers, she'd say, if anyone asked, but she didn't like to think of me home alone. Now, both Robyn and I were coming to tea. And that was that.

In front of the stove, Edna unwrapped the fancy candles.

'They're lovely, Fi,' she said. 'You're a darling girl.'

'They're not very imaginative,' I said.

Robyn rolled his eyes.

'They will work just as well lit as a thousand new ideas,' Edna told me.

She touched her hand to the kettle. The room was warm but it was another cold day that raged outside the big, double-glazed windows. The tractor pulled into the yard. A few minutes later, Karen looked up in surprise as she came in from the garden.

'You're here?' she said.

Karen hung her oilskin coat on the peg and left her boots on the newspaper pad. She saw the framed Pekingese pictures on the sideboard and took out each one, peering at the sweet face of her neighbour's little dog. 'Thanks,' she said. 'They're good. I'll make the tea.'

'I'm already making it,' said Robyn.

'Are you sure you won't crack a nail, now?' she said.

'Do you have any to crack?'

'None of that today,' said Edna gently.

She took the handle of the kettle and gave a stern look to the two of them. Nearest the fridge, I was sent to get the milk, and Robyn to get a plate for the Jenkins and Holster cream cakes I'd brought, and as Grandpa Joe came puttering in from the other room with his stick stabbing at the stone floor, we each found our places around the long kitchen table, Robyn taking a seat as far from me as he could get without moving his chair on to the muddy field outside, Karen doing the same to him.

In a desperate attempt to lighten the party, I grinned at Karen, who looked back at me as if I was a failing ewe in a puddle of slurry.

Fake cheer, as they say, was as painful to bear as true delight. From Karen's grumbles about a neighbour's rotten fence to my tale of photographing an aging Labrador who closed his eyes with every flash, we each tried our best. With a single tiny birthday candle lit on one of the chocolate éclairs, we sang away to Edna in our ropey, merry voices, and once the last of the gifts was displayed on the dresser, we sat together in an uncomfortable silence.

I picked at my nail.

'Don't,' Robyn hissed.

'I'm not.'

'You are.'

'Don't what?' said Edna. 'What are you grumbling about, love?'

'She's at it again. No, you are,' Robyn said to me. 'I can see it on your face, Fi, written as clear as those wrinkles you pretend you don't have.'

'Shocking grammar!' I tried to laugh as if he were teasing me.

'Fi is doing what?' said Edna.

'She's strung out about Eve,' said Robyn. 'The one who died.'

'I never mentioned her,' I said. 'You told me not to raise the topic, so—'

'Why not?' said Karen. She turned to Robyn. 'Why wouldn't you want us to talk about that, Rob?'

'It's hardly the occasion,' he snapped.

'It's OK,' I said quickly. 'I wasn't going to talk about it anyway.'

'She said a whole bunch on her blog,' Robyn muttered.

Karen tugged her hands through her hair. 'I don't care what we talk about. We can talk about it, or not, or whatever. I don't care. I'm sure as hell—'

'Karen!'

'OK, fine, I'm certain Mum doesn't care either.'

'You're being really weird too,' Robyn said to her. 'That's usually Fi's job.'

He met my eyes and, for a split second, I thought he really was joking. I thought the ice wall that had appeared between us since Eve's death might have melted. Then the wall closed. No one was laughing.

Grandpa Joe looked between me and his grandchildren in confusion.

Pushing back from the table, Karen stood up. As the door rattled behind her, Robyn's teacup shook in his hands and he gripped the fragile china too hard, his fingers white, and I realised his nails weren't pretty like they used to be. They were bitten and sore.

In the field, the tractor started up again.

'Don't you mind Karen,' said Edna. 'She's been a bit upset since . . .' She leaned over to squeeze Robyn's arm. 'Don't let it bother you, lad. It's not easy, you know, working the hours she does, and now she's running Tom's land as well as ours.' She smiled at him. 'He's such a beautiful boy, isn't he, so?' she said to me. 'And now a beautiful girl! I said to Joe, just this week, I always longed to be beautiful, and now look, I have a beautiful girl—'

'Aw, Mum! I'm not a girl!'

'Oh, I know, dear,' she said. 'But even part-time, it's still nice. You should have seen my face when Fi sent the photo,' Edna said. 'My darling boy, you were a picture as Mae B, I was so proud. I only wish your father could have seen. We so wanted to be there, didn't we, Joe? But stuck out with the lambs all night, I don't think Karen's had a night off in a month. We couldn't ask her to drive. We barely know her. You saw her more than we have the other week, with that dog picture of yours, Fi! Still, the lambs have a fine mind to be born when they're ready and even if we weren't there for Mae B this time . . . well, we have our little spy here, to let us know what's happening, don't we?'

She took my hand, drew it close, then took Robyn's. He shot me a stare of betrayal and sorrow and I felt the last tiny scrap of hope fade away that there, in his mother's kitchen, our friendship might heal. I had hoped that it was a good thing we were there together and not a bad thing, and that, really, I wasn't losing them at all, and I wasn't losing him.

I was wrong. I could see it in the way Edna consoled me. I'd already lost him.

'Now,' said Edna, as if she stole the thoughts from my head. 'We can't help it if our little star here is born to shine.'

'Ma . . .'

'It's been a big month for all of us,' said Edna.

She touched her hand to the back of my head and brushed my hair with her fingers.

'Your sister took it hard,' she said to Robyn. 'What happened to Eve. She was worried. We were all worried after we heard. After all, that young lad was killed right behind the club.'

'It was an accident,' said Robyn. 'Eve slipped and she'd been drinking anyway, and—'

'Be gentle, lad,' said Edna. 'It's not difficult to see what might have happened, against what did.'

◆　◆　◆

We stayed until it was right to leave, but however many times I tried to chat to Karen, she was clearly too stressed about the whole situation and in his turn, Robyn was impatient and cross, and too quick to see his own position. On the fields or in the house, Karen kept herself to herself the whole time we were there. Once we'd moved into the front room, she closed the kitchen door, muttering about batch baking for some cake sale for the local shop.

I found her with her hands deep in the washing up. I reached for the tea towel, started on a mug, slid it into the cupboard.

'I can manage,' she said.

'Your mum said you're running all of Tom's land now, next door?'

'It's a job.'

She thrust a deep pan under the bubbles.

'The commute is handy?'

I took a plate and started to wipe it with the towel when she whipped the cotton from my hand, and set the plate back on the draining board. Her hair was damp where she'd run her fingers through it again, catching it back behind her ear.

'I'd love to be on the fields all day,' I said. 'It's so pretty here.'

'It's Ireland, Fi. It rains every day and even if it isn't actually raining it's thinking about raining, and then, when it does stop, like last April, it dries out the land until the earth becomes a solid plate of clay and it bakes thick and hard and then it floods again.'

She stopped. A wash of fear rattled over her, and she gripped the edge of the sink. She darted a look back at the door.

'It's OK,' I said. 'Really. He's fine. He's not hurt.'

Karen shook her head. Her eyes were framed by deep shadows of exhaustion, just like her brother's. In her rush of panic, I thought how like Robyn she actually was, however much each would insist that wasn't the way. She had the same high cheekbones and the same tall, skeletal frame but where his arms and legs were slender, hers were strong, her long muscles tough and toned from years of working outside on the land with their dad, and now at only thirty, running the farms herself. She put her hand over her face.

'Karen,' I said. 'It's OK. Robyn is perfectly safe at the club. They look after one another, it's like—'

I bit my tongue. It was probably best not to say how TRASH was like a family, or how he had these lovely new drag sisters, and a drag mama, now. That was taking insensitivity to a whole new level, even for me.

'He was good up there onstage,' I said instead. 'You could pop in, if you wanted? I can come with you.'

She inhaled, hard.

'I know how you feel,' I said.

'You don't, Fi.' She wiped the sponge around the taps. 'You're like everyone else. You seem to think he's some kind of wonderful just because he said he's gay, and now . . .'

'No.' I nudged her with my elbow. 'Right now I don't think he's that bloody wonderful at all. But come on, eh? I know you guys had an up and down back then but all that was ages ago. This is different. And seriously, he loves it! He was really good onstage,' I said, pushing on. 'His Mae B thing was hysterical, and honestly he lip-syncs really well already, and—'

Karen set her hands down on the rim of the sink.

'I'm sorry, I can't stand here talking all day,' she said. 'I have two more sets of queen cakes for the church sale and the iced fingers . . .'

She plunged the next pan into the suds, splashing water over the sides of the sink.

'Let us help you. I can mix and Robyn's a dab hand at icing,' I said. 'It's about the only cooking he can do, but it involves sugar, of course, so—'

'I.' She whooshed the pan from the water. 'Can.' She set it on the draining board with a thump. 'Manage,' she snapped through her teeth. 'Just bloody fine.'

◆　◆　◆

Edna looped her arm through mine.

'You'll keep a good eye on my boy,' she said. 'He tells me you've been to the club again?'

'Just once,' I said. 'Look, I'm sorry about Karen. I think I said something . . . weird, or . . . I upset her. That is . . .'

'She doesn't have it easy,' said Edna. 'The extra land now, she works hard.'

We both nodded as if that were the reason.

'So,' said Edna.

'So,' I agreed.

We stood together by the rambling marigolds. Down the lane and over the wall, the railway platform was nearly empty, just one man with a suitcase and a rucksack, as if neither were quite enough without the other.

Edna squeezed my arm, the old lady iron-fingered grip.

'You were always such a good girl,' she said. 'It'll work itself out when all this silly argument settles.'

She looked back for Robyn.

'I'm not sure,' I said. 'Not this time.'

'He will come around.' She patted my hand. 'You two have always been close, but perhaps now is the time for you to find other friends as well?'

I watched the man on the platform.

'There's no rule to say you're only allowed one friend,' said Edna.

'Oh, I do have other friends,' I said. 'I mean, there's—'

'What about that nice chap you used to see at college?'

'Henry?' I pictured my ex-boyfriend, Henry Chandler, the man who had managed to shag every one of my female classmates in one university term.

Edna frowned. 'Was he a Henry? I don't remember him looking like a Henry. The scientist guy,' she said. 'Robyn knew him.'

She stood back and I recognised the look in her eye, the same one as Robyn had when he was trying to tell me something by not telling me anything at all.

'Patrick,' she said, as if she might not have already known the name perfectly well. 'That was it. I have it now.'

I nodded. I remembered Patrick.

'The one who was sweet on you,' she said. 'They all seem to run away, though, don't they?' Edna chuckled. 'He was a nice fellow. I liked him. He came here once, for Robyn's nineteenth, I think?'

Patrick Midda. His face sharpened in my memory – glasses, a scrub of grey-brown hair, a kind of gangly youth – tall, as if his legs had been stretched a little too long for his body.

Behind us, Robyn's grandfather swamped him in a thick hug, carefully instructing him on every way to keep safe at night and how, now he was a girl, he had to be more careful, and Robyn took out his phone, showing the old man the pictures from the club. 'See, I'm still a guy,' he said. 'But I get dressed up, and I go on to the stage.'

'Well, sonny, now you like dressing up as a girl—'

'No, you see, it's a job, it's onstage, and—'

'But drunken eejits on the street, they don't see that, Robbie,' said the old man. 'They see a beautiful woman and with tits out like that, I mean—'

'Daddy!' Edna chided.

'Just because they're not real, doesn't make him any less attractive to that sort,' said old Mr O'Neil. 'They've never been the brightest, those kinds of men. I'm just saying, that if he has the option to be a little less chesty, then it might help the poor lad not get murdered?'

'He's not going to get murdered,' said Edna. 'You hear me, boy? You're not to get yourself murdered. You promise me, now,' she said.

Robyn kissed her. 'I promise,' he said.

Edna walked us both to the end of the garden path. She kissed Robyn again, and told him she loved him, and she did the same with me.

'You call that Patrick,' she said to me. 'Smart girl like you, you need a nice smart boy in your mind.'

'Oh, I'm not smart,' I said.

'You got that right,' snarled Robyn.

◆ ◆ ◆

Patrick Midda.

I stared out of the window on the train. His name rattled over my tongue like the wheels on the track. Pat-rick. Pat-rick.

Robyn sat on the other side of the carriage, his fingers tapping at his phone screen.

Whatever had happened to Patrick Midda?

Taking out my own phone, I rumbled through Facebook until I found him. I clicked on his photos. His profile picture was a plastic human skull – or I hoped it was plastic – wearing a red knitted bobble hat. I clicked some more, fishing, until I found him.

The glasses were still there but they looked good. He had a strong jaw, and he was clean-shaven. His hair, once thick with grey so early, was still messy but swept back from his face. In the picture, he stood alongside someone who could only be a brother, maybe a cousin – the same jawline, the same shape of eyes, the two of them towering over a young woman in a bright blue dress.

Patrick Midda.

I wondered if the woman in the blue dress was Patrick's girlfriend. Not that it mattered – of course it didn't matter, I wasn't going to call him anyway. I could see what Edna was up to and I wasn't a puppet for the playing – first by Del's ma and now this. I didn't need their help. I was quite happy with the friends I had, thank you very much.

I clicked on the link. Patrick Midda. Pathologist. Dublin.

Edna had always been canny.

I stared out of the window again, at nothing.

Patrick Midda, the scientist guy who had switched to pathology in his last year, and was now working here, in Dublin. Funny that. I wondered how long it had taken Edna O'Neil to find a pathologist I might have known, and if it was just me she was setting up, and if she and Del's ma were in cahoots, an army of wily little old ladies. A gingham mafia.

Still, Patrick Midda.

It probably wouldn't hurt to say hello.

Chapter Fourteen

The mortuary had been built to look exactly like someone would expect of a house of the dead. Dark grey with tiny windows, it stuck out from the fading lines around it. The parking spaces had filled from back to the front and the path was empty, as if death were catching.

I neatened my hair with my fingers and pushed away the notions of anything spooky, and strode in.

Unlike the outside of the building, the reception room was peaceful – still grey but with soft tones of violet and pink, a warm blush in a painting of flowers, and a faint green in the comfortable chairs under a lamp. Behind a desk, a woman dressed in black scrubs was filling out a form. She made quick marks with her pen. She looked up at my cough. Her eyes were the same green as the chairs and she wore no jewellery and no make-up.

'Can I help you?' she said.

'I'm here to see Patrick Midda?'

'Is he expecting you?'

'Not exactly.'

Not at all. Not unless he was psychic, which I imagined would make his job very difficult.

I started to give the line I'd worked out in advance, the line about interviewing him, writing a piece for my blog. The woman's green eyes were already scrutinising my face. I stopped.

'My name is Fiona McKinnery,' I said. 'I'm ankle-deep in someone else's drama and I thought I'd cash in on a tenuous college connection and ask him a question he might not want to answer.'

Behind the closed interior door, there was a soft chuckle.

'Patrick only sees dead people,' said the woman.

'I considered killing myself to get his attention, but I thought that might have its own complications.'

'Please don't make jokes about suicide,' she said.

Horrified, I put my hand over my mouth. 'No. I'm sorry.' I shuddered. 'You're right. That was crass of me. A terrible thing to say, especially here, only—'

The door opened.

'It would probably have been worse if you'd actually done it, rather than just saying it,' said Patrick. 'Great headline, though: *Woman Kills Herself To Get Midda To Touch Her.*'

The mortician lady scowled. 'Pa, that's really not OK,' she scolded.

'Oh, on so many levels,' he told her breezily.

He wore the same black scrubs as the woman but on his feet he had mismatched woollen socks and no shoes.

I started to ask. Then closed my mouth. It was absolutely none of my business.

'We have to wear wellies,' he said, gesturing behind him at the row of white rubber boots in the open changing room. 'Sorry. My sock collection is somewhat depleted at the moment.'

'No, they're great,' I said. 'I'm wearing something very similar myself.'

Raising one eyebrow, Patrick looked at my skinny-heeled suede boots, chosen for neither warmth nor comfort.

'Nice to see you, Fi,' he said. 'It's been a while.'

Suddenly my plans for asking sensible questions about the process that the guards would have been through with Eve, and about if Patrick could tell if she'd been hurt before dying – or, of course, if she really had just slipped over and dropped dead – vanished. All sensible words and questions disappeared from my brain and the only thing I could think was how I wanted to make him smile again and how nice it was just to be there . . .

In a mortuary, I reminded myself. In a house of the dead.

I set my shoulders back. For all Edna's mama-manipulation, I was definitely not there for anything like that, and anyway, he was probably married.

He wore no ring and there wasn't one on a chain around his neck either, but maybe pathologists didn't wear rings when they worked, or maybe he was someone who lived with their partner, like the girl in the photo with the bright blue dress – and maybe they weren't married, or if they were, then maybe they hadn't changed their names or worn rings or—

He pushed his hair back from his eyes and my brain switched to offering me cartoon bluebirds.

'So, umm . . .' I started. 'How's work?'

'Ridiculously busy, actually,' he said.

I took a breath. That was one of those hints that other people gave me when they wanted me not to outstay my welcome and probably to leave.

'Um, I was wondering – that is, if you're not too busy – which you just said you are, so – but if you weren't, I was wondering if . . .'

Ten more seconds and I'd be scribbling Mrs Fiona Midda on my notebook.

'If I can buy you lunch?' I said.

'Lunch? Oh, um . . .'

The mortician coughed.

'I think I'm working through lunch?' he said, checking with her.

'Just a coffee, then?' I said. 'Or a tea? A hot chocolate? A packet of fruit pastilles?'

Patrick hesitated, and then smiled again. I reached for the wall behind me.

'Is this business or pleasure?' he said.

'Purely business.'

Ish.

'And would that thing you're working on involve questions about who killed a certain dead drag queen?'

I looked over at the reception woman. She raised her eyebrows.

'I love a bridge,' he added dryly. 'I'm not entirely against a blog about dead drag queens, either. The thing is . . .'

Ah, and there it was. The thing. The thing would be his wife or his eight perfect little children, all tiny versions of him like elongated bespectacled Russian dolls, or a time-consuming hobby – an obsession with train sets or philosophy lectures at Trinity, or dubious French movies.

It would be a thing that said, *Hey, Fi, back off.*

'I'm not sure how useful I could be,' he said.

Give me ten minutes and a piece of paper and I'll give you a list, I thought. However, he hadn't closed the door on me. He hadn't run away. The woman at the desk was giving him all kinds of get-outs and he was still there, still talking to me.

'Just a coffee,' I pressed. 'Three minutes of your time. A scalding hot coffee in the hospital canteen, which is probably utterly undrinkable, and then I will leave you alone.'

'I really can't help you with the case,' he said. 'Or if I could then I won't, and to be honest that's not going to change with the offer of terrible coffee, Fi. But sure, I can eat dinner?'

'What?'

'Dinner?' he said.

'Oh.'

Dinner. That was like a meal. That was so much more than lunch.

'Can you eat dinner? I mean, I'm working all day and if you still want to ask me your questions, and—'

'I-I-I can eat dinner.' I nodded, my head bobbing up and down like a drunken frog. 'Yeah, that would be . . . sure. Yes.'

I gripped my jaw to stop it moving, then dropped my hand and blushed deep red.

'Pa?' said the lady on the desk. 'Your twelve o'clock is—'

'He'll still be dead when I get to him,' said Patrick.

I giggled, and Patrick winked. The single most gorgeous wink any one person had ever given to anyone else.

I'd lost all respect for myself, and I no longer cared.

'How about six fifteen tonight?' he said. 'I'll meet you at The Hungry Ogre, if you know it? Just past the Unitarian church on St Stephen's Green?'

'Six fifteen,' I said.

It wasn't a date. It wasn't anything, except the very respectable asking of a few questions, so there was no good reason why I shouldn't meet with him, whether he was married or not.

He smiled again and my face went from beetroot to burgundy. Stumbling, I thanked him, then I thanked the woman. Then I thanked Patrick again. Then, before I turned back to the woman, I stumbled backward out of the door.

It was only when I'd made it back to the bus stop that I remembered The Ogre was the restaurant where Ben worked.

◆ ◆ ◆

I ran up the stairs and into the apartment. Giggles came from behind Robyn's closed door. I let my keys rattle against the bowl as I dropped them.

145

The laughter stopped.

I closed my bedroom door. I set my coffee on the windowsill and put on the radio. I didn't want to know who was there, or why. Robyn was entitled to live his private life in his own private way. I just didn't care, I decided. I turned down the volume, wondering if it was Del behind the door, although Del would have come out and said hello, and not hidden in the room. Also, I didn't recognise the laugh – it was deeper, more manly, and—

I sat down. It was nothing to do with me.

The take-out coffee was perfectly dark and creamy, the kind that filled my soul from the bottom up. It wasn't as good as the Jenkins and Holster coffee, but it had come without the irritation of seeing Mr Jenkins or Mickey on my day off.

I sipped slowly and watched people cross the bridge. I leaned out with my camera, catching two young boys, no more than seven or eight, as they pointed away, east, over the side of the bridge, cheering something as it flowed down the river.

Racing sticks. It was the Liffey, after all.

I checked the pictures. There was one without their faces and I saved it. I scratched at the furrow between my eyebrows. There was nothing wrong with writing about bridges, I told myself. Nothing at all. Some people liked bridges. Bridges were just fine.

I scowled as I opened my laptop.

There were a hundred and eighty-one new messages on my piece about Eve.

I said a very bad word, the kind that Edna would have come after me for with her frying pan in her hand.

A hundred and eighty-one messages!

I stared at the number, blinking.

I'd never had a reaction to anything like that. I had followers, sure, but they were quiet. One or two would speak up regularly, and every now and then some troll would drag itself from the mud to try to stir up trouble where there wasn't any, but my posts were innocuous – my pictures were Easy Listening for the eyes. If I was lucky, I might get three comments telling me how someone liked the picture, blah blah, how the sky looked good . . .

I read each new reply. In the most, people were kind.

It was funny how life went on. I sat back in my chair and watched my corner of Dublin. Whatever happened, that bridge was there, unchanged by someone else's tragedy. A tour of people wearing matching lanyards swarmed up and over the steps, each taking their own photos, seemingly without the slightest notice of the actual bridge or the people, or the buildings – merely ticking off the next in the list of Irish Things To Have Seen.

Well, I'd seen a new thing too. I'd seen a Patrick.

It was just dinner but the more I thought about it, the more normal it felt, and the more I accidentally-on-purpose let myself forget about the woman in the blue dress and that I was meeting him professionally.

Sure, I decided, Robyn would be happy for me. He'd be delighted I was seeing someone else, someone different and new and hadn't that been what his mum told me to do? And who cared if Patrick ran away after one night, like all the other men in our lives?

It was still dinner.

Robyn would want to be told, so. I nodded as I made up my mind. After all, I wanted to know who was with him in his room, so it stood to reason that he'd be interested in my news too.

I waited until I heard him in the kitchen.

'I have a dinner,' I said from the door.

He scooped ice cream into a bowl without looking up.

'That's nice,' he said.

'It's with Patrick Midda, from college.'

Robyn squeezed a long swirl of toffee sauce over the ice cream. He took two spoons from the drawer.

'Mam told me she'd issued her instructions to meddle.'

'I'm not meddling.'

'If you say so, Hagatha.'

'Oh come on, Rob—'

'So, you're going to dine out on the death of one of my friends?' he said. 'Nice.' He scooped another plop of ice cream. 'Classy, Fi.' He stalked through the room to his door. 'You're making it weird,' he said.

'Will you let that go already? I'm trying to help.'

'Help who?' he said.

'Whom,' I corrected him.

The air cut as he slammed the door. Furious whispers burst through the quiet. I scrunched up my face, rubbing my hands over my eyes at my bullish words.

I'd still hoped that I could fix things. I thought maybe we could find a common ground again, and that he'd sit with me, like he used to, and he'd help me choose an outfit to wear. And, sure, I knew he might still be a bit cross under the surface, but for a second there, I'd thought that we could get past all that, and if I told him about Patrick then maybe he'd tease me like he used to, but . . .

And yet again, I was monumentally wrong.

In Robyn's room, the two voices cut.

Was it so bad to want to know who was with him in there? I'd tell him if I had a friend over, after all. I told him everything.

Back in my room, I sat down on the edge of the bed.

Robyn's laugh suddenly rumbled through the walls, but it was a fake laugh, like the laughs we'd all given at Edna's tea. I wanted to know if he would be working that night in TRASH, and if he'd ever go back to putting his make-up on in the sitting room with the good lighting, like he used to. And I wanted to know if I'd messed things up too badly to make it right.

Chapter Fifteen

The Ogre was a thin building, tucked in-between two hulking great stores on one of the side roads that led from St Stephen's Green. I walked down Grafton Street, dodging tourists. However long I lived in Dublin's city centre, heading anywhere that way was always further than I remembered. My silk-mix trousers clung to my bottom, swishing around my legs. Paired with a light shirt, I looked more like I'd dressed for a job in a bank, but with no time to shop I was not about to show up in my jeans and t-shirt. My boot heels clicked on the pavement, too tight, each tap an aural reminder of how much my feet would hurt on the way back to the flat.

I was only just late. Patrick had taken a table by the wall. He held his phone in his hands. His fingers were long, his knuckles wide, but he touched the phone with a careful delicacy. I tried not to imagine him at work with dead people in the same vein.

I brushed my hands over my hair and checked my lipstick in the door glass, then gathering every scrap of confidence I had, I strode in as if I went to places like The Ogre for dinner every day of the week with handsome men.

'Hi.' Patrick stood up straight away. He leaned down to kiss me, his cheek connecting with mine. I set my right hand on his chest. I didn't mean to. It just sort of gravitated to the muscles under his light blue jumper and shirt.

I whipped back my hand and sat down. He still wasn't wearing a wedding ring, I noticed. Ben drifted toward us from the bar, his shoes barely making a sound on the polished wooden floor.

'Good evening. Can I get anyone a drink?' he said.

Ben smiled and waited with perfect professional calm. I was unsure what to say. I was, after all, sitting at a table in a very expensive restaurant with a man who – by then, Robyn would have told everyone – was a pathologist, being served by the one who – I was also fairly certain everyone would have known by then – was top of my list for having knocked over and drowned a drag queen in the gutter, only a matter of weeks before.

'Wine,' I said suddenly. 'I, umm . . . A glass of wine, please?'

Patrick's eyebrows raised, just a little. He hid a grin, and coughed.

'Wine it is,' he agreed.

'Any particular kind of wine?' said Ben.

'Large wine?' suggested Patrick.

I giggled, and nodded.

'Two large white wines, coming up,' said Ben.

Walking away on the same, soft steps, Ben went to the bar at the other end of the room. As I was watching him, Patrick watched me. I scrambled in my mind for something intelligent to say.

'So, how are you?' I asked.

'Overworked, underpaid and hungry.'

'Of course.'

I picked up the menu and dropped it on my knife, sending the cutlery clanging to the floor and me following it. He was wearing different socks and nice black shoes. Really big black shoes, for really big feet.

'How're you?' said Patrick, when I returned.

'I'm fine. And you?'

Too late, I remembered I'd already asked that.

150

'So fine,' he said. 'You're fine, I'm fine. Now, what shall w—'

'Two large wines,' said Ben, setting the huge glasses in front of us. 'Are you ready to order?'

Barely able to focus on the menu I stumbled and stuttered through picking something, instantly forgetting what it was I'd asked for. A second later, I was wishing I'd ordered whatever it was the next couple were just being given, as it smelled amazing – and also wishing I'd met Patrick again, after all these years, without the weight of a dead drag queen, between us, and—

'So?' he said.

Ben had disappeared to the kitchen.

I nodded.

Had he asked me a question? I set the knife back into place and dipped for the napkin.

'So, um . . .'

'You have me for an hour,' he said. 'Martha will need to go out then, and . . .'

Ah.

Of course, there was a Martha. There had been a Thing, a legal Thing, and now there was a Martha. There was always bound to be a Martha. Patrick was a good-looking guy, and, more than that, he was a nice, decent and intelligent guy, and that kind of guy usually has a Martha of some kind or another. Of course he had a bloody Martha.

I pulled myself up, my friend-zone smile stuck firmly in place. I could totally do this.

'An hour is very kind,' I said.

Kind.

I swallowed hard.

'I'll keep it simple.' I pushed away all thoughts of inappropriate things, of dinner, and of anything other than the matter in hand.

'Noting the importance of confidentiality, I have a question about someone who died,' I said.

'A drag queen friend?'

I considered the word. 'A drag queen, yes. She was someone I knew. Someone connected to friends of mine.'

Patrick sat quietly as I told him how I'd been out to the club with Robyn for his first time, that night, and how Eve had upset so many people. I paused when Ben brought the food.

I waited until we were alone, and then went through how I left TRASH, how I'd walked around the corner. How I found her.

Patrick set down his fork. 'People often come to me when they're trying to make sense of the passing of loved ones,' he said gently. 'It can be a difficult time, Fi, especially when the person lost was so young.'

'Oh, I couldn't stand her,' I said without thinking. 'Sorry, I mean—'

He grinned.

'How's everything?' said Ben, appearing at my side.

I jumped, rattling my fork against my glass.

'It's grand,' said Patrick.

'Can I get any—?'

'We're fine,' he said.

I waited again, until Ben had gone.

I took a big mouthful of the goat's cheese tart that I'd thought by my rubbish Italian might have been some kind of chicken pasta dish, trying to both swallow the spinach and give myself time to work out how to say the next bit of my story.

'Someone killed Eve,' I said in the end. 'And I know they will already have finished the autopsy and the guards said it was an accident, but—'

'I really can't comment on a particular case, Fi.'

'I know, but—'

'Even if it wasn't my case,' he said. 'Not that I have . . . you know . . . cases, or anything – not that I'm like a guard, or . . . or a detective, or . . . But even if the body in question wasn't under my knife. Or, the file in question wasn't on my desk . . .'

He left the sentence hanging and broke the bread in his hands, dipping the crust into the pepper sauce around his chicken breast. I tried another piece of the goat's cheese tart with the surprisingly tangy cranberry sauce. I sucked my cheeks over my teeth and felt my eyes open wide. I darted looks at Ben, watching him when he wasn't watching me. Patrick ate quickly, drinking between, and at the tables around us, other people talked about normal things that didn't leave them staring at how their dinner guest was cutting up his meat.

'How can you tell?' I asked, after a minute.

'Tell what?'

'You know, dead people.'

'They're usually dead before I get them,' he said.

Ben drifted past our table, again. After the fourth time, Patrick leaned across to me and whispered, 'Is he waiting for me to stab you with my butter knife?'

I grinned. I considered telling Patrick that, actually, it might have been our waiter who'd killed Eve, that I wasn't sure because it still didn't really make sense, but of all the people who knew her, for Ben and Del, ridding themselves of her might have made things less complicated. After all, people killed for three reasons, so the stories tell us. For love, for money, and to cover up another crime. Love would make sense for Ben – his love of Del – and for Del, with his love of Ben. But it still wasn't enough. No one killed someone for being a nuisance. It had to be more than that, and if no one had truly loved Eve, and she didn't have any money, then what crime had she committed?

I tried the carrots. I wondered what his Martha was doing for dinner and if it was right that we were there together, without her, considering he was clearly committed, and if I should have invited her, or if he should have invited her.

'Fi?' he said. 'If you have something to ask me, just ask. I can always say no.'

'I think someone held her down and drowned her in the water,' I said. 'The guards brush me off when I call.'

'And then you went and wrote a blog asking who killed a drag queen?'

'I did.' I shrugged. 'I can't settle with it.'

He sat back in his chair and rested his fork on the side of the plate.

'It wasn't my case,' he said. 'You want to know if I think someone killed Eve, drowned her intentionally, or if it was an accident?'

A waitress came up from the bar. 'Your waiter just had to slip out, but any problems, just give me a wave,' she said.

I looked around the room. When did Ben leave? I thought I'd been watching him.

Patrick leaned over the table toward me. 'Even if I had the answers to your questions, I really couldn't comment,' he said.

I looked away.

'If they say it was an accident then . . .'

'But it wasn't,' I said. 'I had her head in my lap and she was dead, and I saw the look on her face, and—'

'Fi, the face changes after someone dies.'

I tried to find the words in the scramble of emotions that ran around my head. My glass was barely touched and Patrick's was empty. For all the excitement of the afternoon, thinking we would be deep in conversation there, imagining myself on an actual nearly date – maybe a bit flirty, and maybe he would be able to tell me yes, he'd checked Eve's body and she was fine, she really did just die by accident, and then maybe I could actually relax for the first time in ages, and maybe in my mind, he hadn't had a Martha, and—

It didn't matter.

I cradled my wineglass with both hands. I'd hardly touched my meal and Patrick was nearly done with his. I'd been talking too much.

'It sounds like the whole situation is a mess,' he said. 'And you're better off out of it. Go back to the bridges, Fi. Bridges don't keep you up at night.'

'You read the blog, so?'

'Of course I read the blog. I read it since the beginning.'

I lifted my glass.

'This is . . . different. It's complicated,' he said. 'There are many factors, and really, even though it's lovely to see you and to catch up, as I warned you, there's nothing much I can do to help or s—'

My phone buzzed in my pocket. I turned it off without looking.

'And in death,' he said, keeping his voice low, 'our faces relax – maybe you were just seeing something you weren't used to seeing, and—'

My phone rang again.

'I'm sorry,' I said. I pulled it out to reject the call. My thumb was over the red button as I read the name.

It was Robyn.

I blinked at the phone screen, watching it ring.

'Do you need to take that?' said the waitress pointedly.

'I'm sorry.' I rushed up to my feet, heading for the porch entrance. The line connected.

'Hey, Robyn?'

In two words, I sounded anxious – I felt anxious. He'd been so mad at me only an hour or two before, and now he was calling, and—

'Fi?' It wasn't Robyn's voice. 'Is that you? This is Del. You weren't answering my calls.'

'What's happened? Is Robyn hurt? Is he OK?'

'It's OK . . . No, girl, he's OK,' said Del quickly. 'He's here, but something's happened. Can y—'

I crashed out of the fancy little restaurant into the street.

'W-where is he?' I stuttered.

Behind him, I heard Robyn wailing.

'We're at mine,' said Del. 'Please. Come, now.'

The phone line went dead.

'Wait – Del?'

Ben jogged around the corner of the building. He must have heard me. Pale and drawn, he saw the phone in my hand. The look on my face.

'What's happened?' he said. 'What's going on? Is it Del?'

Patrick was at the bar, his credit card in his hand. I'd meant to pay for the meal – I'd meant to ask real questions and make the most of my time with him. I'd meant so many other things and now none of them mattered. Robyn was hurt or something had happened, or I didn't even know – I couldn't think – I couldn't shape my words.

'What's happened?' said Patrick, as he came out on to the street.

The other couples at the tables were looking at us through the window.

'It's Robyn,' I said. 'Or . . . or it was Del. I mean—'

'My Del?'

I stared at Ben. What had he done?

Ben grabbed for my arm. 'What happened?' he said. 'Is someone hurt? Who's hurt?'

Why did he need to run out all of a sudden and leave the other waitress covering for him, and why was he now looking at me so guiltily? Where had he been?

'No, no one's hurt,' I said. 'Or I don't think so. Del rang and just said something's happened. He said to come right away – that doesn't mean anyone's hurt, right? Does that mean anyone is dead, Patrick?' I turned to him. 'Does—'

'Where are they?' said Patrick.

We moved together, a pack of three. I forgot my pain from the high-heeled boots and I forgot that Patrick wasn't part of our tribe, that he had to go home to his Martha, and I forgot that I was meant to pay for dinner, because that's what I'd set out to do—

I forgot everything, except Robyn.

At the last corner, Ben started to run. Patrick caught the door before it closed. He stopped me at the bottom of the stairs.

'Should I leave?' he said.

He stood so close to me I wanted to cling on, and I wanted to ask him to go up there for me, instead of me, and to tell me it was all fine, and that no one else was dead.

A desperate cry came from the top landing. We let the front door slam behind us as we ran up the stairs. Robyn was shouting, 'What were you thinking?'

Another scream, a high-pitched wail of anger, frustration. No one could scream like Robyn.

'You used my phone?' he wailed.

'She wasn't answering to mine and—'

'Well, you can go out there and tell her to f—'

'Ben!' said Del, relief written through his tone. 'Thank goodness, is—'

'What the hell were you thinking using my phone?' Robyn shouted.

'I was thinking this bloody happened, Rob, and—'

At the top landing, I leaned on the stair rail, panting heavily. Patrick was barely breathing harder than before. He turned to me but before he could ask, the door swung open again. Del stood in front of us, his face fully made up, his wig on the kitchen table behind him. He stumbled forward.

'Fi—'

'Who is dead?' I said.

'No one is dead.'

'You can go home,' said Robyn. 'There's no story here.'

He stepped out from behind Del.

'I called her,' said Del. 'Like it or not, she's involved with this mess, and this is my flat and I called her, Robyn, and—'

'What happened?' I said.

'Why do you care?' said Robyn. 'So you can write it in a blog?'

He had on his good orange shirt, and his black-and grey trousers, and the runners he only wore when he was on a second date. Suddenly, the giggling in his room earlier made more sense.

Del's apartment was jammed full. I looked around for someone who might have been with him on a date, but I knew everyone there. In the background, Ben paced the kitchen. Mark sat on the antique chair by the window, making the elegant carved arms look spindly. Behind him, the bedroom door swung on its hinges and Thora – her wig askew and her dress half falling off – and Miss Merkin burst into the room.

'I just can't!' said Thora. 'My babies – my girls – I just can't! None of you understand! None of you—'

'I think Gavin understands,' said Mark. 'He's in hospital right now, understanding that what happened – happened to him and not to y—'

'Oh do shut up,' said Thora. 'You're not paid to have an opinion.'

'Another month like the last one and none of us will be paid for anything,' Mark retorted.

'So that's it?' said Thora. 'We're attacked again and you're raging for your pocket?'

'I'm going to the damn bathroom – do you have a problem with that?'

Storming through the others, he pushed to the back of the room.

'It's first on th—' Del started, but Mark was already there.

'Look,' said Ben. 'Everyone here is fine, and if y—'

Thora put her hand to the heavens. 'They're coming for us, I just know it,' she wailed. 'Oh, my babies, my babies! What will happen to us?'

'It was an accident,' said Robyn. 'There's nothing to worry about.'

'You have no idea,' Thora snapped at him. 'No notion of the responsibility.'

With a long eye roll, Del pulled us into the flat and closed the door.

'Who's this?' said Merkin, turning with a snap.

'This is Patrick,' I told them. 'Patrick this is . . .' I swept my hand over the crowded room.

The queens stood like a pageant display. Thora, her face caught in horror; Merkin, pursing her lips, her ripped tights and torn skirt thick with dirt; Del, wrapped in PVC, one arm up, perfect lipstick, boy hair flat to his head.

Robyn struck out his chin.

'Everybody,' I said.

'Gavin is in hospital,' said Thora. Her eyes burned with fury as she glared at me. 'I hope you're proud.'

'Me?'

'You made it a thing.'

'Who's Gavin?' said Patrick.

'Made what a thing?' I said.

'You said someone was trying to kill us!' Merkin screeched, shedding sequins as she wafted her arms. 'You told people that someone was killing drag queens, and now everyone is trying to kill us!'

'It's open bloody season,' Thora cried.

'Can anyone here tell us what actually happened?' said Patrick. 'Who's Gavin?'

Mid-squeal, Merkin stopped. She put her hands on her ruined hips.

'A car drove at Robyn and his new boyfriend,' said Del.

'Gav isn't my boyfriend. We're just—'

'It went for Robyn and—'

'It wasn't going for me,' said Robyn.

'Who was driving the car?' said Patrick.

'The driver took the corner too fast,' said Robyn. 'That's all. They were driving too fast, and Gavin tried to pull me away, and then Del had some kind of episode and decided we all had to come up here just in case—'

'I could have died!' Merkin cried.

'You? You think this is all about you?' said Thora. 'Have you even seen my wig? This is a thousand-euro wig!'

'It's a forty-quid wig from the dressing-up shop around the back of Connolly Station,' said Del. 'And neither of you were anywhere near Gavin or Robyn when the car hit.'

'But I'll be next!' Merkin wailed.

'Keep going and I'll throw you down the stairs myself, Baby Jane,' said Mark, reappearing.

'I still don't see why you had to get her here,' said Robyn, sneering at me. 'She is obviously busy!'

I started to push back against the door, but Patrick stopped me.

'Since we're here, can I help anyone who is hurt?' he said.

'We're not dead,' snapped Robyn.

'Clearly,' I said. 'Dead people aren't so rude!'

'Have the man come in,' said Thora with a long sigh. 'Dear Lord, at the very least we must surround ourselves with beautiful things. Come here, my beautiful thing. Tell me something soothing.'

'Which one of you was hurt?' said Patrick.

'I was,' said Merkin. 'My legs are all kinds of broken.' Standing nearly seven foot tall in her platform heels, she towered over even Patrick. 'My skirt!' she said. 'This . . . have you any idea how long this took to make? How many needles I broke on the machine?'

'I'll put the kettle on,' said Del heavily. 'Fi, I'm sorry to call you o—'

'And are you Gavin?' said Patrick.

'DO I LOOK LIKE A GAVIN?' Merkin screamed. 'Did I spend hours painting my face, twisting into this goddamn corset, for you to call me Gavin?'

With a long sigh, Ben ducked through the others.

'Merkin,' he said. He put out both his hands and led her to the sofa. 'Darling, I can't imagine the shock.' Setting her down, he turned, already taking hold of Thora. 'And Mama Thora, please, sit down, my precious, take the w—'

'If you use this opportunity to tell me I'm fat then I swear I will not be responsible for m—'

'Take the delicate elegance off your feet, darling, and please sit down and let this nice man here take a look at you. Who are you again?' Ben asked Patrick.

'Patrick Midda,' Robyn snapped.

'So much clearer straight away,' said Ben, shaking his head.

'Patrick was at UCD with us,' I said. 'We were—'

Thora eyed me suspiciously across the room. Suddenly I didn't want to say out loud what we were doing, especially since I couldn't quite figure it out myself.

Ben's phone rang. Without flinching, he handed it to Del, who lowered his voice as he crept back into the kitchen.

'. . . yes, Ben is really very sorry, we had a family emergency . . . Nothing he could do . . . yes . . . he, he will be back in as soon as he c—'

Abandoning the boiling kettle, Del picked up a bottle of gin from the dresser, gestured to me and to the tonic on the side. I took eight long glasses from the shelf and ice from the freezer. We worked as a team. As soon as I had two mixed, I handed them to Ben.

'They're like babies,' he whispered. 'They need something in their mouths.'

Gin. Tonic.

Del took one and I passed Mark another.

I leaned to Robyn.

'Are you OK?' I said.

Reaching over me, he took a glass from the table.

'What actually happened?' I asked.

'Why?'

'Gavin was run over,' said Del quietly. 'The nice young man who has been entertaining your little friend here while you two have been feuding – he and Rob were walking down the street and they just turned in from the back road and some car, for no good reason, sped up and—'

'They might already have been speeding,' said Robyn.

'And Mark was on the door.'

'He wasn't,' said Robyn. 'He was halfway down the road, on the phone.'

'I don't remember,' said Mark. 'Someone rang for the club. I saw the car coming and then the cute guy with the red shirt pushed Robyn out of the way, just in time.' He nodded at Robyn. 'And the car still veered toward them.'

'It didn't veer.'

Mark shrugged. 'And it hit the young guy, clear on his legs.'

Patrick looked up from checking Merkin's pulse.

'What did the driver do?' he said.

'Did you get the number?' I asked him. 'Did you see who was driving?'

'Everyone asked me that and I was too busy calling a bloody ambulance,' said Mark.

'What kind of car was it?' said Patrick.

Thora scrubbed the air with her hands. 'Calm down, action man,' she said. 'And you' – she pointed at me – 'I don't care what we said. I have no idea why Del called you—'

'Because Fi is Robyn's best friend,' said Del. 'And because we don't yell at family.'

'She—' Robyn started.

'She's your best friend, you idiot, even when you're both being ridiculous about it,' Del added.

'Oh, so now it's my fault?'

'Shut up and drink your gin, petal.'

'As far as I can make out, no one saw the driver,' said Mark. 'I didn't even get the make. I barely got the colour.'

'It was silver,' said Del.

'Grey,' said Robyn.

'Was the driver a man? A woman?' said Patrick.

Robyn shook his head. 'I didn't see, and then I was face down on the road.'

'Sound familiar?' I said.

'Not helpful, Hagatha.'

'I could have died,' said Merkin, her voice shaking.

'You ran to see what was happening, tripped over your heels and fell out of the door,' said Mark.

'I fell headlong into the car!'

'The car was already half a mile away by then.'

'It's my babies,' said Thora, holding a tissue to her mouth. 'Oh my poor drag babies.'

'Was Gavin—' I started.

'HE'S NOT DEAD!' Robyn shouted.

'Sorry,' I said. 'Is Gavin a drag queen?'

'Not technically,' said Merkin.

'Not at all,' said Del. 'He's a nice lad who works as a barista at the new café just past the gay SPAR.'

'Oh, my poor pet!' Thora cried.

'He's not yours,' said Del. 'He's just some guy who hooked up with Rob here last week, and now—'

'Now you're getting your coffee at the Orange Place?' I said to Robyn.

'Well, I'm hardly going to drop in to Jenkins and Betrayal-Are-Us, am I?'

I crept back until my hands met the door.

'Fi is just as much a part of this family,' said Del.

'It's not your fault, Fi,' said Ben. 'It's just not your scene, that's all.'

I looked from him to Thora, back to Robyn.

It had always been my scene. My friends, my place, my home. Not as much as Robyn, sure, but as much as anywhere was my home.

'Ben doesn't mean that,' said Del gently.

'I imagine Ben doesn't mean a lot of things,' I snapped.

Del's face fell.

'No, no, I'm sorry,' I said. 'I shouldn't have said that.'

'Why not?' said Thora. 'You seem to make a habit of saying what you think.'

Tears flooded my eyes. I blinked them away. 'I just wrote one stupid blog about how anyone could kill something so beautiful.'

'Eve wasn't beautiful,' said Del. 'She was poison.'

Thora and Robyn nodded. Patrick looked up from checking Merkin's bony ankle. I held the door, wishing above all things that it was Robyn who would leave the flat with me, and who would link arms and stumble around the little gated square, down past Trinity, back home.

As if knowing my mind, Robyn walked to the window. He turned his back to the room.

Had I really ruined everything? Was that one question on my blog too much? Had I crossed a line I could not see?

Patrick checked Thora's pulse.

'Should I call someone?' said Thora. 'I can't breathe. I think I'm having a heart attack.'

'Loosen the corset,' said Patrick. 'Maybe switch the gin to water, and—'

'Dear Lord, man, I'm not dying!' Thora shook her hand free but as she sat back, she nodded to Ben, who moved to top up her glass with more gin.

'I'm sure I'm bruised,' said Merkin. 'I have such tender skin. Right here, see,' she said, running her hand up her thigh. 'Any pressure at all, and . . .'

Patrick patted Merkin's calf. 'I think you're OK,' he said with a grin. 'Nice deep breaths now, and—'

'Oh, don't you be worrying, everything about Merkin is deep,' said Thora.

'It's a life skill,' Merkin whispered.

Chapter Sixteen

I walked home the long way, past Trinity. The green was well lit. It was so long ago that we used to meet there, well away from UCD. Not that it was any different to hanging out on the little mini-park near Christchurch or up by the Botanic Gardens, but it was green and the birds would land down near Robyn and he could throw them biscuit crumbs. The wind would whistle through the plane trees and, for an hour or two, we were away from the endless tapping of the other students on their phones and on their laptops, and the squeak of pens on whiteboards, and the rumbling lectures through which neither of us could stay awake.

It was no different there by the lawn, but like bunking off study periods and climbing up the hill to the farm gate, it was just us. At Trinity we could be quiet, and Robyn would stretch out in his one-strap dungarees with his hair swept to the side and no one we knew called out words we didn't want to hear. We both drank more and more coffee and I leafed through comic books and magazines about photography.

And it was easy.

◆　◆　◆

'How is Gavin?' I asked, as he closed the door.

Barely looking at me, Robyn went into the kitchen and took out the breakfast cereal, filled a bowl.

I pulled the blanket over my legs. I yawned. It was cold. Not the dark, damp cold of the winter, but a threatening, bitter meanness in the air.

Robyn stood at the kitchen door.

'Are you working on Wednesday?' he said.

I nodded.

'And you won't mind if Gavin comes here?'

'Why would I mind?'

Robyn had always brought friends to the apartment.

'Because you're being weird,' he said.

'I'm not.'

'You've sat up there all night?'

'Because your friend—'

'But you don't even know Gavin,' said Robyn. 'That's what I mean. This is nothing to do with you.'

His words cut through me like a blade.

It never used to matter that the people who came over were Robyn's friends, or that the bars we went to were gay bars. It never mattered that our friends were his friends more than my friends and that the arrangements came through his phone, and not mine, and that his world . . .

His world was my world.

Back then, when we'd curled up on the doorsteps in Trinity grounds, it was the gay bars we'd talked about going to and the gay shows we'd saved up for, and when we got back to the little room in Stanhope Street and he chose what to watch on my laptop, it was drag shows and gay shows and—

And it never mattered. It never bothered me.

We'd go to a straight bar at some point, but I wasn't troubled as long as we had a laugh and as long as he was happy.

I closed my eyes. Again and again, I thought back to the evening when this nightmare had started, but each time I tried to remember it, there was a piece missing, like a jigsaw without its middle. Something in my mind just would not settle about Eve's death, any more than it would about Gavin being run down. It didn't make sense. People didn't just die in the gutter. Young men were not mown down.

Robyn was right about one thing. I was pushing. I couldn't let it go. And I could see by the way he looked at me while he munched his chocolate loops, he thought I was making trouble or being nosy or inventing a story – but he had no idea how, like a dog with a bone, my brain simply could not stop gnawing at those worries. Every time I thought of Eve, all I could see was Robyn. It must be the same for Edna and Karen, the same for Del.

There were so many unanswered questions. Was TRASH really failing as Mark had implied? How much had Eve stolen from Thora, and why hadn't she just called the guards herself? Why were they holding Eve's gathering when they couldn't stand her? And why, if they were all so keen on celebrating her life, would none of the others admit this was clearly not an accidental death?

Robyn tipped out another bowl of chocolate loops and splashed them with milk. If things had been normal, I would be in there with him, one of us sitting up on the counter and one at the table, both crunching, slopping milk, but then if things had been normal, I would have slept all night on my bed and not dozed on the couch and I would be just about waking up for work and Robyn would be tucked up in bed, with or without Gavin, and my blog would still be the same dull series of people on bridges without faces.

And Eve would be alive.

Again, I'd rung the gardaí, and again I had short, sharp thrift from the woman on the line.

'You really need to stop bothering us, Ms McKinnery . . .'

And if Robyn had been acting normal, I would have told him how the woman had lectured me on wasting their time for three times the length of my original query, and how she still, in the end, refused to answer any of my questions about whether Gavin's case was being looked into, or if they'd released Eve's body for burial.

But he wasn't. Robyn wasn't being normal about anything at all. Nothing was normal.

◆ ◆ ◆

I left on time for work. At the corner, I bumped into Mark on a run. He looked up with a start, and stopped. Sweat clung to his tight running top; his legs were like solid tree trunks, carved with perfect lines of muscle.

'Any news?' His voice was dull and tired. Deep black shadows hung under his eyes too, as if none of us had slept.

'Gavin was staying in overnight. They're going to reset his bones and stuff, Del said, but he'll be OK.'

'I meant did he see who it was who was driving?'

'I thought you told me no one saw?'

Mark shrugged. 'It was dark. It could have been anyone, Fi.'

I felt an itch claw under my hairline, over my neck.

'So,' he said. 'Ben told me you had a date at the restaurant with the tall Patrick guy? Been there long, had you, when Del called?'

'No, not really, actually, but—'

'What time did you get to the restaurant?'

'Sorry?'

'Never mind, it'll be on the phone log,' he said. 'It must be so hard when someone threatens the things you love.'

I frowned. It was too early and Mark was making less and less sense by the minute.

'Del called—'

'Did the date go well?' said Mark, cutting through me.

'Not really,' I said. 'I was my usual, socially uncomfortable self, then I asked him a bunch of inappropriate questions about cutting up dead people and we'd barely finished our first course when Del rang – freaking out because someone is trying to kill Dublin's drag queens, even though no one had died and the only person attacked, or not attacked, wasn't a drag queen at all – and after we left, Patrick went home to his wife.'

'I've had worse dates,' he said.

'Really?'

'You'd be surprised.'

I grinned. 'It wasn't really a date,' I said. 'It was just two old friends.'

'Did he iron his shirt?'

I thought back. 'Yeah, I think so,' I said.

'A straight guy irons a shirt, it's a date.'

I jogged the last two blocks to Jenkins and Holster. The shop was already buzzing with early customers.

'I am not late,' I said, as I pushed past a customer at the door.

Jenkins didn't answer. His face was dark with fury. Mickey shot me a look of warning from the station behind the coffee stand. I stayed out of the firing line. Without taking off my coat, I dealt with two customer queries, steering a man toward the sugar-free biscuits and an older woman to the organic flour.

I crept in behind the till.

Seeing the apples, I wondered how Del's mum was doing. If she too had mentally timed how long it would take Ben to leave the restaurant and drive around the corner, mow into Robyn and Gavin . . .

But there was no reason he would do so. Why would he hurt either of them? Maybe the car wasn't actually speeding at all – maybe we were just all really jumpy? Sure, every one of them was

170

bitching at Del in the end, for pulling them over to his flat, pulling them offstage and away from danger, and every one of them had different reasons to be scared. Was it, like Thora declared, an attack on the drag queens of Dublin, the bad guy just happening to hurt someone who wasn't a queen – or was it simply coincidental?

But I'd never believed in coincidence.

'Psst.' Mickey leaned over. 'Here.' He handed me a small cardboard cup filled to the brim with thick black coffee. 'Don't say anything,' he whispered as I snuck it down to the shelf below the till. 'The boss is in a real state.'

I whispered my thanks. The coffee was strong enough to strip away my stomach lining.

I turned for the next customer.

'Good morning.' I set my face to a friendly, slightly manic, smile. 'That's six forty, please?'

Jenkins waited until the customer had gone, then bustled over to stand in front of my till.

'You were late,' he said.

I was a minute and a half late.

'I'm sorry, Mr Jenkins,' I said. 'It won't happen again.'

'It happens every morning.'

'Not every morning,' I said.

'She was on time last Wednesday,' said Mickey unhelpfully.

Jenkins thumbed through the display of handmade cards. On the front, a sympathy card wobbled and fell from its rack, and he bent to snap it from the ground.

I worked without thinking, bleeping the food over the scanner, taking money, giving change, making nice, vague comments. When we switched for lunch, I took my sandwiches outside. I had thirty minutes, which was easily long enough to get to the Orange Place and back.

I stood in line.

The shop was tiny. If I'd been unkind, I'd have noted that their coffee machine was the baby version of ours. So, Robyn had chosen this place over mine now. In a matter of weeks, he'd gone from my friend, my coffee buddy and my confidant, to someone who spent actual money on their own coffee and cakes.

The woman smiled, ready to take my order. She was younger than me, thinner than me and prettier than me, and I loathed every part of her from her perfectly messy hair to her well-worn Doctor Martens boots.

I was possibly not being my best self.

'Double shot latté, please, and a cream slice,' I said with an over-enthusiastically warm grin. I wasn't even sure what I was out to prove but I would verify that their coffee was worse than ours and that their food was inedible, even if I ended up shaking with caffeine and sugar. There were worse ways to go, as Del would have told me.

The bill was less than Jenkins charged. Not by much, but enough to be annoying. The cake was amazing. Light, fluffy and creamy. Steaming with exhausted resentment, I lurked in one of the side streets under the lip of a building, licking cream from my fingers. The base was heavenly and even the jam was perfect.

To my relief, the coffee was nearly as good as ours, but not quite.

Regally pertinacious, I nursed my envy to my chest.

I glowered into the milky remains of my nearly perfect latté.

Things change, my dad used to say.

I wished I could have called him, asked him what I did that was so wrong. On an impulse, I flicked my phone to Edna's number, but you don't call a friend's mammy. Not even if the friend was being an eejit.

My hands shook behind the till when I got back. Everywhere I looked, the Jenkins and Holster logo seemed to swim in front of my eyes. I pinged each item without thinking, my brain running the same damn loop as always.

Eve was dead. Eve was dead. Eve was dead.

I counted out the change. I smiled.

Now Gavin had been run down by an unnamed driver.

I nodded. I said it was brightening up.

Eve was dead. EVE WAS DEAD.

I was losing it and I was boring myself.

At closing time, I took a minute to tidy my space in the back room, trying to get my head to calm the hell down. Mickey came in.

'No little friend again tonight?' he said, nodding to the window.

He's not little. 'Not tonight.'

'Have you had a row?'

I looked up. 'What makes you say that?' I asked.

'You look sad. I figure, OK, so our Fi, she is sad, and usually when our Fi is sad, her little friend, he comes to the window in the evenings, and you buy your coffee in twos before you leave. But this week and last week . . .'

'Yeah,' I said.

'So I thought,' said Mickey, 'that maybe I, here, could buy you your coffee today?'

'No. No, it's fine.' I looped my bag over my shoulder.

'Or, if you like, maybe dinner?' said Mickey.

The very last thing I wanted was to go out for dinner with anyone after the debacle at The Ogre. I would survive on Pot Noodles, and that was just fine.

I touched his arm as I slid past him. 'I'm fine. I'm not sad.' I smiled to prove it. 'I'll see you tomorrow?' I said.

A strange look passed over Mickey's face. It was nearly an hour later, alone, in the apartment, when I realised that maybe he wasn't just being kind, and maybe he was asking me out on an actual date. Not as two old friends where one's a desperately good-looking pathologist and the other trying to get information for a case that wasn't even a case because it was none of her damn business – maybe Mickey wasn't thinking about any of that, but of an actual, actual date?

'You're a fool, Fiona McKinnery,' I said out loud.

My phone bleeped. As if picking himself from my thoughts, Patrick's name was displayed on the screen.

Hey Fi, I've been thinking. I'm going for a walk with Martha. Meet me on Ha'penny Bridge in an hour? Patrick x

Before I could answer, the phone rang in my hand.

The line connected, but Del hesitated. 'Hi?'

'What's happened?' I said. 'Who's dead?'

'Umm . . .'

I was joking, and then suddenly I wasn't joking. 'Del?'

'No,' he said. 'Robyn's fine. We're all fine. Look, can I – I mean, if it's not too much, and—'

'What's up?' I said.

'Would you fancy a drink?' he said. 'If you're not too busy or anything.'

I drifted to the wardrobe as we talked, starting to think what I should wear to meet Patrick.

'Of course,' I said. 'When were you thinking?'

'Are you at home?'

'I am.'

'You see the taxi outside your window?'

Chapter Seventeen

Del was easy to like. Dublin born and raised, he was old enough to remember how the city used to be and young enough to enjoy how it was now, and unlike one or two of the other drag queens, he only held himself up when he was in heels.

The taxi driver nodded as I opened the door. In the back, Del's face was entirely surrounded by ruffles of silver tulle and net, his legs and feet all but lost under the huge ball of fabric. His wig was new, gold ringlets sticking from his hair like angry silk snakes, the ends dipped in silver, and he had mock-diamond earrings and a sparkling choker around his neck, but the taxi's interior light was hostile and whilst I could see that his make-up had originally been spotless, his eyes were red and the liners were streaked and smudged, his cheeks dusted with what now looked like a multi-coloured bruise.

His hand shook as he stretched it toward me. I gripped his fingers and lurched forward into the mess of net, throwing my arms around him.

'Twenty past,' said the driver.

Del nodded. 'We'll make it,' he said.

'You were meant to be onstage at five past, lad.'

'It's OK, Dad.' Del wiped his hands over his eyes again, then looked up. 'Oh, and this is Fi. Fi, this is my dad, Ned.'

Reaching over Del's costume, we both waved through the plastic divider.

'Twenty-one minutes past,' said Del's dad, tapping on his watch.

I pulled the door closed behind me and we slid forward into the traffic. With Del's help, I found the seat belt and, striking blind between us, finally located the holder.

'So,' I said. 'Wh—'

I wasn't sure how to ask but Del was already shaking his head. 'Nothing wrong,' he said, grinning through the tears. 'I'm fine. We're going to get drunk and forget all about it, and—'

'Honey, are you sure?' I said.

'It's bingo tonight,' he said, his voice cracking. 'At The Maple Leaf. And more importantly, I'm getting paid for this and they are not going to see me cry – Fi, please, don't let th—'

His chest heaved and I nodded, taking hold of as much of his arm as I could find, patting him and soothing him as he tried to regain control.

It would be about Ben, I figured. That bloody man. He'd have done something – or someone – or at least said something.

Del's bottom lip wobbled but he snapped his head to the side and whipped back the front of his wig. 'Nope,' he said. 'I'm not doing this. I am not crying.' He wiped his eyes on his fingers. 'How do I look?' he said.

He looked like he'd been painted in watercolours and left out in the rain.

'Oh, um . . .'

He dug into the side of the seat and brought out a make-up bag. Peering into the mirror, he blanched even paler under the thick lines of base.

'Christ,' he hissed. 'I look worse than Merkin on a Monday morning.'

'Slap on the silver cream eye shadow your ma got you,' said his dad.

I looked out of the window, watching the lights on the water. The night sky was pretty again, layers of red and blue, and no hint of the day's grey clouds. Patrick would have a nice walk by the river.

If we were lucky, maybe the weather would break at last, and we'd finally be into summer. Dublin usually delivered a decent few months of heat once it got itself going but the Irish sun was unreliable, reluctant to rise before noon, often peeling away just before I left work.

Along the bank, the weeds and tufts of grass were bright green against the mottled earth tones of the slimy mud.

Del drew out an eyeliner but his hand shook. He passed it to me. I leaned closer, peering at the damage. The upper colours were OK, the eyebrows still in place, it was mostly just his lower lid lines, his lashes on one side, and the curls –

I've got this, I thought. How hard could it be, anyway? I'd watched him make up his eyes a hundred times over the years and, anyway, I was a girl, wasn't I? This stuff was meant to come easy to me, and I'd been doing the black lines around my own eyes for years.

I took each colour he passed me and worked through the base, then the powder. When he started to shake again, I gently prodded his chest. Tough love, I decided, as I drew the gold curl up to the left eyebrow to try to make it look the same as the right. I added a bit more. Then a bit more of the blue cream stuff.

I wondered if Patrick was on the bridge already and if Martha was smiling as she walked with him, hand in hand down the Lovers' Lane, if her heels clicked as she walked, just loud enough to be sexy without echoing along the walls like mine did, and if the evening light was picking up the copper in her hair – not that she would have to be a redhead, of course, but that's how I pictured her: tall, svelte, intelligent, some kind of scientist probably – someone he would have met at a conference in Galway in one of those posh hotels. She'd be neat and clean – naturally, not having to work at it – and she'd be the kind of woman who didn't fall over her words but picked and chose what she said and made sure each comment made perfect sense before she opened her mouth.

'How busy is bingo?' I said. I took the lash glue and tried to stick down the long blue top lashes over my wobbly line.

'It's usually rammed,' said Del. 'Are we done?'

The taxi turned the last corner and Del's dad pulled in behind a tall, square building. I held the mirror in my palm.

'Before you look—'

'Dad?' said Del.

His dad turned in the seat. 'Holy Mary Mother of God,' he said. He bit on his lip. 'Your mother and I love you, son, and—'

'Christ, it must be bad,' said Del. 'Fi, you're fired. Come on, girl.'

With help from his dad and me, Del squeezed himself and his costume out of the taxi. Stopping only for him to kiss his father and to promise he really was fine, we ran across the road and under the mock-Canadian veranda of The Maple Leaf Inn.

I'd never seen so many check shirts in one place. The walls were log-lined, the floor dusty. In the far corner, a group of men sat around a long table, their plates filled with steak and chips, and burgers and chips, and the three-piece mix of undressed lettuce, cucumber and tomato that my dad called 'plastic greens'. To my disappointment, the only Canadian man seemed to be the barman. On the dance floor, Irish accents mixed with Polish and Japanese, and women thronged together, some in what might be loosely be termed as drag make-up, some in sparkly dresses and some, like me, wearing old black leggings and a plain t-shirt, and probably feeling just as out of place.

From the second he was through the door, Del was onstage. He flung his hands into the air, launching into a ridiculous story of getting stuck in the wake of a hen night from Brussels, and as he greeted the manager and ordered the drinks and took up the microphone, he was absolutely in charge. Only when he beckoned me to sit right next to the stage where he could see me, and he gripped my hand, squeezing my fingers with his, could I see the heartbreak and fear in him.

'Fi,' he said. 'If I get fired because I look like a human toffee wrapper, I won't be able to pay the rent, and I'll be moving in with you. Just so you know.'

I nodded and grinned.

A click sounded and the house lights dimmed. Lady Gaga's voice burst out of the speakers and Del took to the tiny stage. I moved my shoulders in time. With a huge kick, Del launched into the chorus. He twirled, he twisted, he threw himself backward, he death dropped, he lip-synced every word without fail, his eyes sparking and burning through the lyrics, his hands flickering over his heart.

I sang out 'Born This Way' with the others.

Del slid to the very edge of the stage and leaned forward into the small audience and it didn't matter that his eye make-up looked ridiculous or that his wig was higher on one side, and as the song came to the end, Del spun on the stage, his arms bent at the elbow, his hands in the air, and the giant ball of net that was so crumpled and messed in the taxi opened up into a million petals, sparkling ripples around his body.

He finished with a final death drop and I clapped and cheered. He looked for me.

I handed him a vodka and tonic, letting my fingers brush his.

'You're slaying it,' I said quietly.

The bingo game was ridiculous and just what I needed – just what everyone there needed, I imagined, seeing the laughter and the bright eyes, and the enjoyment of finding each number. At the back of the stage, a screen hung from a long pole. The numbers rolled down so quickly I was still looking for the last one when the next came along.

Every twenty minutes, I collected drinks from the bar and brought them to Del's little table. I needed one more number for a line when the shout came from the back of the room and a tall, bearded man came forward, delighted with his win. The game was over.

Two more songs, each one with just as much life and fight as the first, and we were done, the stand and screen were put away, the money was handed out, the glasses collected, and the bar faded back into its pre-show slumber.

I reread the message from Patrick, and my lame excuse that actually I was sorry but I had to pop out. I pressed my thumb to the screen, as if I could reach through the glass to touch his name.

Outside, Del sat alone on the bench. The light caught him, casting his delicate, handsome face into shadow, the dark night more sympathetic to my attempt to fix his eyes. Unable to resist, I took a photo.

'Hey gorgeous.' I showed him.

'A portrait in nothing,' he said with a sad smile.

'Want me to delete it?'

'No, stick it on your blog, I could use the pity publicity,' he said. 'Maybe I'll get Merkin's Tuesday night bingo as well.'

'She'll never give that up.'

'Shit, I'm sorry,' he said. 'You obviously had an evening planned and I called you all the way over here, just because me and my misery needed a babysitter, and now I'm sat here and—'

'It's fine.'

'It isn't,' said Del. 'Can I tell you something?'

'Of course.'

'I thought Ben had actually killed her.' He put his hand over his eyes. 'I actually thought the man I love, the man I married, had somehow bashed that stupid bitch over the head with a brick or something.' He gave a soft, huffing laugh. 'The worst bit . . .'

The lights of his dad's taxi picked out the car park.

'The worst bit,' Del whispered, 'is I could forgive him that in a heartbeat, and yet, the stuff I could not forgive . . .'

He stopped, and I nodded.

'So.' He pointed a long finger at me. 'My question for you, dear Hagatha, if you're such a sleuth—'

'I hate that name.' I screwed up my mouth. 'Don't call me that.'

'You can hate the name but you can't deny the calling. Put me out of my misery, Fi. Who killed Eve? Because if she was killed,' he said, 'and then whoever did it ran their car at Robyn and Gavin . . . ?'

'It was definitely aimed at Robyn too?'

'Sure,' he said. 'The car went straight at them, and the driver only missed Robyn because Gavin pushed him out of the way first. So, unless I misread every detective novel on my mother's shelves in my teens, we have three questions.' He held up one finger. 'Who killed Eve Harrington?' Two fingers. 'Who was driving that car?'

'And three,' I said, 'who's next?'

The night curled around us.

'And Ben was really with you when the car came for Robyn?' said Del.

I stood up, turned away toward the taxi. I could tell him the truth, but what good did it do? I could be wrong. I could be monstrously wrong.

'He was working at the restaurant,' I said, choosing my words.

'Then he couldn't have driven the car.' Del breathed out a long sigh. 'I shouldn't even say it,' he said, 'but I keep looking around me and thinking, *Which one of them was it?*' He shook his head, his spiral hair shimmering in the low light. 'Is it worse to be thinking these things of someone you love? I mean, it's easier to assume the killer was a stranger but why would a stranger bother killing us? What you said in your blog, right – why would anyone kill a drag queen?'

'Why would anyone kill anybody?' I said.

'Yes, but a drag queen? I mean, we're useless.'

'You're not. You're fabulous,' I told him. 'You make people laugh, you make people feel better. Look back in there at that audience. You gave every one of those people a good time tonight.'

'And not once was I on my knees.'

'Exactly. Every night at TRASH it's the same – people can escape, they can laugh, and sing along. You matter.'

'Yeah, but enough to kill?' he said.

We squeezed in together in the back of the car, holding hands. I let my thoughts rumble through my mind. At my corner by the bridge, I leaned in to hug Del, putting everything I didn't know how to say into gripping him around as much of his middle as I could find through the fabric, my face buried in the yards and yards of sparkling tulle.

'There is no other way than to go on,' he whispered.

I thanked his dad for the ride and climbed back on to the pavement, shedding sequins.

I closed the car door but then turned back.

'Hey – hey, Del?'

He edged over to the window.

'Don't die, OK?' I said.

He blew me a kiss and the car rolled away.

Chapter Eighteen

I was nearly an hour late to work the following day.

'I'm so sorry.'

'Remind me why I don't fire you,' said Mr Jenkins from the tills.

'I have no idea,' I said truthfully, as I ran my cardigan and bag into the back room. 'It won't happen again.'

'It will,' he sighed.

Mickey looked up. I tried to smile, but my eyebrows shot up too high and I could feel the sweat already beading on my forehead from having run the last hundred metres.

'Morning,' I said.

He set a coffee on to the little shelf.

'Ah, you're sweet,' I told him, trying to forget the weirdness of the other night. After all, I'd never been any good at getting dates and things, so the chances were, as I had told Del, I'd probably misread the signals and he was just being kind.

'I am that,' said Mickey. 'You should make the most of me, Fi. Jenkins really will fire you one of these days if you keep on being late. You might not know what you missed.'

Nope. I wasn't wrong.

I worked through the morning. In my break, I flicked through the photos I'd taken of Del, and a little voice in my head reminded me of Mrs Harper's words.

That camera of yours, she'd said. *It might make it easier to keep it between you and the world, but don't forget that the world can see you perfectly without a lens.*

Well, fine, I thought, as I went back to counting the packets of overpriced organic tea. *The world can see me as they like.*

But then there was Robyn.

Mrs Harper was right there too. Robyn could see me just fine, but what he was seeing wasn't who I was. It was like he'd lowered a filter over me, a glaze, and although he saw me, he somehow heard another voice as well in his head.

Mickey grinned at me. He had never liked Robyn. Whether it was a snarky comment or a soft insult, Mickey never lost a chance to take another dig at him either in person or, more usually, behind his back.

Mickey wore big boots too. Had he really heard something from his uncle's friend, or whatever the tall story was, or was he there? Every time I'd asked him he'd shrugged and muttered about Jenkins being right, that gossip was toxic.

The world can see you perfectly, Mrs Harper said, but didn't that depend on what the world was looking for?

I made my own coffee that afternoon and before I left, I picked up an extra carton of soup and two Holster and Jenkins cream cakes, and a few bits of fruit from the organic aisle – nice things that I knew Mrs Harper didn't buy herself. As I trudged up the stairs, her door was open. She liked the through draft, she used to tell me, with a canny smile in her eyes that said she liked to know exactly what was going on, just as much.

'Hello?' I called.

'All quiet,' she said, pointing at the next landing.

'He's away with friends,' I told her.

'I met the new young man last week. He seems very nice.'

Even our landlady had met Gavin.

'Here, so.' I held out the box with the food. 'These were looking for a good home.'

'I'll get my purse, dear.'

'No need.' I waved away her protests.

'These biscuits are the good ones, these are expensive. You have—'

'My treat, Mrs Harper,' I said.

I leaned back against my door, closing it with a soft click. Saturday night. I refused to feel sorry for myself. I put on the radio. I washed my hair and changed into sweats, and I sang along to Christina Aguilera as if she didn't remind me of a million memories with Robyn. *I'm a strong, independent woman,* I told myself. *I'm not afraid of the dark. I don't need ANY man or any woman in this apartment with me right now. I have a job, I have a hobby, and I have friends.*

I have a friend. One single friend.

The radio switched to Aretha, then to Kylie, completing the triangle.

I did not need Robyn.

Eve had never been my friend so why should I care if she was dead? No one else seemed to be that bothered about how or why it had happened, and even Del – the nicest person in the known universe, Del – was more bothered about whether his husband was the killer than about the witch Ben might have actually killed. So I was done. Finished. Over it.

Oooover it.

I turned up the radio.

I would put it out of my mind, I decided, and think about other things. I would think about dinner and bridges, and maybe some new shoes, and I would text some of my college friends I hadn't seen in ages, and—

And while the microwave zapped the packet dinner, I sat up on the counter, scrolling through Robyn's Insta posts.

On the radio, the nice-spoken DJ was working through the classics. When he finally reeled around to Nancy Sinatra, I was still staring at the phone screen.

These boots are made for walkin'.

Hadn't I heard footsteps, though? That night, in the alley. I'd heard someone running away, I was sure.

Heavy footsteps.

I slammed the phone down on to the table, pushing away. It was ridiculous, the whole thing. It wasn't worth it. The cost was too—

I remembered the look from Mark to Thora, and the look between Ben and Mae B, but when I thought about that night it was like I had my own filter on the lens and I remembered them all through gauze, through a thin veil that didn't quite make sense. I thought I remembered everything so clearly, but what if I was making up the memory without meaning to, just to fill the space in my head?

I'd been chasing the wrong thread. I was so sure that Ben had killed Eve, or that someone I knew had killed her, that one of us had killed her. But what if, in trying to protect the people I love, I was simply pushing them away?

I had to stop. It was too much.

◆ ◆ ◆

I didn't see Robyn for days. He came in while I was at work, and I stayed at home while he was at the club. Instead of chatting and gossiping and watching Netflix together, I advertised my pet portraits and I set about fixing my blog, ignoring the one piece I was proud to have written and instead keeping up on the vapid descriptions of friendship and love. I took some decent pictures but they were all the same thing. They were safe.

However much I tried to focus, my mind strayed, over and over again to the empty alley, the gutter, the scraps of crime-scene tape. I found myself running through old pictures I'd taken at the club, anything with Eve in them, as if they could hold a clue in other people's faces. I fell asleep at night with a thousand Eves running through my mind: Eve wild and wicked, Eve with blond hair, Eve with long black hair, Eve with a short red bob, not a million miles away from the colour she'd died in.

Eve face down in the water, dead.

I wondered who had to clean her face that night and bring her back from girl to boy, how it might have felt for them to see first the queen with her long, wet hair and fake pads, and corset and silicone breast padding, and then, when they were done, to see a man. Liam. A young dead man who had all the world to live for and none of its scruples.

At work, I smiled and talked and laughed, and I tried not to say anything too uncomfortable, and when five o'clock came around, I trudged back up the stairs and closed the door of the apartment behind me, and I sat at the kitchen table in silence.

Again, the song ran through my head. *These boots are made for walkin'* . . .

Who was I really hurting? And worse – so much worse – if I didn't do something, then who else was out there to do it? Who else, if not me?

I stared at the condiments.

No. I wasn't wrong.

Nancy Sinatra wouldn't have sat back. Aretha Franklin wouldn't have let anyone tell her what to think.

I picked up the saltshaker, fiddling with it, rolling it in my hand, careful not to spill.

My dad used to work on his house if he needed to think. I didn't have a house, or any land on which to start building, and, without selling a kidney or my firstborn, I couldn't ever see myself buying property in Dublin. I'd never seen the need. If I was honest, I'd always assumed that Robyn and I would carry on living together forever, and I'd tease him for being messy, and he'd still leave his feather boas on the couch, and then he'd pay the rent on time if I forgot, and I'd get supper for us both, and—

I sat bolt upright.

I'd accidentally presumed I was married to Robyn.

I shook my head.

He was right. I really had made it weird.

In my comfortable state, I'd forgotten that it wasn't enough. Robyn was my friend – no more and no less – and one day, maybe even already, for all my moaning at him about it, he really would find a husband and settle down, and when that happened, there wouldn't be a spare room in that apartment with my name on the door in mismatched wooden letters.

I was on my own, but Eve wasn't.

The next day, I got up early. I dried my hair, and I put on make-up and earrings, and I wore an actual dress – not for any reason other than I was trying to encourage summer, I told myself, and if it also meant that the deep V neckline made my boobs look amazing, that was absolutely nothing to do with it.

I reached Jenkins and Holster with fifteen minutes spare.

'It's a miracle,' said Mr Jenkins. 'Praise be to God.'

Mickey rounded the corner of the shop, behind me.

'She's early?' he said in his clipped accent.

'I'm on time,' I told him.

'Exactly! Wow, you look . . . What's happened? Is something wrong? You're dressed as a girl, Fi.'

They nodded to each other, clearly humouring me in their mockery, and I laughed along with them both as if they were funny. 'Onwards and upwards,' I muttered under my breath. Even if the hill was actually a mountain.

I liked taking pictures. Whatever Mrs Harper warned me, I understood the world through my lens. I took a good picture too, of Pekingese or Labradors, or bridges, or drag queens.

At lunchtime, I ate my lunch as I walked.

The car had come from nowhere, Mark said, but when I paced the street, there was a clear, straight run up to the club with no major junctions, no cameras. It wasn't far but a decent car could have made it to forty or maybe fifty if they'd been trying.

I dipped back into the shadows to take the long shot, and then I looked up.

The next corner was turning to a stop sign, so they should have been slowing down, not speeding up. There was no reason to speed up, except—

It was so easy.

There were no cameras there. None at all. The driver could see the entire stretch from the club: the street and the thin alley, peeling away to the city centre.

189

That night, I wrote a new blog post.

Thora had been so cross when she'd come storming around to the flat, and Robyn was still cross. Even Merkin, who barely knew me, had made her views very sure up in Del and Ben's apartment that night.

I typed slowly, certain of each and every word. I read it back. I checked the spelling, checked the photo and looked at the title.

I was convinced, whatever the guards said.

Robyn would be furious, and he wouldn't understand, but at the end of the day, I was done with apologising for myself. Thora and Del were right – we have to own up to not just our actions but who we truly are. Robyn was not my fake-husband. He was my family, and I would stand in front of any fire for him, whatever the cost.

With the sinking knowledge that I was bringing the world down around my ears all over again, and that in posting this piece, I would probably never repair the damage done between Robyn and me, I pressed 'Publish'.

I had to say something. I had to at least put it out there. No one else was listening and they were wrong. There was someone in Dublin killing or trying to kill drag queens, and if no one else was prepared to say it, then I had no choice. If Robyn never spoke to me again, at the very least I did this for him. My love for him and for Del and for justice was deeper than the fear of losing him.

I watched the blog ripple on to the page.

A SECOND ATTACK ON DUBLIN'S DRAG
COMMUNITY – IS NO ONE SAFE?

Chapter Nineteen

There used to be days when life would pass so quickly. It had been a rush every January to get the little attic apartment clear of Robyn's Christmas decorations before the summer came around. Then to get my sandals back in the wardrobe before the fake pine tree took its place, after Halloween. Even long past May, I would find a scrap of tinsel stuck in the vacuum cleaner, and my sunhat on the fat, twinkling tree-angel in New Year, and as each month spun away with itself, I barely noticed the days.

After Eve's death, there were times when every hour peeled back so slowly I might have lived three lifetimes by the time I'd finished one shift at Jenkins and Holster.

Judging by his mood, Mr Jenkins was finding the long hours equally trying, and behind the coffee bar, Mickey wasn't much company either. Between us, we busied around the little store, being nice to the customers but barely looking at one another as we lived inside our own worlds.

As we finished up that Friday, I stuffed the last couple of cream cakes into a plastic tub and left a two-euro coin on the till to ring in. I slung my bag over my shoulder. I was nearly out of the door when Mickey caught me.

'Swap?' he said.

'Sorry?'

'Coffee for a cake?'

He held out a tall cardboard coffee cup and nodded to my bag.

'Unless your friend is meeting you, or . . . ?'

'Robyn? Oh, no. No, he's not coming.'

And yes, I didn't add, *both cakes are for me*. This one is my dinner and this one is my dessert. So bite me.

'He's not been by for the last five weeks?' said Mickey.

I tried to keep the hurt from my voice. 'He's busy.'

Even if that busy was simply watching old movies from Del's sofa.

'I have an hour, if you're free?' Mickey looked at his watch. 'Shall we take a walk, maybe down to St Stephen's Green? I know you like the Green?'

Nothing could go wrong with a walk.

We turned together. It was a nice evening for June, and the sun was high enough in the sky to kid myself it was still mid-afternoon even as my belly complained it was not. As we neared the end of the long road, I found myself wondering if the Pride march would go along Dame Street, as had been mused that year, or if it would take the recent diversion. Not that it mattered, of course. I wouldn't be walking behind the TRASH bus with Robyn like I had in the past few years. I'd be on the pavement, on the edge, watching them from the crowd as Mae B – my Mae B, my Robyn – would be at the very front of the bus with the other queens.

I realised too late that Mickey had asked me a question.

'You still go to that club down the alley there, right?' he said.

I nodded vaguely. I thought of Del. Of Thora. And of Ben.

We were just down the road from The Ogre. What had he been doing, while Patrick and I were in the restaurant? And why had I lied to Del, suggesting Ben had been there all evening, when he clearly hadn't? He deserved the truth, if only I was sure what that was.

'You heard about Mr Jenkins's son, then?' said Mickey.

'Hmm?'

'His son? He was run down there.'

'Jenkins's son?' I said.

I vaguely remembered a pale, skinny type in his early twenties with a long face and shaggy hair, helping out at the shop. He would come by on a weeknight sometimes, to wait for a lift home, but that was four or five years ago now.

Suddenly a cold wash ran over my skin.

It couldn't be . . .

'What's his name?' I said.

Robyn was never one to go out with guys who were younger, it wasn't his thing.

'It's something English, or is it Welsh?' said Mickey. 'No . . . not Gareth, not Gwynne . . .'

'Gavin?' I stood still, on the corner by the park.

'Yes,' said Mickey. 'That's it – Gavin. Nice guy, actually. He broke his leg.'

I barely moved. Gavin was Jenkins's son?

'Funny old world, isn't it?' said Mickey.

'Dublin is a small town,' I said.

I crossed the street ahead of him and walked between the open gates. The night was somehow less friendly. The ducks pecked at the bread, stabbing the soft lumps. The gulls screamed and cried. The tiny sparrows darted from fear, not from delight.

'Here,' said Mickey. 'There's this bench down here. Look, it's empty.'

'Gavin, Jenkins's young son . . . Gavin is gay?'

Mickey waited for me to sit first. He frowned, a sharp look to the side.

'I did not ask if he was gay or bi,' he said. 'Just that he was run over. I think that is more important. You want that cake, then?'

I took the plastic tub from my bag and passed it to him. The cream inside the slice had smeared against the side of the tub.

I turned the cardboard coffee cup in my hand without comment.

Mickey started talking about the bench again, and about how when he first came to Ireland he would sit there in that very spot, every night after work, and how he would look around him at the flowerbeds and the long paths and the people crossing the ornamental bridges, moving from one side of the city to the other, from one world to another, between the trees. I wondered if he knew what else would go on, between the trees. He bit into the long patisserie and the cream came spilling from the end.

'Mrs Holster makes a bloody good bun,' he said, wiping the back of his hand over his mouth.

Conversation was all about taking part, I told myself. I should say something interesting. It wasn't difficult, surely? I chattered all the time with Robyn or with Del without having to consider what I was saying – what was the big difference? Mickey was nice enough. Sure, he wasn't exactly handsome like Patrick, or funny like Del, and he didn't catch my thoughts and make me laugh like Robyn did, but he was sweet.

I needed sweet.

And he almost certainly hadn't murdered anyone.

'It's a grand day,' I said, realising too late, as his words jostled into place in my brain, that he'd just told me about his uncle's funeral.

I sipped at my coffee. The cup was empty but I lifted it to my mouth, filling the space where I should have put words.

Two small boys ran over the grass to the water, pointing into the rushes. A woman called them. At the bridge, a runner stopped to stretch his legs. My hips suddenly ached from sitting down all day, from being stuck in the shop there.

Mickey was rattling on and on about how he was going to learn baking skills with Mrs Holster, and how he was going to become a chef, and how he was going to get promoted in the shop, and

Mr Jenkins had promised him they would consider promoting me too, if I just got there on time a bit more, and how as Jenkins was getting older he'd need a manager.

'Sorry?' I said.

'Isn't it great?' He grinned. There was jam on his lip.

The last dribbles of cold, milky foam stuck to my teeth.

'Are you not going to eat that?' He pointed to the other cream cake.

I shook my head. I couldn't remember why I'd bought them.

'We will share it,' he said.

There was nothing wrong with working at Jenkins and Holster. It was a job. It paid the rent. I got up, I got dressed, and I pinged food over the little red light for people.

It was an in-between job, that was all. Like Robyn at the phone job. It wasn't forever.

'We'd be like them,' Mickey went on. 'Me at the kitchens, and you in the shop!' He laughed. 'Like them, only us!'

I blanched. I saw myself at the counter. I saw the lines on my face, the shadows that framed Mr Jenkins's eyes, the hard-worn pockets of dry skin on his hands, on mine.

The way he greeted each new customer the same, with a smile and kind word, and a readiness to find what they needed, if he could, and—

Nausea rippled through me.

'Mind you' – Mickey patted his flat, toned belly – 'I would want to be careful. We can't be eating these all the time now, and—'

My phone pinged in my pocket. It was an online order being delivered; a second-hand DVD I'd bought weeks before, thinking Robyn would like it. It was not important. It was nothing.

'I should really take this,' I said, standing, as if the text was a call, as if the call was a key. As if it was anything at all I could use as an excuse to get out of there, to run away.

I walked a few paces, trying to unscramble the mess in my head. Mickey seemed to like me, and what was the harm in working at Jenkins and Holster, anyway? Why was it upsetting me so much? It had only been—

Six years.

I grabbed at the railing.

Had it really been six years I'd worked there?

I rubbed my hand over my eyes.

'Everything OK?' he said.

Was it really six whole years? I only took the job to see myself through until my real life took off, until the English degree finally started paying for itself, in whatever way I could imagine that doing so.

Was this the thing I wanted to do?

'Fi?' Mickey called. 'Did I say something?'

I could see the look on his face. Well done, Fi. Captain Weirdmaker.

'Sorry, I—'

I clamped my lips closed, suddenly aware that every other word I said was an apology.

Had it really been six years? I'd always told myself it was temporary. I was just waiting for the right kind of job to come up, something creative, somewhere I could write and think, and make things that mattered, and yet I'd spent six years taking money and giving change and talking about the weather, and about nothing.

The church bonged the hour. Pigeons rushed up from one of the beech trees and my life spun in front of my eyes – not the past, but the future. How many more years until it was Mickey and me there in the shop, with him making the cakes, and me eating the cakes, and with both of us looking forward to our packet dinner at the end of the day, picking over the reduced vegetables, the nearly-out-of-date puddings—

I edged back toward the main path. 'I should, umm . . .'

Mickey stood up. He took a step closer. He had that look in his eyes. I thought for a second that he was going to attack me and then I realised, too late, he was going to kiss me. He dropped his head to mine, he put his hand on my shoulder . . .

I darted back.

'I'll see you tomorrow?' I said. I ducked away and stepped into the path of an older woman, catching her arm with mine, sending her bag spinning to the ground. Blushing madly, I picked up the lady's things, apologising over and over again, but also moving around her, using her, keeping her between Mickey and me like I'd watched Thora and Del many times, switching the person who was trying to get to them with another member of the TRASH family.

I waved, apologising again to the lady as I started to walk away. Then I looked back.

'Hey Mickey,' I said. 'You remember the other week? After Eve was killed and you were going to tell me something. We were just getting ready to leave, and you said . . .'

He frowned. Then the frown deepened.

'What was it?' I said.

'My brother-in-law, my sister's husband, he said the chances of the young man dying like that were very slim. I thought of your little friend, that was all. I thought that he might want to know, and—'

I was halfway down the road when I heard my name.

'What about the other cake?' Mickey called.

I held up my hand in a wave, and kept walking.

I sat at the kitchen table. I set out the condiments, in place. Eve was in the gutter. I laid the chilli sauce on its side in the middle of the table.

I closed my eyes and mentally walked out of the club, turned down the alley. I was an Oxo cube. The three men, drunk and staggering, who had come up the street toward me, were packets of pub ketchup.

I set an Earl Grey teabag on the side. That was Thora in the club. I could not have missed her in the dark. A saltshaker, that was Del. A badge for Robyn.

Who else?

Mark, Ben . . .

I focussed on the table.

Who else could have been near the alley when she was killed?

I cradled the saltshaker, Del. He was up with the DJ. It wasn't him, and he didn't see who was there. He'd have told me, I was certain.

The pepper, Ben; the jar of coffee, Mark . . . I moved each piece to each corner, to each doorway. And the one I had not matched, the one who was in the alley with Eve; I took the mustard from the shelf. The murderer.

I tore an old envelope in half, started a list. Then I wrote another. I tried to remember where Ben had been, if he was inside or outside at different times, how I could account for Eve's time once she'd been thrown from the club, and who she was talking to, where she was talking to them. I wrote down each person's journey in a line, their positions in each place.

I stared at my kitchen crime scene for an hour before the doorbell rang.

I looked out of the window. I didn't recognise Karen at first, with her hair cut short and her coat collar turned up. I threw down the keys so she could let herself in and hurriedly plumped the cushions, threw the empty Pot Noodles away. The door opened just as I pulled a comb through my hair. She brought a scent and a feel of the fields with her.

'Fi, how are you?' she said.

'I'm fine.' I grinned. 'How're you? Are you—'

In town, I was going to say, which was the single most stupid thing I'd said all day and I'd said a few contenders.

'Am I what?' she said.

'Are you . . . well?'

She scowled, the deep furrow between her brows marking the glooms under her eyes. She looked different. Away from her comfort of the little country farm, she stood like a heron in an IKEA store.

'Grab a seat,' I told her. 'I'll put on the kettle.'

'I'm not staying,' she said quickly. 'I needed something from Rob's room.'

'Oh, he's not in.'

'He's not?' she said. The frown lessened. 'You don't mind if I . . .' She went to open his door, but the lock held.

'Can I get his room key?' She held out her hand.

'I don't have it.'

'What?'

'I don't have a key,' I said.

'How can you not have a key to a door in your own flat?'

'It's his room,' I said. 'If I had a key, that would kind of be beyond the point.' And up until recently, he'd never once had to use the lock, I thought. I'd only put it in there to comply to some stupid regulation – and as a joke. We'd laughed about it, back then. He'd hung the key up on the wall, and we'd laughed, and—

And that was then. Now was now.

'Tea or coffee?' I asked, brushing away the rock of sadness that had fallen into my belly. I went into the kitchen.

'I said, I'm not staying. He, umm . . .' She closed her fingers around nothing. 'Well, he borrowed a book from me,' she said. 'I could really use it back. It was a library book.'

'Which one?'

'What's this?' she said, pointing at the condiments and lists on the table.

'Oh, nothing.' I whipped the lists away and stuffed them into my pocket. Karen looked at me. There was something strange to her eyes, as if she were accusing me. As if she would launch into a Robyn-like tirade about my meddling, about my opinions.

'It's nothing,' I said again. 'Just a shopping list. You know.'

She picked up the packet of Oxo cubes.

'Knight takes queen,' she said. She smiled. 'Checkmate.'

I rolled the pepper jar in my hand.

'The book?' she said, reminding me. 'If I could just look into his room. It won't take a minute. My mum would really like it back.'

'I'm sorry, I really don't have a key,' I told her. 'But he's been spending a fair bit of time at Del and Ben's. It might be there? It's not that far.'

Karen walked back into the main room. I took two mugs from the shelf, opened the fridge. 'Go on,' I said. 'Grab a seat for a minute and I'll make us a cuppa and I can call Del, and—'

The door closed. The flat was empty, Karen's footsteps disappearing down the stairs. I went to my window, leaned out. As she stepped into the street, she looked up.

'I'll call him now,' she said, waving her phone. 'Sorry to have bothered you.'

'Oh, no, it's fine, it's—'

She scuttled away over the bridge.

I stood in my room, holding the teabags.

It was only when I lay in bed, just drifting off to sleep, that I realised I'd forgotten to take my house keys back from her and now, on top of everything else, I'd have to go all the way over to their farm, just to get them back.

Chapter Twenty

The train took ages, crawling down the line, rammed with commuters, stopping everywhere. I stood by the toilets and tried to breathe through my mouth.

It was early, not long past eight, but Edna met me at the station. We walked back down the lane together.

I'd been to Edna's house almost as often as my own back when we were young, but never without Robyn's friendship. Even at Edna's birthday I'd assumed it was a spat, a silly argument, not a forever.

'Fi.' She smiled, blues written through the green in her eyes.

'I'm sorry to bother you,' I said.

'It's Karen should be sorry, walking off like that with your keys. Silly girl. Her head's in the clouds at the moment. It'll be the lambs, you know. Her daddy was just as bad.'

'It's my fault,' I said.

Edna gripped my arm. She leaned closer. 'Never take the blame for another's mistakes,' she said. She raised one eyebrow, just as her son would. She handed me the keys.

'Ah, that's great,' I said. 'I should go.'

'Would you have a cup of tea?'

'I should get to work, really, I told them I'd be a bit late but—'

'There will be another train in half an hour, and another again, half an hour after that one,' said Edna. Enfolding my arm with her trademark steely grasp, she led me inside. 'Karen is already out in the fields, of course,' she said. 'And Grandpa Joe doesn't do mornings, so it's only me you'll be having the tea with, and you can't let me be lonely, now.'

'I should probably—'

The kitchen was bathed with morning light, the table already set, the plates ready, the air scented with newly baked bread.

'That's really nice of you,' I said. 'But—'

'How's my boy?'

'He's fine, I think? I mean, I haven't . . .'

The ache of our lost friendship cut through me. We'd been in that house together so many times it was another home for me. So many Christmases and birthdays and Sunday dinners, and yet it was his home, not mine. It had never been mine. I had my own place to go, and my own life. I'd just forgotten that.

'The keys,' said Edna, squeezing my hand. 'You have them safe, there? Before we forget, now, and get chatting, eh? Why don't you take your coat off?'

The tea was already on the table. Ushering me further into the room, Edna set the cast iron frying pan on the hot plate and opened the fridge.

'Actually,' I said. 'I really should g—'

'How many sausages?' she said. 'I'll put a couple extra for Karen. She's so on edge at the moment. I tell her, it's too much, working for Tom as well as managing our land, she's out at all hours and his cattle they have no manners on them, and . . .'

I tried to subtly look at my phone. I'd missed the first train for sure. I had no chance of getting to work by ten now, and even less chance of getting out of the farm without a full Irish grilling, one way or another. With the lines of sausages filling the wide pan,

Edna leaned back against the stove. She held the towel between her hands like a bishop's robes.

'She's so pale,' she said. 'You could take a wander up to the top fields if you'd like to see her?'

'I really should get b—'

'I was so glad she came into town last night to visit you.' Edna smiled. 'She's never had that many friends. It didn't matter so much when they were younger. It was always Robbie who needed to get out into the city and to see people – all that driving I did, heavens be to God – and the theatre school and the choir and the discos. Of course, we knew, back then, he was destined for greatness.' Edna nodded to the photograph of her husband on the dresser. 'Pat was the one who saw it. He knew, by the time our Robbie was walking, that we had a little star.' Edna took up the teapot but the first splash came too light and the pot was set to the corner of the stove. 'Sit down, would you, Fi?' she said. 'I'm not having you traipsing all the way out here without giving you a decent breakfast at the very least – not after it was my girl who went off with your keys last night, and you kind enough to give Robbie a room in your home, and—'

'Well, he pays the rent.'

I set the keys on the table but Edna whipped forward, casting them back into my hand. 'No keys on the table. It's bad luck.'

'Oh. Right. Sorry, I—'

'Now, so.' She set to the teapot with a spoon. 'Tell me, Fi, what's all this about you and my boy falling out over your little blog, then?'

The blush reached my ears before she'd finished stirring the teabags.

'I shouldn't have written it,' I said.

'I don't see why not. It's not like it was the front page of the *Tribune*.'

'Yes, but—'

'So why is Robbie so upset with you? What else did you do?'

'I said . . . well, that is, I . . .'

'You insulted him?'

'I did, and . . .'

'And he insulted you back?'

'Robyn believes that Eve tripped and fell,' I said.

'And that nice man who writes for the *Irish Times* – he did that little piece in the Wednesday paper – and he said it was an accident too?'

'Well, yes, but—'

'But you still believe she was killed?'

I didn't answer.

'Well, Fi?' said Edna.

'Yes,' I said quietly.

'Good girl,' she said.

I blinked.

Edna turned her back to me and started to cut bread in thick slices. She had four pots on the go and bacon in the oven. She'd called me a good girl. She wasn't one to hand out rewards lightly. My head itched, sweat beading on the back of my neck. My insides squirmed and wormed.

'You may be right, of course,' she went on. 'I was up all night worrying about him, I can tell you, and I know Karen has been jumpy as anything, but she doesn't understand his world, that's all. No more than he'd have a clue how to put up a fence.' She chuckled. 'It's harder to worry about something unknown.'

I nodded.

The danger was too close. Robyn couldn't see it because he was determined not to, but those of us who loved him, we saw it sure enough.

'He's really angry with me,' I said. 'I probably shouldn't be here now.'

'It'll be a fine day when I let my son tell me who I can and cannot see,' said Edna.

'He called me Hagatha Christie,' I said. 'He told me I was interfering.'

'I heard the latest was Herlock Scones,' said Edna, laughing to herself. 'Here.' She set a plate in front of me. 'Don't you worry about them. You start on that lot.'

The plate was enormous, two fat pieces of bread, both buttered, with rashers and sausages and beans and mushrooms and three pieces of black pudding and a tomato, cut in half and seared to within a quarter inch of its previous life.

'Don't bother arguing with me,' she said. 'I raised two fussy eaters, so I did, and I have no time for it. I won't be taking no for an answer. Now you eat that up and let's see what we can do about Robbie.'

At a loss to what else I could say, I stuffed a big piece of bacon into my mouth. Edna picked up her mug of tea and stared through the window, over the fields.

We sat together, just the sound of my chewing and the cutting of my knife on the plate. The meat was divine, the homemade sausages clearly not long from running about in the yard. I tried not to think about it. It was the most I'd eaten in one go in many months and I felt the stabbing pains in my chest start to ease – the worry that had been so deeply carved in there, the loss of not just Robyn and TRASH and the scene that I had once assumed to be a little bit mine even if not a lot, but also the loss of the family here at the farm.

'So,' said Edna, pinning me with her eyes as I ate another mushroom. 'How was your dinner with Patrick Midda?'

I was glad to have my mouth full.

'The old lady gossip circle is tight,' she said with a wide grin. 'I have coffee with Del's mammy once a month down in Cow's Lane. Is Patrick still tall?'

'He hasn't shrunk,' I said.

'Marianne knows his mother, you know.'

I stuffed more food in my mouth. Nodded.

Edna chuckled. 'You young ones, you think you're the first to do it all, don't you? Mind' – she nodded – 'in my day, none of us got ourselves murdered.'

She had a point, I thought.

An hour later, she pressed a homemade loaf of bread wrapped in a brown paper bag into my hands, and when I was on the train, I realised there was a twenty-euro note inside the bag, with it.

You're very kind, I texted her. Thank you. And thank you for the breakfast, too. X

The dots played alongside her name. We were nearly in Dublin when her message popped up.

Take care, Fi. X

No chats. No advice. No further missions. No new pathologists for me to see. No cases for me to answer, no old ladies' dogs for me to photograph. She was saying goodbye.

She was telling me Robyn was her son.

Chapter Twenty-One

The next evening, I sat on the end of Del and Ben's bed. Moonlight bathed the smart Dublin square in a warm blue light.

'What is it with you and staring out of windows?' said Del. He threw a bundle of black fabric at me. 'Here, try this one.'

As he disappeared back into his dressing room to find more, I wriggled out of my old jumper dress and pulled on the tight black sheath. At the door, Del whistled, but when he thought I wasn't looking, he glanced back at the little clock on the bedside table and his wide smile disappeared.

'I expect Ben's just working late again,' I said.

'Turn around, I'll zip you up.'

The thin fabric clung to my hips and my waist, and very much to my chest. It wasn't as tight as the purple one, but it was certainly a different shape than I was used to.

'Blimey, Fi! You're a girl!'

'I'm not sure,' I said.

'No, I am really sure,' he said. 'I know what little girls look like and, sweetie, you are indeed a girl. Where have you been hiding those boobs?'

'They've been there,' I said. 'You know . . . just being boobs . . . I'm not sure about the dress. I mean, it's great on you, but . . .'

Del nodded. After the entire evening spent trying on everything Del had in my size, he knew.

I stood in front of the mirror. 'I look like a nineteen-fifties mistress,' I said.

'Your bottom looks biteable.'

'Are bottoms biteable?'

Del rolled his eyes. 'Try it with the shoes. You need the right shoes. The wrong shoes and you're charging by the hour; the right shoes and you're running Clark, Wilmot and Arnolds from a window office in Abbey Street.'

I slid my feet into my court shoes. On his gesture, I walked up and down the little bedroom floor.

'It's a job interview,' I said. 'Not a mob funeral.'

'I imagine it will come as a shock, but you are an actual woman, Fi, not a fleece-covered blob. You have curves.'

'I know. And I don't just wear fleeces. I wore a dress the other day. To work.'

'Name one day this week when you went the whole day – the entire actual day, Fi – without a fleece on your body.'

'Do pyjamas count?'

'Were you wearing them while you ate your dinner?'

I turned to be unzipped. As the fabric slipped to the floor, I breathed out, feeling my insides relax. I rubbed my belly, apologising to my internal organs.

'This dress works,' he said. 'You could team it with a short jacket, something that comes together under your boobs with a deep V, and some decent shoes—'

'These are decent shoes.'

Del pointed at me. 'Final warning, McKinnery.'

'I could wear my boots? They're flat but . . .'

'Don't be ridiculous.'

'People wear boots with dresses.'

'Not since nineteen ninety-eight.'

'It's an office job, Del.' I grumbled. 'It's a shit job. I'll be sat behind a desk, and I probably won't even get it anyway.'

'I've seen *Mad Men*. I know what those places are like. OK,' he said. 'I can do clothes and shoes, but if we're getting into self-depreciation and misery, I'm going to make another round of margaritas. That's the last one – I give up, you take a look.' He gestured to the dressing room. 'Try anything from the left rail. The rail on the right won't fit.'

I padded over in my bra and knickers. Inside what used once to be their second bedroom, every man-made fabric known to drag queens clamoured to be the loudest. Del's pink-and-white striped candy frock was hung on the end rail, in pride of place, the skirt fluffed out. The latest silver creation was at the nearest end, ready for the weekend's show. At the back and at the top, shelves of wigs waited in line – blond, pink, jet black, icy blue – and on every surface jewellery and glitter shone in the bright mirror lights.

'How do you make any money at all?' I said. 'This stuff is amazing.'

'I sometimes think there's three of us living in the flat,' said Del from the kitchen. 'Me, Ben and the drag.' Holding a full glass, he rested on the edge of the bed. 'And Eve,' he said.

I sat next to him.

'All that, it's over now,' I told him. 'He's said so, hasn't he? And she's gone, anyway. He's probably working late. You know how it gets at the restaurant.'

'He's not there tonight.'

'Not at all?'

'I just checked. This is what I have become, Fi. I just called his boss and asked if he was on shift. Terrance hasn't seen him all day. Or yesterday, for that matter, when Ben told me he was doing the early. I even cooked for him in the middle of the afternoon so he could eat before he went. And we ate together and—'

He took a breath.

'I was going to check his phone but he keeps it with him all the time now,' he said. 'It was just like this when Eve—'

I brushed a tear from his cheek.

'Eve is gone now,' I said.

'So why aren't things better?' said Del.

We sat together on the bed for another hour but as the night wore on into the early hours of the morning, the shape of Ben not being there had become as big as if he'd been sitting on the chaise with the huge pile of dresses, testing me on my future goals as a junior advertising creative.

Del yawned.

'I can't drink any more,' he said. 'Not even tea. I can't fit it in.'

'Shall I call Ben?'

His name echoed between us. Del shook his head.

'I'm not running after him like some jealous leading lady.' He stood and stretched. 'You need to sleep,' he said. 'What time is the interview?'

'Nine-fifteen.'

'Eight hours' time.'

'It'll be fine.'

'Wear the black,' he said.

I started to reply, but the memory of talking with Robyn only weeks ago cut through me. He'd worn the outfit I told him to wear. He'd worn the red. Then Eve took it from him.

Del touched his finger to my chin.

'Earth calling Fi?'

'Sorry,' I said. 'Just thinking.'

He nodded to himself, and scooped up the black dress. 'Dry clean only,' he said. 'Wear simple stud earrings and a long necklace that brings the eyes to your shape.'

'I'm not trying to advertise my boobs.'

'Of course you're not. You're trying to get a job in a city filled with people who are also trying to land a job. So wear the dress.'

I gave in. 'Thank you,' I said. 'I don't know what I'd have done.'

'You'd have asked Robyn to go shopping with you, like you usually do?'

I thanked him again, and slung my bag over my shoulder, the dress tucked carefully inside wrapped in tissue paper, with strict instructions to hang it only by the tabs. The night was old, but I didn't have far to go. I took out my phone as I stepped on to the street, checking the time.

I barely saw them move. Two men, sliding back into the dark. One tall – dressed in a black shirt, short hair, hugely wide shoulders – and one shorter, slight, built like—

I blinked, my eyes blurred from the light of my phone. The shorter one, I could have sworn was Ben.

I kept walking.

It could have been anyone, but it looked like Ben.

Why was I protecting him?

At the flat, I texted Del. Safe at home. Thanks again xx

I was just turning off my light when the reply came.

Lovely to see you. Ben just back, late night helping Thora with the bar. I'm such a daft cow! Good luck tomorrow x

I let the reply stay empty. Some lies could not be written down.

Chapter Twenty-Two

I'm not sure which was worse – the interview, with me perched on the very edge of the chair and trying not to breathe in case the tight black dress split and cast me tumbling from its hold, or the look on Mickey's face as I slumped back into Holster and Jenkins, an hour later, sticking firmly to my excuse that I'd been to the dentist and looking more like I'd been to the premiere of a seedy movie.

It would have been OK if I hadn't worn the boots. Somehow, the big clumpy black boots and thin black tights made the dress look even tighter, the neckline lower, and the waist more sculpted than it had in the court shoes.

'A new look for you today,' said one older lady.

'It's warming up out there,' I said, nodding to the sun that baked the busy pavements.

I pinged her overpriced organic wholemeal flour through the scanner.

How did Del and Robyn and the others do it? How did they peel away their outer selves like that and walk with such confidence in dresses and leotards – and, in some cases, in bikinis and underwear? I could happily wander around the apartment with Robyn in my bra and panties, or in front of Del – but in front of strangers?

The interviewer had stared at me, his mouth open. He hadn't even tried to hide how he saw me, and when he'd come to say goodbye, he held my hand too tightly, and he leaned . . .

I'd kept my gaze on the pavement on the way back to the shop.

Well, it was an experience if nothing else, I figured. I'd been lucky to get an interview right away for the first job I'd applied to, and maybe I'd be lucky again. And next time I was going in a shirt right up to my neck and a boxy all-encompassing shapeless jacket, and long, loose, not-at-all fitting trousers, with my most sensible flat shoes, and—

'Fi?'

Patrick laid a packet of wrapped sandwiches on the belt and raised a takeaway cup of coffee.

'Oh. Patrick. Hi.'

I scanned the packet too fast. I did it again but by then the little red laser had already decided I was having a laugh. I typed in the number.

'How are . . . um . . . ?'

I swallowed, hard. I wondered if it was good manners to ask after his wife, or girlfriend. His Martha. I got the number wrong, my fingers clumsy on the keys. The till beeped, demanding I start the whole process over. I was making it look difficult. It was hardly rocket science, or medicine, or—

My fingers slipped and I dropped the packet on to the glass scale. The red light pinged, the price popping up straight away on the screen.

'That's three sixty, please,' I said.

Again, he lifted the coffee. I started to add the number.

He was wearing a white cotton shirt, open at the neck, and his chest was lightly covered in dark hair. Not a lot, just a little.

'Fi?'

'Sorry?'

'The coffee?' he said.

'Of course.' I checked the price on the card and coded in the number that I knew by heart any other moment of the year.

Patrick said nothing. Even as I squirmed, his eyes never strayed from my face.

'How have you been?' he said.

'Me? Oh yes, great . . . Yeah, really good, actually. I'm doing really well, actually.'

I had to stop saying actually.

'Yes, fine,' I said. 'Grand, actually.'

I gave him the new total and a bright, breezy smile. I took the money, gave the change. I smiled again. I wondered if he'd been working long hours, or reading papers, or whatever it was that pathologists had to do when they weren't cutting up bodies, and I wondered if he'd cut up his sandwich into two halves . . .

'I wanted to let you know,' he said quietly. 'The toxicology report came through.'

The next man in the queue quietly picked up his cream cake box, and went to the other till.

'Eve's?' I whispered.

Patrick nodded.

I stood up. 'Mr Jenkins, I'll just be a minute,' I called.

Ignoring my boss's short reply about having only been back twenty of those minutes, I followed Patrick out into the sun.

'What did it say?'

'You look amazing,' he said.

I blinked.

'I mean, it didn't say that – and sorry,' he said. 'I know I'm not meant to notice stuff like that. We're not meant to, any of us, are we? And—'

'I had an interview,' I said quietly. 'I wanted to, you know, maybe look for something else.'

'Oh, good luck!' he said. 'Did it go well?'

'I think I can safely say it didn't. I should have worn one of my own dresses, rather than borrow Del's.'

'Del the drag queen in the pink stripes? This is Del's dress?'

I nodded.

'Well, then it could have been a lot worse,' he said. 'That shiny pink number would almost certainly have given a different impression. And to hell with the interview – I think you look great.'

He smiled.

Patrick had always had the most incredible smile. I think that was the first thing I'd noticed about him all those years back when we'd started meeting on the green in Trinity, away from UCD, drinking coffee and pretending we were like the smart kids and the posh kids and the pretty kids – when he and Robyn played chess and I lay there in the sun, watching them both.

'The report?' I said, suddenly remembering.

'It's not my place,' he said. 'And I shouldn't even have read it, but—'

'But you did and you have, so.'

'I wanted you to know.' He rubbed his hand over his mouth, the humour gone. 'I'm not messing here, Fi. I mean it, I want you to be careful. And Robyn, I want him to be careful.'

'I am careful, but—'

'Liam Flanagan. Her drag name was Eve, is that right?'

I nodded.

'Eve had maybe drunk two or three shots of vodka. That was all.'

'No drugs?'

'No drugs,' he said.

'Not even cocaine?'

He shook his head. 'Although frankly I would have expected something more like an opiate if we're saying that she – is it she? Is that the correct pronoun?'

I nodded.

'If we're saying that she slipped and fell and was too out of it to . . .'

He didn't finish the sentence. People walked past us, around us, but I didn't see them.

'So she was killed?' I said.

'She drowned. The water killed her. There is no definitive answer as to whether she was conscious or not, when she lay there as the water filled her lungs. There are no defensive wounds but then she was face down, so . . . and I'm not getting involved.'

He'd rested on my school bag once, his head against my files, leaning on my writing, my notes. The sun had shone on his hair and even then he'd had flecks of grey, even when we were eighteen, nineteen, and he'd stretched out his long legs and stared at the chessboard, and I'd watched them together – Robyn in his skinny jeans and a tight black shirt and Patrick in his loose blue jeans and his ancient Nirvana t-shirt and his old-man glasses slipping down his nose, and his head leaning back on my bag like it was my lap.

He held the coffee and the sandwiches in his hands, his thumb on the lip of the coffee, just the tiniest bubble at the top.

'I didn't want to write it down, but I couldn't live with myself,' he said. 'If I hadn't said something to you, and I know you and Robyn are pretty much joined at the hip.'

'Not any more,' I said.

'Still not?'

'I upset him. I said something I shouldn't have said.'

'So can you apologise?'

Had I? I tried to remember if I'd apologised for calling Mae B stupid, or if I'd just become swept up in wanting it all to go away, presuming I'd said and done all I needed.

Had I been so obsessed with what had been done to Eve that I'd forgotten what actually happened between Robyn and me? I

216

remembered the argument but had I really just walked away and assumed it would all be fine?

Patrick had said something. I looked up, started to ask.

'It doesn't mean anything,' he said quickly. 'Nothing I am saying to you here means anything.'

Nothing anyone was saying meant anything.

'Unless a toxicology report clangs, no one cares,' he said. 'They take forever anyway and by then you've mostly already come to one conclusion or another and you're just waiting for confirmation. The coroner's report is accidental death, as previously estimated by the guards. Eve fell, hitting her head, she knocked herself out, she drowned. Maybe they have more information than I do . . .'

'But?' I said.

'There were no marks of conflict on the body but they noted recent bruising on the forehead, under the make-up. Possibly at time of death. It was enough bruising to be consistent with falling, but . . .'

She didn't trip.

She wasn't drunk and she wasn't off her head. And in the unlikely event that she had slipped, chances were that she'd have fallen with her hands out. There were no defensive wounds, and no abrasions.

'The car speeding toward Robyn and Gavin was no coincidence, was it?' I said.

'A coincidence is rarely a coincidence,' said Patrick.

Chapter Twenty-Three

The apartment was empty. On the kitchen table lay a note from Robyn, with his half of the rent in cash. I opened the piece of paper beside it.

> This is my last month's rent. I am giving one month's notice. Will be moving my stuff tomorrow morning while you're at work. Thanks for everything, R.

Thanks for everything?

I read the handwritten words again.

And again.

Years of perfect friendship and that was it? That was how he signed off?

I left the money on the table.

I let the shower run hot.

I stood in the water. I was shaking. I was spitting mad and yet I was shaking, and I felt sick, and—

Thanks for everything? After all this time? And where was he going? Was he not even going to leave a forwarding address?

With a gulp of tears, I leaned against the cold tiles.

Edna. Karen. Old Grandpa Joe. I was losing Robyn and I was losing them too. And all for one stupid argument and a silly little blog post about Eve. It didn't make sense.

I washed my hair. My face.

Robyn knew me better than this. One argument shouldn't bring us to this, surely? I scowled at the shower curtain. We'd had disagreements before, of course. We'd both said stupid things or insensitive things but neither of us went stomping off like this. It was ridiculous. It was . . .

It was too much. Not just too much in a huffy I'm-over-this sense, but it was actually too much.

I opened the bedroom window. A hen night group came staggering through the thin, cobbled street, shrieking and laughing and calling out nonsense.

I was missing something. The puzzle didn't make sense because it wasn't complete. Robyn was smart. For all he played the ditsy bimbo, he was way more than that. He had a degree, for goodness' sake. He understood people. He understood me – or he used to. A sharp pain stabbed behind my eyes. I rubbed my hands over my face again. My stomach griped and growled. I couldn't think, no one could think on coffee alone.

I had firm ideas about cheese on toast. Thin, evenly cut wholemeal bread, with a smear of tomato purée and then a thick-cut layer of Cheddar – not grated, never grated – then tiny chopped pieces of onion and a splash of hot chilli sauce, and eight slices of cucumber on the side.

My dad always told me there was nothing in life that couldn't be helped by either cheese on toast, zip ties or duct tape.

I wandered into the kitchen. The saltshaker was still on the table, and the packets of ketchup. Karen was right. It was a chess game.

I set the facts in my head.

1. Eve wasn't drunk. I'd seen her drink half a bottle of vodka, straight down, more than once, and still go onstage. She might have wanted them to think she was drunk or high to get away with half the stuff she said, but she wasn't.

Again, I set out my condiments, one by one.

2. Del hated Eve, but he was gentle. He was kind. He was the first to tell Thora that she had to be stopped that night and to insist she was removed from the stage. And sure, he'd found Eve and Ben in bed together but that was over a month before, and he'd forgiven Ben and they were trying again. He'd put it behind him. Del was the most obvious killer but there was no way in hell that he'd done it.

3. Thora knew that Eve was toxic. If Mark was right and Eve had been stealing from the club, from all of them, and if TRASH was already broke . . .

I twisted the pepper grinder over the cheese.

And 4. Ben loved Del, sure, but I couldn't let their relationship cloud me. It was always the quiet ones, they said, and Ben was sure quiet. Was it really him there, making out with the other guy in the street the night before? Maybe I'd just thought I saw him making out in the square because I was thinking about him. Maybe it wasn't him, at all?

Patrick's words spun through my mind: *a coincidence is rarely a coincidence.*

Then Robyn?

My ex-best friend, Robyn.

5. Eve took on Mae B that night. In mocking her the way she did, Eve made sure everyone would remember not the first performance of Mae B, but what happened after. In Mae B's performance, they'd remember Eve. Robyn had been working on that act for months: the iconic red dress; red hair; the high, high shoes; the slow song; Julie London's voice.

Eve had not just mocked Mae B, she'd stolen her entire drag identity and ridiculed her. Ruined her.

And then again, 6. There was the car. Gavin, the cute lad from the coffee place.

If there were no coincidences, then what connected the two incidents?

There was only one name that connected them both.

I gripped the counter.

The only thing that connected the two events was Robyn. And he still had no idea how much danger he might be in.

A true, cold certainty rippled through my bones like ice on the metal poles at the station.

It was all about Robyn.

I called him three times, letting the phone ring out.

I had to tell him. It didn't matter if he never talked to me again, it didn't matter if the guards thought I was crazy, if they arrested me for pestering them. If I was right, then none of that mattered against keeping him safe.

I left a message. Then I left another.

'Robyn? Call me. It's not about the money or whatever. That doesn't matter – please, this is important. Call me.'

I called the guards again. I left messages for the detective. I asked to be put through to his superior.

Queen of Petty strikes again.

The phone cut off.

I called Del. No answer. I called the club. I called again and again until the woman on reception put me through and Mark finally came to the phone, his voice sharp.

'Fi. I hope there's good reason f—'

'Mark, I'm sorry to bother you,' I said. 'I'm looking for Robyn and—'

'We're all looking for Robyn, honey. Mae B is meant to be onstage and her drag is untouched up in the dressing room.'

'But—'

'Try Ben.' Mark sighed. 'As far as I know, he and Del and have taken your little queen back to the flat under yet another drama – and if you get through to his highness, tell him Thora is on the warpath. She's got Pride next week and Mae B's still missing half the cues, and—'

'So Robyn definitely isn't at TRASH?'

The line went dead.

◆ ◆ ◆

I paced the apartment.

On the one hand, even if something did happen that didn't mean it would be immediate. There was no need to rush over there.

But what if I was wrong about that and it did? What if it was tonight? What if I stayed quiet, trying not to make any more trouble, and Robyn was killed next? If his body lay there in the gutter and his face became closed, like Eve's, unrecognisable in its death.

If Ben had done it once, what if he wouldn't stop? If he'd already tried to kill Robyn with the car, what if he tried again and again? What if that was why he had taken them back to the flat? What if he was trying right now? If Ben was the killer, then Robyn and Del were walking right into evil's lair.

Robyn was moving out of the flat. He was already not talking to me. How much worse could it be?

But I knew how much worse. I'd found her.

My phone rang. I leaped to grab it, but it was Del.

'Hey, I said. 'I've been—'

He was crying. 'Fi, can you meet us at the flat? Come quickly, yeah?'

'What's happened?'

There was a crumpling sound, and then Ben took the phone.

'Fi?' he said. His voice cracked. 'I have Robyn here. Can you meet us at the flat? This is important. Please. Please come.'

I didn't think.

I ran.

My feet pounded the streets. I ran too fast, stumbling and falling at the kerbs, skimming around the cars, pushing past the night walkers, the street revellers – those who fumbled along with no more of a care than for their next pint.

I made the corner of the square as I saw a flicker up ahead in the dark. The three of them were already at the steps: Del, Ben and Robyn. The streetlight on the green was out but the porch lit them from above. The three men were arguing. Ben had hold of Del's hand, but tears ran down Ben's face. Robyn stood between them.

'Please,' Ben said. He was crying. Even from where I stood, I could see his shoulders shake, the grief rip through him. 'Please,' he said again. 'None of that is an issue any more. Just get inside!'

'You want me here, a pretty bird in a cage,' Del snapped back. He had on the candy pink dress and a curly blond wig, high bunches in insane ringlets, waving in the air. 'You want to go out all night, doing whatever it is you're doing,' he said, 'and I have to stay at home here like some trapped animal. I'm not going inside. You have something to say, you say it right now – you say it in front of Fi, and—'

Robyn turned. Had he heard something? He looked back to the green.

I hesitated.

'Please.' Ben reached out to stop Robyn from leaving, his other hand to Del, gripping his arm like Edna had gripped mine. 'Del, darling,' he said. 'I know who killed Eve. Just get inside, OK? And I know who ran into Gavin, and—'

Robyn spun around, his face unpainted, lit clear by the porch light. He saw me on the corner.

I froze. I lifted my hand.

I wanted to walk forward. I started to move.

'Just go!' Del shouted to Ben. 'You bastard, you haven't changed – you will never change!'

'You have to listen to me,' said Ben. 'All that – it doesn't matter. We have to go inside – please, just go inside. It's not—'

'Doesn't matter? You stand there and tell me.'

'Just get in the house, please.' Ben stared around them, his eyes darting from place to place, unseeing. He started to push Del toward the door. 'Please, love, please. I love you. Just . . .'

Again, I saw the movement, the glint of light on something. Del turned. He saw it as I did, the flicker of light, the tiny silver speck in the dark. A long barrel, lifting . . .

The shot boomed through the air. Then another.

I started forward.

Ben fell. Blood poured from his shoulder, from his chest. Dark, heavy blood, thick against his shirt. Blood on his hand, on Del's hands. Blood on his lips.

Robyn screamed. The scream pierced the night.

I ran at the green – I ran at the movement. I crossed the road, still running. I shouted.

'Hey! Hey, you!' I yelled. 'You coward!'

I tore at the gate, pushing forward.

'Show yourself! You killer! You coward! You hide in the dark! You—'

Robyn caught my arm. We rolled together on the ground as the third blast of the shotgun spun past my cheek, past his arm. He threw his arms around me, pushing me into the darkness, under a van, squeezing down.

Another shot boomed into the small square, too close. Someone shouted.

Then nothing.

I held my breath.

Del was crying. I could hear him punching at the numbers in his phone, begging them to come quickly. I started to move. I had to get up. I had to go to him. But Robyn held me still. I lay under the van, my face inches from its oily guts, and I listened, my heart tearing apart as Del sobbed, telling them to come now, to come quickly.

Telling them Ben wasn't moving.

Telling them the blood was too much, it was seeping out of him, Del said. It was flooding his lap.

Telling them, in broken, stuttered sobs, that Ben had stopped breathing.

The dark, greasy smell of the van was thick in my throat. I wanted so desperately to call out to Del. I wanted to go after the man in the bushes, to find him, to stop him, and to grab the gun from him, to yell.

I wanted to hurt him. I realised, even against the terrible madness, how much I wanted to go after whoever it was there in the bushes.

I wanted none of this to be happening. I started to cry.

Slowly, Robyn put his hand to my face, a finger to my lips.

The person in the green was moving. The bushes parted, rustling. The fence clinked, then hard steps as they landed on the pavement, so close. Big boots.

We didn't move.

They were coming.

Would they drag Robyn out first and then me, or kill us both where we lay? Was this it?

I was shaking – my heart crashed so hard against my throat I thought I was going to be sick.

A door opened, down the street.

The person was leaning down. They were looking.

'Hey!' At the back of the square, someone else shouted. 'Hey, you OK, there?'

'I've called the guards,' said someone else, leaning out of a window.

More people were coming closer. People who were not afraid.

The shooter ran. Footsteps, running fast. Light footsteps in heavy boots.

They were getting away.

'Hey?' said the neighbour again. 'Shit? Did someone—'

Robyn was shaking. In the absolute dark, my breath was too loud. Crammed in the small space, I put my hand up, I wriggled until I could touch him. He laced his fingers with mine.

'He's gone,' I said.

All around us, people were talking. Del was crying more and more, sobbing, retching. I started to move.

'Wait,' said Robyn.

But the heavy footsteps had disappeared into the night. I stretched my hearing, needing to be sure. Somewhere else, a car started. A door opened. A woman shouted out. A siren was on its way. More people came running.

We moved slowly – Robyn first, then me. We climbed out from under the van together.

Ben was draped over the steps, his head against Del's chest, for all the world as if he were sleeping. Del rocked him so gently.

Robyn reached them first.

Ben was dead. His eyes stared into Del's hold, seeing nothing.

'My boy,' said Del. Over and over again he said the same. 'My boy, my boy.'

Still talking, sobbing, his words were only for Ben.

I stood with Robyn, our hands together.

'He's gone,' said Del. He looked up at us, horror written in his eyes.

Chapter Twenty-Four

A coincidence is rarely a coincidence.

Patrick's words rumbled through my mind over and over again as I sat on the pavement. Detective Garda O'Hara, the same irritating man who'd stood for nothing over Eve, now stood with his feet planted, one hand in his pocket. I stared at his expensive leather shoes.

'So there were two shots fired?' said O'Hara.

'I-I d—' Del's voice stuttered and faded, the words lost.

'Three,' said Robyn clearly. Again, he took my hand and squeezed my fingers. I could not let go of him. 'Or was it four?' he said. 'It was loud. Like a shotgun. It was . . .'

I shook my head. I didn't want to remember.

I remembered the roughness of the ground as Robyn shoved me out of the way, the skim, the whistle of something going past me. The sound of Del on the phone.

'Miss McKinnery, again?' said the brown-suited detective.

I was tired. So much of me blamed him but there was no point. It was no more about blaming the detective than blaming a magpie that sat on the fence watching a fox take a lamb.

'And where were you when—?'

'Are you going to investigate Eve's murder now?' I said. 'Now another young man has been killed?'

'I don't appreciate your tone.'

I said a bad word. A very bad word indeed. I starting saying another, but Robyn pulled at my arm, steering me back. I pushed away from them all. The detective could not ignore a man being shot to death in the street, but that didn't mean he was going to let go of his sheer stubborn insistence that he was right, and I could not stand there and argue with him when, even if he had listened, none of us could have predicted this.

I'd had enough.

I muttered under my breath as I walked. I didn't even know where I was going, I was just going.

Bursting from around the corner, Mark came running toward me. Out of breath, his feet clunked in his heavy boots.

'Is it true?' he said. His chest heaved, he fought to breathe. 'Is it true? Is Ben—'

On the other side of the road, the ambulance door closed behind the stretcher.

'Mark . . .'

'No,' he said, shaking his head. 'No, not Ben. It can't be!' He caught his arms around his waist, breathing hard.

It had been five minutes, maybe six. The guards were only just taking Del from the scene, the big-nosed detective was standing over the steps. The guards were searching the gutters.

'Oh, God.' Mark fell to his knees, his shoulders heaving. 'Ben?'

'How did you know?' I said. 'Where were you?'

Mark didn't answer me.

Del gripped the railing. He pointed at Mark.

'Get him away from me!' he sobbed. 'Detective, please, make him go away. He has no right . . . Make him . . . He can't be here. I can't see him—'

Robyn put out his hand. 'It's my fault,' he said. He had his phone in his hand. 'I texted Thora . . .'

'No one texts anyone until I say,' the detective snapped. 'Is that clear?'

I wanted to tell him that many, many things were clear.

'You shouldn't be here, Mark,' said Robyn quietly.

He stepped in front of Del, shielding the place where Ben's blood had drenched the steps.

I looked from one to the other.

I'd got it wrong. Mark was stronger than Ben. He could have overpowered Eve without a second thought. He was one of the last people to see her alive – and now he was suddenly here in the street where Ben had just been killed?

Mark who had wide shoulders. Mark who was with Ben up on the balcony, while Ben said he'd missed Del's performance.

Mark who had taken the drink from Ben without thanking him. Without needing to thank him.

Mark who had looked for Ben, every time.

'Excuse me,' said O'Hara. 'Could you—'

'What's happening?' Del looked up at him, at the guards who swarmed the little space, at the crowd around us, the tape already there, binding across the street, the cars, the uniforms. 'Who would do this?' he said.

Del looked at me.

'Ben said he knew who it was,' he said. 'We were at the club, and he saw someone in the audience, and he freaked out. Robyn was just about to get ready and Ben dragged us both here. He grabbed hold of Robyn and he wouldn't let go, and I thought . . .' Del shook his head. 'And he was trying to find Mark – he was cry- ing – and I came right off the stage in the middle of a number, and he said there was no time and he dragged us both all the way here, and he stood right here and he . . . and . . . and he . . .' Del fought to breathe. 'He was trying to get us inside.'

Behind us, more people were coming out of their houses in dressing gowns, in jumpers and joggers, bare feet stuffed hurriedly into runners.

Someone put up their phone. Behind the guard cars, the first press van pulled up.

'We should go inside,' I said.

'Miss McKinnery?' said O'Hara.

I took Del's arm.

'You can ask your questions inside,' I said firmly. 'All of you.' I bent to help Del over the bloodstain. 'Del has lost his husband, Detective, and this time you cannot tell us it was an accident.'

'I really think—'

'You think?' I snapped. 'Then if I were you, I'd give me a hand here. Mark, go home,' I said. 'This is enough of a show for one night.'

First light was just touching the sky as Robyn and I finally made it home. I could not remember having a normal sleep pattern. Together, we climbed the stairs. Robyn held on to the banister, pulling himself up. If Mrs Harper was awake she didn't bother us, and we did not speak until our door was closed.

The argument between us, whatever it was, was long gone. I fastened the second lock closed and kicked off my shoes. I fell, fully dressed, on to the top of my bed. After a minute, Robyn came into the room and sat beside me.

The air was dull, the flat stuffy and quiet. In all my hurry earlier, it had made no difference. Ben was gone. I was too late. If I'd got there ten minutes before, I might have seen the shooter and I might have been able to stop him. But then, if Robyn hadn't moved so quickly, it might have been my blood on the ground.

'It wasn't Mark,' said Robyn.

'He was there.'

'He was in love with Ben,' he said. 'They've been together for ages – I saw them, when Eve died. It does my head in – they were there, kissing and rowing and yelling at one another, right outside the club, and Del was only just inside, and they expect me to be able to walk in there like nothing happened? They were at me to promise, to give my word I wouldn't tell, and Del's my friend . . .'

I curled my knees up to my chest.

'But Mark couldn't have done it tonight,' said Robyn. 'He loved Ben.'

'He's big enough. And he was wearing boots.'

'Lots of people wear boots.'

I shook my head. I couldn't stop hearing those footsteps coming toward us. Coming right up to the truck.

I shivered.

'Hey, now,' said Robyn. He pulled my blanket over me. 'It's OK.'

'It's not OK,' I said.

'I know.'

'Stay with me?'

'I'm not going anywhere,' he said.

I woke up with my face mashed into Robyn's shoulder, his shirt button imprinted into my nose. I stretched my legs and nearly rolled off the edge of the bed, but his arm clamped around my waist.

'I'm still furious with you,' he murmured into my hair.

'You're cute when you're mad.'

'Then I'm mad,' he said.

I crawled up and slowly unfolded my body and clambered to my feet. My clothes were wrinkled and creased, my jeans biting at my skin, something ugly and stinky on my leg from the road. Slowly, we unpeeled ourselves from the night. We wandered around the small space together, bumping against one another, mumbling. I kept touching him. I held his arm while he put teabags into two mugs, and he smoothed back my hair as I pulled a packet of Jammie Dodger biscuits from the shelf. Neither of us would make it into work, that was certain, and in the end we sat on the couch, clean and showered, both in robes, wrapped in blankets, sipping tea and slowly waking into a world without Ben and without Eve.

Robyn dipped a biscuit into his tea. The silence swamped us. I leaned down for his laptop. Unable to handle anything with police in it, or drag queens, we switched between cartoons, finally settling on *Tangled*.

'Can we talk?' I said after a bit.

'Do you want to?' he said.

The last thing I wanted was to rehash everything that had happened, but I nodded. I would have avoided it if I could, but it was still there, even if it was hiding behind the pain.

'I'm sorry,' I said. 'I shouldn't have said . . . you know. What I said. I'm sorry I called you stupid, because you're not. Not at all. And I'm sorry.'

Robyn nodded.

We watched for some more, until I reached for the biscuits and he caught my hand.

'I'm sorry I called you a little straight girl,' he said. 'I know you hate that.'

'You called me other things,' I said, poking his knee.

He grinned and pulled me into a hug. 'I love you, Fi,' he said. 'I'm glad we're not dead.'

'I love you too,' I said. 'What's Gavin like?'

A slow smile spread over his face. 'Jenkins is his dad – did you know that?'

I took another biscuit, crammed it into my mouth, crunched through the jam and relished the absolute pleasure of its biscuity taste.

We watched the movie. We made more tea, we got another blanket, and finally, eventually, Robyn brushed the crumbs from our laps and turned to me.

'We should go and see Del,' he said.

I nodded. 'He texted to say he's with his family.'

'Yeah, but we're family too,' said Robyn. 'We should call him anyway.'

But neither of us knew what to say and somehow the phones lay dormant on the little table. An hour later, I raised the subject again. A little while after that, Robyn did. Real life was so much harder to go back to when it hurt.

'First Eve, then Gavin, now Ben,' I whispered, the words spilling out of me, unchecked.

Robyn chewed his lip. He thought, and then nodded.

'Ben knew who it was, didn't he?' I said. 'He knew who killed Eve.' I broke the last biscuit, handing over the bigger half.

'I thought it was him,' I said. 'He was being so guarded and strange.'

'So did Del,' said Robyn. 'And he was being guarded and strange because he'd been arguing with Mark.'

'It's all guarded and strange,' I mumbled bitterly.

'When you and that bloke were at the restaurant, Ben had to go out and call Mark and stop him from coming in, because Mark tended to meet him there on his break, and you would have seen him.'

Ben, Mark. Mark, Ben.

'Have another biscuit,' he said.

'We're out. The packet's empty, that was the last half.'

'We could get another?'

'I'm not sure I want another,' I said.

'Of course you do. Then you can give me one.'

It was gone two when Robyn's phone buzzed. He listened, nodding, and in the background I heard Thora crying as she spoke. The guards had charged a man with shooting Ben, she said. A drunk, homeless man who'd been found, hissing and blinding, just waking up on the next street with the gun in his bag.

'So they caught him?' I said, as Robyn hung up.

'They caught someone.'

'Was he wearing boots?'

'Thora said he has an alibi for Eve's death but they're still treating that as accidental anyway, and this as a separate issue.'

'Is it a good alibi?' I said. 'I mean, anyone can make up—'

'He'd been arrested for abusive behaviour or something. He was in the clink.'

'Ah. So.'

The detective had said it was just chance that the man took a pot shot at Ben, Thora told us. It was nothing to do with Eve, or with Gavin, or—

'That's insane,' I said.

Robyn paused the movie.

'The gun matched,' he said. 'Unregistered, but he could have taken it from any farm in the country. He has a history of violent episodes. Detective Darrel O'Hara is certain they have the right man, and Thora says they don't even think there is any reason to cancel Pride.'

I waited.

Robyn was pleating the cashmere blanket between his fingers, thinking.

'So we're saying he did it?' I said slowly. 'This bloke. He shot Ben?'

'The gun shot Ben,' said Robyn. 'The man was found holding the gun, with no memory of shooting anyone, but no memory of not doing so either.'

'Who is he, though? Why did he kill Ben? What—?'

Robyn gripped the blanket. His knuckles were white, his nails bitten down to the quick.

'Sorry,' I whispered. 'I should—'

'We're meeting Thora at ten tomorrow morning,' he said. 'I told her you'd be there.'

We sat together, watching the paused animation stuck mid-song.

'Is it time for another shouty blog post?' said Robyn.

I smiled. 'No, I'm done with that. I'm done with blogging,' I said. 'No one blogs anyway, nowadays. It's all Insta stories, and—'

He gave me that look, raising one eyebrow. 'I was thinking that maybe you should.' He sat up, pushed back the blanket. 'Look, it's insane,' he said. 'But if the person who is doing this knows us, and we all follow your blog now, and—'

'Robyn?' I said. 'Do you know who killed Eve and Ben?'

He looked down at his lap. 'I don't know for sure,' he said. 'And don't ask me because I'm not saying anything out loud until I know I'm right, because if it is who I think it is . . .'

'Rob?'

He shook his head. 'If I'm wrong, I don't ever want to have said the name out loud, Fi. I can't live with that.'

'You have to go to the guards.'

'If I'm right, the only person in danger is me.'

I knew that look. He got that from his mother. I pushed back from the couch.

'Trust me,' he said. 'It's rough, but I think I might have a plan.'

'Whatever it is, it sounds like a terrible idea,' I said. 'Tell the guards. Have them sort it out.'

'No. No, I can't.'

'Why not?'

'In case I'm wrong! Christ, I . . .' He pushed up from the couch and started pacing the floor. 'Fi, trust me. Please. I'm done playing games in the dark. I'm done with being afraid. With being' – he trembled – 'hunted. I can feel it when I walk around in town – I can feel it when I'm onstage. If I could just see them, see their face . . .

'If I'm right,' he said. 'They will kill again, and again, until it's me on those steps – and maybe after. Either way, it's time to drag them into the light. Once and for all.'

'Blimey, Robyn.' I laughed, my nerves rippling into giggles as he strode across the floor, but he didn't laugh with me.

'It started with Mae B,' he said. 'Not Eve, but Mae B. Eve thought she was stealing my act, but it was so much more than that.'

'But—'

'No, I get it now. And I get why I was so mad at you, and – oh!' His face lit up. 'Hang on, do you still want to do that photoshoot on the bridge?' he said.

'What? I don't really think now is the t—'

'Because there is one fact that no one else knows,' said Robyn. 'Throughout all of this. No one outside our group knew that Eve died dressed as Mae B. Not the guards, not the press. I never told them. No one except us, and the murderer. So let's lay the trail, Fi. Let's set a trap.'

'And if we lose?' I said.

'Then we lose together.'

'I'd rather not lose.'

'Me too,' he said.

Chapter Twenty-Five

It took three hours for Robyn to do his face and another for him to decide between the dresses we'd hung from the tops of the doors. After lengthy phone discussions between Thora and Robyn and the others, I was sent to collect a long, sweeping cape from Miss Merkin's house, on the promise that I would take excellent care of it.

'I'm giving you four outfits to choose from,' said Merkin. 'I have complete sets for all the queens. Please take better care of these than you do of your friends.'

'I think she just wanted the one cape,' I said.

'Don't be ridiculous, Fi, a drag queen never wants just one of anything.' Merkin flicked invisible dust from her arm. 'I need them back in perfect condition,' she said. 'I have no idea what I'm going to wear now. The Pride gown is the very pinnacle of the drag queen's year. The zenith of the creator's season.'

'It's not the Met Gala,' I muttered. I folded the first cape and started to tuck it into my bag.

'What are you doing?' she screeched.

'I was—'

'Oh dear Lord, child, that's silk!' She whipped the cape from my hold and draped it over her arm.

'Oh, I—'

'You will bring each piece back in exactly the condition you borrowed them.'

'I'll wash them all,' I said earnestly.

'You won't, you'll tell Mae B to keep them safe and completely unharmed, and she can bring them back to me herself, with a decent bottle of rosé.'

Behind her, a muffled sob echoed through the long hall from an open door. Merkin pushed me out ahead of her, back on to the street, and pulled the front door closed. In the light, her clear skin shone, her grey hair lifted and played in the breeze.

'Mark,' she said quietly, gesturing at the closed shades in the window.

I craned to see past her.

Was he there when Merkin got Robyn's text? Was he really arguing with Ben and watched by Robyn when Eve lay drowning, unnoticed in the gutter, or was that a careful play, a sleight of hand, of dead drag queens?

'It's funny, isn't it?' said Merkin. 'Del's phone will have rung off the wall by now, but what of the others who loved young Benjamin?'

'Del was his husband,' I said.

'Ben was everyone's husband, if he was in the mood,' said Merkin.

Eve. Ben. Mark. Around and around the carousel went. Del said that Robyn once had a fling with Eve – had he also been with Ben?

'All that effort not to be seen and, at the last minute, we wonder why,' said Merkin.

'Where were you last night?' I said suddenly.

'Between the hours of nine and ten, you mean?' She fixed her eyes on mine. 'I could ask you the same, dear.'

'I was with them. I lay with Robyn under some stinking van.' I took a breath. 'I didn't kill anyone,' I said.

'I didn't kill anyone, either.'

'Ben said he knew who killed Eve. Did he tell you?'

'No. And yet, now we mourn another.' Merkin's deep brown eyes filled with truth. 'And you?' she said. 'Are you keeping safe, child? Or are you writing another toxic blog post?'

I didn't speak. She knew the answer.

'So now, Robyn's little friend,' said Merkin. 'The numbers are closing in. We surround ourselves with the only people we can be sure of, with our family, and yet, somehow, we are never sure, are we?'

She looked to the house. The weeds in the garden clambered thick and untamed, so unlike the perfect order of the inside of the little house. Brambles fought against nettles and the walls were grey with time.

I walked down the steps to the pavement.

'And you, Fi,' she said, following me. 'You have never been sure of any of us, have you?'

As she started down the stairs, one of the capes slipped from her hands, curling under her feet. She slipped, tripping and falling toward me, her hands outstretched. I caught her, falling back to the pavement as she tumbled on top of me, squirming and screeching, her arms flailing as she cried out.

The door banged open. Merkin howled and wailed, and Mark rushed down to us, heaving her from me.

'Are you OK?' he said. 'Are you hurt?'

I lay on the ground, staring at the sky. I wasn't honestly sure I was OK. There was a great deal of Merkin to be under.

'Tell me, are you hurt?' he said again. I realised he was talking to Miss Merkin.

Surplus to requirement. Once again, I was to be left lying in the dirt.

'Oh!' cried Merkin. 'Oh my head!'

'What happened?' he said. 'I saw the sequins go flying!'

'These bastards,' she whimpered. Tugging the mess of fabric from underneath her, she hurled the long capes at my body, covering me. 'I spend my life caring for them, and that's how they repay me? By trying to kill me?'

'Fi?' said Mark. 'Are you under there?'

He reached down, offered me an arm.

What was the socially acceptable greeting when you think someone has killed one of your friends? Or at the very least, when someone's illicit affair is discovered by the shooting of their married partner, right in front of his husband?

'How are you?' I said.

'Grand.'

'It's, um . . .'

'Yeah?' he said.

'I'm sorry for your loss.' I had to say it, I thought. He may have pulled the trigger but I'm still human, still mostly Irish. 'May he rest in peace,' I said.

'Thanks.'

May he rest in peace without you, I added in my head.

I dusted down my jeans. The capes were crumpled, one of them had ripped in a corner. I turned the fabric in on itself and carefully laid them in my bag, zipping up the top.

'So,' said Merkin. 'Mae B is really doing this?'

'It's a terrible plan,' said Mark.

It was better than killing people, I thought.

'Are you in?' I said.

'He's driving the bus, of course,' said Merkin. 'Mark always drives the TRASH bus.'

240

Mark picked at a freckle of dirt on his arm.

'And I'm in, if that's what you're really asking,' said Merkin. 'But it's all change now, eh? We're all in, little Fi. All ready for the big plan.'

The inside of my head was ringing and fluttering as if a synchronised fleet of bluebirds had taken up a performance somewhere near my medulla oblongata. I blinked.

'Take the capes away,' said Merkin. She put her hand to her forehead. 'Tell Mae B I'll have the other dresses finished by tomorrow evening and if anyone wants me after that they can book a damn appointment. They don't understand – honestly, they think it's just a flick of the sewing machine and out it comes, like I'm giving birth to the damn things! Come along, Mark. You can make tea – I need to lie down. Go away, Fi, darling. My head hurts from all this chatter.'

'Thank you for th—'

Ignoring me, Merkin took Mark's strong arm.

'They tried to kill me,' she said to him as they turned for the house. 'Honestly, I take one step out of place and the capes tried to trip me up. I can't do it, I really can't do it!'

I rode back on the Luas. I wondered how many other people were getting ready for Pride with no notion of murderers or secrets or lies. Painting signs, painting rainbows, fixing costumes, smiling, sharing pizzas late into the night as the glue dried on a headdress or a skirt, or inflating fifty rainbow balloons with helium as we had one year, only to lose them in the trees behind Trinity on the way to the march.

◆ ◆ ◆

Two hours later, I stood on the bridge with my camera in my hands.

'Fi?' Mae B hung back from the top arch. Balanced on the spiked rails. 'Are we making this weird?'

'You're asking me because?'

'Because, honey, you are the queen of making things weird.'

'Only one queen here today, gorgeous.'

I watched her reach up to the sweeping arch, her heels stuck in the very top of the railings, the sparkling red gown and long train sweeping back behind her, the sequins catching in the evening light, bouncing the shine from the water. Most people waited but two men stormed past, pushing against my shoulder. One of them muttered a word to Mae B. A bad word, a word that dug under skin. I riled, turning to defend her, but behind me a low voice called out.

'Want me to take this one?'

Patrick stood in the way of the men. Beside him was a large dog, all teeth and phlegm, straining at the leash toward them. The men stuttered and snarked.

'Can we just do this, Fi?' said Mae B.

Patrick didn't move.

'I imagine they're sorry about now,' I said.

The people either side of us hung back as Mae B swayed on the railing, looking horribly like she was about to fall, gown and all, into the dark, murky water below.

'What of it?' said one of the troll men. 'You got a problem with what I said?'

'Fi?' said Mae B. 'Can we take the damn picture?'

I grabbed my camera. 'Turn a bit more,' I said. 'Just a little bit more . . .'

'If I fall off here and drown . . .'

'Then I'll chop you up myself, gratis,' said Patrick.

'That's disgusting!'

'Just get the shot!' Mae B laughed.

I moved again. Taking three more, four more, letting the lens find the light, the silhouette. Another three, another five, moving one more fraction. Then the sunlight beamed down over her, and she put her face to the sky.

I had it.

She was the absolute beauty of drag. Her long gown sparkled and shone, the lights catching every shadow. Her expression, tipped to the evening sun, her dress incredible – her body inconceivable – and the long, long train, sweeping away from the twisted iron and over the river. The crowds eased and started to move past and there she was, Mae B, above them all, one hand gripping a chain from the overhead arch, the other stretched up to the sky – so graceful, so beautiful. Rising like a phoenix above the mud, above the undercurrent of pain and loss that slid through the city.

I checked the shots. Against the setting sun, Mae B's face was nearly obscured. Nearly, but not quite; the high brows, the lips, still undeniably hers.

'You look awesome,' breathed a young woman.

Another lady lifted her phone to Mae's face. I put out my hand.

'Sorry.' I kept my hand in the way until they'd walked past.

'Guys, I'm coming down,' said Mae B, 'one way or another.'

'I'll catch you,' said Patrick. He passed me the dog's leash. 'Fi, can you take Martha?'

The dog looked at me. I looked at the dog.

Martha was a dog.

'Robyn?' said Patrick. 'If you'd just try to fall this way?'

'Hey, dude.' Mae B grinned as she leaned forward, gracefully lowering herself into Patrick's arms and away from the high, pointed rail.

'Is this another photo for the infamous blog?' said Patrick.

'It might be,' said Mae B. 'It depends if I look cute.'

'Looked cute, may delete later?' I said.

'Sick on so many levels . . .' said Mae B.

I gathered my bags together, looping them over my shoulder. The giant hound sniffed at my camera. Without thinking, I took her picture, her nose right in the middle of the shot, her big dark eyes gawking up at me as she sniffed the lens. She was gorgeous. She sat, her mouth open, her tongue out, and she grinned at me, wagging her tail, a perfect model, without having to nearly fall off the bridge to get the shot.

'She's a terrible flirt,' said Patrick. 'Don't let her take advantage of you, Fi, or you'll never get rid of her.'

'I could say the same about Mae B here,' I told him.

'It's all true,' said Mae B. 'Blimey, doc, you put on some muscle since UCD? Any chance you slipped to the other side?'

'None at all,' said Patrick. 'But if it was going to be anyone . . .'

He winked, and Mae B grinned. I fumbled with the strap of my camera bag. So, Martha was a dog. Martha was not a wife or a girlfriend. She did not wear a blue dress in a photograph. She was not a blond, or a redhead.

'If you're done,' said Patrick. 'Can I buy us all a drink?' He nodded to the bar just down the river.

Mae B started to answer, then looked at me. She turned her head, an imperceptible question. Behind Patrick's back, I nodded, also barely moving.

'Why don't you two head on,' she said. 'I'll put things back to how they're comfy, and see you in there?'

Without waiting for either of us to reply, Mae B gathered her skirts in her hand and swept down the steps to the road. She stood at the traffic lights, nearly seven foot tall in her heels, her gown clinging to her tiny waist and round padded hips and boobs. As the light turned to green, the others held back and she stepped forward with a slight dip of her head, acknowledging her absolute queenliness.

'Robyn looks good,' said Patrick. 'What do you call her now?'

'Mae B.'

He nodded. 'And she can really walk in those shoes? Blimey. How can she do that when she could never kick a football in a straight line?'

The dog pushed in between us, leaning against my legs. I rubbed the top of her head with my fingers.

'So this is Martha?' I said.

'She likes the river. So many grim smells, I guess.'

'A bit like pathology?'

Patrick grinned. 'Of all the women I've ever known, Martha is the only one for me,' he said. 'Or the only one not to run away, anyway.'

'That will make Robyn happy.'

He laughed, a deep belly laugh. 'Come on,' he said. 'Let's get those drinks.'

Taking one of my camera bags, Patrick matched my step, but at the bar, the seats outside had all gone and the tables were stacked full of pints and overspilling tourists.

A drunk man staggered back, knocking into Martha before I could pull her away.

'Do you drink terrible red wine?' I said.

'Absolutely – often by choice.'

'And do you like takeout noodles?'

'More than words,' he said.

'I have the perfect place.'

Chapter Twenty-Six

Pride Saturday dawned bright and sunny, the rains of May long forgotten. I woke slowly, dragging myself from my dreams. As Tina Turner filled the small apartment, I opened my eyes. My bedroom door creaked and Robyn peered in.

'Are you awake?'

'Was "Proud Mary" really necessary, this early?'

'She was.'

'You'll get us thrown out of here.'

'Mrs Harper is with her sister for the morning – I helped her into the cab. She's getting the early train.'

Robyn came in slowly, holding two mugs of tea. I pushed my sleep-ruined hair from my face and scrabbled up against the headboard.

'Patrick left late again last night?' he said.

I blushed. 'We were just talking.'

Robyn nudged me. 'There was quite a bit of not-talking time too,' he said. 'I mean, not that I was counting the hours.'

'Not at all. We were catching up. We used to be friends, you know.'

'Mmhmm.' He nodded. 'I remember who used to want to be more than friends with him, too.'

'We were practically kids, back then.'

'He's all grown up now, though, isn't he?'

I grinned, as I wriggled under the covers.

'Oh darling, you're sleeping in a fleece again,' said Robyn, picking at my sleeve. The bed lowered as he sat down. 'What does this one have on it? A kitten? Fi, how old are you? Are you really sleeping in a tent of manmade fibres, covered in cartoon kittens?'

Tina rang from the stereo and Robyn moved his shoulders in time. I straightened my nightshirt, wishing a little bit that I could pull myself back to my dream, away from a world where best friends thought it was acceptable to play lively music at volume before breakfast.

'It's beneath you,' he said, nodding at the fleece. 'Really, it's—'

'It's all around me. And anyway, I sleep alone,' I said. 'And don't you give me that look.'

'Not at all.' Robyn hugged my knees through the duvet. 'No, I'm sorry. Christ, no. I can't, it's too much! The kitten is looking at me. It's hideous, Fi. Please burn it.'

'I love it, so shut up.'

He stopped moving. 'So we're doing this?' he said.

'You don't have to.'

I sipped on the tea. Tiny flakes of leaf floated up to the surface. Real Earl Grey leaf tea; he'd used the good stuff.

'Neither do you, but someone has to do something,' he said. 'It's a start.'

But it could so easily be the end.

He was right. I didn't have to do it but then, neither did he – neither did any of them – but if we were right and the killer was still out there, which one of them would be next? Would it ever be safe outside the club again?

All over the city, hundreds of thousands of people would be getting ready to celebrate Gay Pride. They would look to the drag queens to lead the march as they did every year. They would be laughing and cheering and smiling and very much alive, with no idea.

I hugged my fleece around my middle.

Whoever it was, I desperately wished Robyn could be wrong. I wished more than anything in the world that the man who had been found with the gun might have been the one to pull the trigger. That it was no less, but also no more, than a psychotic rage against humanity. That it wasn't personal.

I wished so hard that Eve and then Ben had been killed just because they were in the wrong place at the wrong time. Not because they represented the core of someone's hatred and fear.

As Thora had pointed out in the family meeting at the empty club the day before, if a death wasn't personal, we could forgive it. We can forgive mental illness, and we can forgive chance, and we can forgive nature if she comes to call for us, when it's our time. But this was never nature. This we cannot forgive. Eve was dead. Gavin was hurt on purpose. Ben had been killed, so close to both Robyn and Del. And it wasn't just the death of two young gay men. With their loss, there was a space left where they should have been, and the grief that cut through their families – both kinds of families – was too much.

'Evil walks amongst us,' Thora had said. 'And this evil is not wearing heels.'

If Robyn was right, then by making our point, we would drive the killer into the light – and we would all be there. Eve's family. Ben's family. Del's family. My family. Each and every one of us, from Mama Thora to Merkin to me – the little straight girl who just could not stop asking questions. And if I was wrong – if we were all wrong . . .

Tina switched smoothly to Beyoncé. My phone buzzed. A message from Edna.

Hope you have a wonderful day. Happy Pride! Karen is stuck with the sheep, she can't get away, but Grandpa Joe and I will be there – we will be waving from the usual place. Kisses to our Mae B, I love the blog post. Lots of nice comments.

I whimpered. I pulled my laptop from the floor, opened it.

'Well?' said Robyn.

'Thirty likes. Thirty-one . . .' I never had that kind of numbers. 'Thirty-two . . .'

I scrolled through the comments. The picture looked good. The first portrait I had ever posted with the face of the person in the shot. Mae B looked amazing, of course, and the bait was right there in black and white.

> Come and see the queens on the bus at Pride,
> this Saturday, dressed to kill.

I pulled my blanket around me. Had I done the right thing? What if we were wrong?

But 'what if' could be a thousand things. What if we had laid the trap, not for the killer to step out of the darkness, but for Robyn? For Thora? For Merkin?

What if they took another shot? Another try? And we weren't quick enough?

I picked up my phone again, to read Edna's soft message.

We can't wait to see you both after. Love Edna xx

Thora's words rumbled through my fear: 'It's OK to be afraid,' she'd said.

'So we die afraid?' Merkin had said.

'No. We set the trap,' Thora had told her. 'And we hand over the monster to the guards, and then we do exactly what we do at Pride every single year.'

'What's that?' I'd said.

'We get very, very drunk.'

I pushed up from the bed. Staggering into the little sitting room, I ground to a halt. The entire room was filled with every dress, every wig, every gown – every scrap of sequins and shine and fluff and drag Robyn owned.

'How the hell long have you been up?' I said.

Beyoncé slid into Danni Minogue, and as Robyn's arms came around my waist, I leaned back against him.

'I hope I'm wrong,' he said.

'You were wrong about that yellow leotard.'

'I cannot hide my shame.'

'If I were you, sweetie, I'd try.'

By nine-thirty, she was ready. We stepped up, into TRASH. The others were on time too, showing if nothing else, the strangeness of the day – if a drag queen was on time, Robyn once told me, it was either because she was getting laid or getting paid.

Merkin looked me up and down. 'I see you brought your friend,' she said, glancing behind me.

'Patrick mentioned he'd give us a hand, and—'

'The cameras are all in place,' Thora announced. 'Fi's hump boy's h—'

'Hey!' I said.

'OK fine,' she said. 'Fi's somewhat attractive, single, straight male friend that she fancies blind but hasn't as yet got around to shafting, or being shafted by, is fixing the last one on the front. I imagine it is looking up our skirts.'

'It's looking up at the buildings,' I told them. 'There are eight cameras in place, and bulletproof glass at the front and back, so if anyone does anything, to anyone, then it should be caught on film. Whatever happens, we have proof.'

'Every view around us should be covered at least once,' said Mae B. 'The lower side of the bus is protected. We're exposed on the top but if you see anything at all, you shout, we retreat as fast as our little heels will carry us down below.'

'Everyone got that?' said Thora.

'I can't see to drive.' Mark stormed in through the open door, throwing the bus keys on to the bar. 'Have you seen what they've done to the cab?'

'It's protective plasticky stuff,' said Thora. 'I had them fix it in case of b—'

'I can't drive a bus like that!'

'Why not?'

'I can't see a thing.'

'It's no different to normal,' said Thora. 'You just point it forward and people get out of the way.'

'I'll end up taking a wrong turn and mowing down a fleet of glorious lesbians. I can't do it. I don't know what you were thinking.'

'Well, then I'll drive,' said Mae B.

'You can't drive a bus,' I said.

'How hard can it be? I've driven plenty of tractors and stuff.'

'You're there to be seen, pet,' said Thora. Her mouth set in a firm line. 'That's the whole bloody point. Although, really, we'd all be better off tucked away behind the plastic stuff, but—'

'These shoes are killing me,' Merkin muttered.

'Saves anyone else doing it . . .'

'D'you have a corn plaster?'

'I don't know why you didn't wear runners,' said Thora. 'No one is going to see your feet.'

'And have them carry out my corpse with a pair of gym shoes stuck over my tights?' Merkin wafted away her words. 'I have standards.'

'Really?' Thora snapped. 'Name one.'

'No one's going to carry anyone else's corpse,' said Patrick at the door. 'The bus is fixed exactly like you said and there are guards on every corner, and lining the fences at sensible intervals throughout. I've said this to Fi and to Ro— sorry, to Mae B, but I'll say this to you all. You don't have to do any of this. The guards will help you. You d—'

Del strode in through the open doors. 'Yes, we do,' he said.

He wore the same bright red sequin gown, the same long black train, as the others.

'You came?' said Thora. She put out both hands to Del.

'Of course I came. Some nutter is taking us out – I'm going to be part of putting them away. But I'll be honest, girls, I'm freaking out.'

'We're all afraid,' said Thora. She drew herself up to her full height. 'Come here, my pets – and you too, little straight girl and your big, tall man there. I want to say this before we go out as bait on the line – beautiful bait, of course, darlings, but bright red, sparkling bait nonetheless: let's be clear about what we're doing here.'

The queens drew into a circle. Mae B, the baby of the family, her wig set perfectly, her face painted to the gods; Merkin, every inch the statue of camp royalty; Del, his dress hanging too loose at the back where he'd lost weight, his long purple wig shining, his eyes fixed on Thora. Mark slipped in beside them and reached out his hand, drew me in with a squeeze of my fingers. His eyes shone with something I couldn't place as he looked at me.

'We are afraid,' said Thora. 'Of course we're afraid! We're smart, strong people, but we know the evil that lurks out there in the shadows. We can name that fear a thousand times over, but we are not going to let it tell us what to do with our lives.'

Del touched the back of his hand to his eyes. The others nodded.

'We are drag queens,' said Thora. 'We throw the first brick. We stand at the front of the line. We take the words that hurt us and w—'

'We dress up in fancy costumes and mouth along to other people's music,' said Merkin.

'And we do it beautifully,' said Thora.

Chapter Twenty-Seven

In the end, Patrick drove. After an hour of screaming arguments between Thora and Mark, Patrick took the keys from the bar and strode between them.

'Your friends are high maintenance,' he said to me.

'It just seems that way because you're used to dead people,' I told him.

'True, my lot aren't known for their conversation.'

'Conversation?' Thora snapped. 'There's no time for a conversation. The bus should have been parked in place an hour ago, but it's been sat in the bloody road all bloody night. We still have to finish up here. Fi, you go with him, we'll meet you at the stand.'

'You have any paperwork?' said Patrick. 'Or do we just show up and say hi, drag queen transport here, mind if I slip in between you?'

Mark snapped around. 'What is your problem?' He swore, hissing the words through his teeth. 'This place is turning more like a straight club than a gay club. At this rate—'

'Do try not to insult the only person here with a licence to drive a bus,' said Del. 'I take it you have a licence?' he asked Patrick.

'To drive you, and also to chop up anyone we accidentally mow down in our way.'

'So sordid,' said Merkin. 'Are they, like . . . ?'

'Often gross, yes,' he said. 'And always dead. Fi, are you coming with me? You can point out the likely suspects.'

I matched his pace.

'You owe me for this,' he muttered.

'I could walk Martha?' I said.

'I'll think of something.'

He pulled himself up into the driver's seat of the old bus. In fairness to Mark, the cab windscreen was thick with the bulletproof plastic, and the whole of the downstairs was hot and stuffy with the windows closed and barred.

'Is this even legal?' I said. 'He's right, I can hardly see.'

'Almost certainly not legal, and definitely not sensible. Couldn't you have been friends with a chess-playing group or something?'

'They're OK.' I smiled. 'They're not always like this.'

'I bet they are.'

'Usually no one's trying to kill them.'

His face darkened. 'Do you really think they're at risk today?' he said.

'I don't know. No, that's not true.' I frowned. 'Yeah, they are. We all are, but they are the most. I'll be looking at every corner, every balcony. They're so vulnerable. When Robyn told me his plan, I didn't really think he meant it.'

I left the rest unsaid.

Patrick started the engine. I stood, tucked into the door. He held the steering wheel with both hands. His shirtsleeves were pushed up to the elbow. He drove slowly, easing into the traffic heading for St Stephen's Green.

'So,' I said. 'How come Mr Patrick Midda, pathologist and dog owner, can drive a bus then?'

'Just one of the many things you don't know about me, Ms Fi McKinnery,' he replied.

I grinned. The warmth grew up from my belly, making my heart bounce around.

He stopped for a traffic light.

'Do you think it's weird that Mark wouldn't drive, when he drives every year?' I said.

'Do you?'

I scratched the back of my neck. 'I'm not sure I trust anyone at this stage.'

Pulling into the right space, Patrick put on the brake. He took my hand.

'You can trust me,' he said.

The warmth that had already started in my belly suddenly swamped me, setting alight to my face. Time slipped away. I'd just pulled back and started to speak, when the back door clunked open.

'We took our time,' said Mae B.

'All ready and correct, ma'am,' said Patrick.

'Right,' said Thora. She dipped her head to keep her huge wig from catching on the low ceiling. 'Up we go, ladies!'

She led the way. Del followed.

'Are you OK?' I whispered.

'No. But the show must go on.' He held the banister as he stepped up. 'Fi?'

'Yes?'

Del reached forward and kissed me. 'You did good, girl.'

He turned and flicked back his long purple hair, and set his face to his professional, wide smile. Merkin came next, still muttering about her shoes, and then there was just Mae B and me, by the stairs. Outside, the crowd was filling the pavements. The guards wandered around, smiling easy. Even the trees seemed greener than before and the sun beamed down, and the birds sat back to watch the real colour of the day.

Ahead of us, the steel drum band started.

'So,' I said. 'I guess it's time?'

Pulling me into a hug, Mae B was shaking. So was I.

'You really think they'll come for you?'

'It's too temping not to.' Mae B kept her arms around me. 'They will be looking for attention. They're getting closer. The street. The square. Closer and closer – if I'm right, they won't be able to resist.'

'What if we don't catch them?'

Fear laced under Mae B's heavy make-up. 'What if we do?' she said.

The parade started slowly but there was nothing slow about the crowd. Pride was more than just another show. Up on the top of the open bus, the queens looked incredible. Each in Mae B's trademark red sequin dress to remember Eve, and the long black trains in memory of Ben. Merkin, Thora, Del and Mae B shimmied and waved and grinned and smiled. Down below, I peered through the thick plastic as Patrick eased us slowly forward. Unlike the queens, my nerves played all over my face. I could feel it in the reactions of those who saw my stares. Everyone around us was so happy, cheering and smiling, waving rainbow flags, leaping about and dancing.

Everyone was so close to the bus.

I started to think that this really was a terrible idea. That this was the worst idea ever. If something happened, if we had trouble of any kind—

A once highly choreographed performance, the queens had decided to wing it, places lost to the worry and panic. Changing the entire plan, Thora had forgotten the original music and instead had botched together a bunch of songs from her phone. She refused any help as she picked her favourites to blare from the speakers on the top of the bus. Ahead, Dublin's more famous drag queens led the parade, their own music young and bubbly and bright, but at TRASH, said Thora, we held our own.

All around us, the parade was beautiful as ever. Lights, music, queens and kings, old and young. A man in a bright pink latex kitten outfit, complete with long tail. Two women dancing together, around and around, skipping to their own music. Companies, groups, huge floats and tiny buses. Steel drummers and disco and classic and pop. The army marched in rainbow wings. The young queer kids together in bright pink t-shirts, led by youth workers, carrying rainbows. Everywhere I looked, rainbows and smiles and strength.

I leaned over to Patrick.

'Have you seen Mark?' I said.

'No, but I'm mostly just trying not to run down these women on Vespas.'

We pulled forward another inch. The crowd were hemmed in behind the railings, but the marchers were with us on every side too – adults, children, dogs – everyone just carrying on, happily celebrating the day: couples, singles, groups, families of every shape and size.

People who might fall. People who might get caught in the crossfire.

Panic rose in my chest, beating at my throat.

'What's wrong?' said Patrick. 'Have you seen someone?'

'I'm beginning to wonder if we're doing the right thing,' I said.

'Too late now.'

I looked again but I still didn't see Mark. Where had he gone? Was he in a building, watching and waiting? Was he hidden from sight?

Heading to check on the queens, I started up the thin metal stairs. The music was so loud, none of them heard me. I kept low. Where usually there would be a crowd of twenty or more people up there with them, this Pride, the TRASH queens took the entire top floor alone. Lights and sparkle filled the space. Each of the cameras had been carefully hidden by one of the hundreds of feather boas, or by a draped string of beads, or tucked inside a stream of flowing pink fabric. Stars and glitter trickled down the sides of the bus, flowing into the air. Never mind using up Merkin's stores, between them, it looked like the queens had emptied every haberdashery shop in Dublin.

I crept up to Mae B, knelt beside her.

'How're you doing?' I said.

She reached down for some water. Fear filled her eyes. 'Nothing yet,' she said.

Behind us, someone shouted. We both jumped, but it was just people having fun.

It was so many, many people having fun.

Merkin took a handful of sweets, throwing them to the kids below. Thora turned and saw me.

'Everything OK?' she said.

I nodded.

'We're halfway through,' she said. 'We have the five o'clock slot onstage, so a while to wait, bu—'

'Oh look,' said Mae B. 'My mum came!'

Her face broke into the first proper smile I'd seen in days. I stood up to wave alongside her. Down in the crowd, Edna and Grandpa Joe grinned and waved in return. Edna nudged a man standing next to her, and pointed to Mae B. I saw her lips move clearly: that's my girl.

'I can't believe they came!' Mae B touched the back of her hand to her eyes, happy tears already threatening to smudge the thin silver line under her lower lid. 'Oh, I wish I could say hi! I don't see Karen . . .'

Edna clapped, harder and harder, and beside her in his wheelchair Grandpa Joe looked like his every Christmas had come at once, sheer delight in his grandson written all over his face.

'Would you—' Mae B started.

'I'll tell them hi for you – I'll be right back,' I said with a grin.

The parade was slow enough and I would only be a minute. I stepped down from the bus and tucked in-between the dancers behind us, squeezing through the crowd. The railings were tied tight but, just a little way behind us, there was a gap. I scuttled back, narrowly avoiding being run over by a beautiful semi-clad lady riding a bright yellow moped.

The front row of people stepped back as I squeezed myself through the gap. I glanced forward. Mae B was leaning over the side and calling with Edna. Behind her, Thora was looking away.

I climbed on to the pavement and slid between two tall men. I was just going to turn—

The knife pressed into my spine. A strong hand gripped the top of my arm, pulling me back. I strained to look, but the knife pressed again, the very tip just piercing my skin. We stepped in reverse, in through a cast iron gate. Someone in the crowd looked over, started to speak. My feet were dragged to the wall, away from the crowds. I opened my mouth.

'Say anything,' said a woman's voice. 'Make any sign at all, and I'll press the magic button in my pocket and your little friends up there in their pretty old bus will blow sky high, taking out everyone and everything you see.'

Chapter Twenty-Eight

'You!'

Karen blocked my way. Dressed in black, with her own hair covered by a grey bob wig, I never would have recognised her. She stood with her feet apart, one hand on her hip. Sickness rolled through me. I suddenly remembered the woman who'd pushed past me as I entered the club on Mae B's first night – the same grey wig, the long black coat – and, worse, I remembered her not just from the club but from the bridge. I'd taken her photograph that night. I'd published her photograph on my blog. I'd stolen her moment on the bridge as she walked down from the Luas into town.

Karen stepped toward me. In her hand, the short, sharp knife looked ugly.

'You?' I said again.

'Of course me,' she said. 'Who were you waiting for?'

A man, I thought.

'But—'

But Karen had just as much strength as Mark, or even Ben.

'You really are the most annoying woman I've ever met,' she sneered.

'Me?'

Coming at me before I could think, she pushed me up the stone steps of the library and in through thick trees and hedges, right up to the wall. She shoved me hard, and I fell against a thin metal pole. She grabbed my arms. I fought her, but she was too fast and way too strong. Before I knew what was happening, she had me tied to the post.

'Let me go!' I pulled back on the binds. 'Karen, what—'

'The more you move, the tighter it'll get.' She laughed. 'Oh, I was so hoping to get you with the others. I wanted you to be in there, when the bus blows.'

Horror filled me, a sheet of cold ice.

A bomb?

'Not exactly my first choice, of course.' Pulling off the wig, she stood back, squared her shoulders. 'I'm not a monster.' She shrugged. 'Thanks to you and your messy little habit of sticking your nose where it isn't wanted, subtlety is lost on that crowd. I told Rob, I told him over and over again this past month, that you're trouble. I told him you only wanted him there because you couldn't pay the rent without him.'

'No,' I said. 'No, not at all, I—'

Karen sliced the knife through the air. 'Anyway, we work with what we have. If life gives you lemons, make lemonade. If life gives you a brother like mine, get Semtex.'

Her eyes glistened with excitement. She was breathing too fast, her chest rising and falling. I glanced past her. We were right behind the parade, behind the crowd. We were barely off the street.

'You're wondering if anyone will come,' she said with a slow smile. 'You're asking yourself why you never noticed this place before, aren't you? Who would tuck an old library in here like this, the garden thick with trees, the walls so solid, so unseen.'

She took a small box from her pocket, not much thicker than an old Nokia phone. On the top, a button stood proud.

'Oh, God . . .' I stared at the box.

'Funny, isn't it?' she mused. Behind us, the music from the bus changed. Donna Summer blared over the crowd.

'A tiny box for a great big bomb,' said Karen. 'And there's my brother, clueless as always, dancing away in those ridiculous shoes. All that attention. It wasn't enough to be the prettiest boy, the sweetest boy, the best boy a mother could ever have. It wasn't enough to be the boy who had dates every Saturday, the boy who took his granddad to the cinema, or who remembered his mother's birthday. None of it was enough in the end, was it? He had to take the only thing I had left.'

A bomb. A BOMB! I couldn't think. I could only stare at the little box in her hand.

'Please,' I said. 'Don't press that button. Don't do it!'

'I don't even have to.' She laughed. 'You'd think it would be difficult, wiring an explosive. You'd think only a nutter could do something like that?'

She touched the edge of the box with the knife's blade.

'It's incredible what you find on the internet now. Blogs about bridges, and blogs about fighting back. About taking control of what's yours.'

The people. All around us. All the people.

'No one needs to get hurt, Karen,' I said.

'Oh, you have no idea.'

'But your mum . . . think what it would do to your mum. And to Grandpa Joe, and—'

'YOU HAVE NO IDEA!'

She stepped into my face. The knife touched my throat. I lifted my chin, but she moved with me. Her eyes were too manic, too weird. Her breath came too fast.

'It could have been so easy if you hadn't interfered.' she said. 'Robbie's little Hagatha Christie.'

I looked away.

'Don't you like his pet name for you?'

Karen's eyes burned into mine, madness no longer kept in check. She was still there. I could still see the woman I knew, but it was like she'd taken off a mask and removed the make-up she never wore, the disguise I never knew was there.

The bus was moving, inching forward. They were all on it; everyone I loved . . .

'*Who would kill a drag queen?* Isn't that what you wrote?' She nodded. 'I'll give you points for that, at least,' she said. 'Who is strong enough? Who deserves better? Who? WHO?'

'But why?' I said. 'Why kill Eve?'

'Who's Eve? Oh.' She frowned. 'The accident.' She brushed it away with a quick shake of her head. 'That wasn't my fault! No one told me Rob would give his costume to someone else. How was I to know that was going to happen?'

'You killed her?'

Karen stared, her eyes still wild, but she bit on her lip. 'He fell too quickly,' she said. 'I couldn't even look. I held his face into the water. It only took a minute. I thought . . .'

The knife shook in her hand.

'It wasn't meant to be him though,' she said. 'That was Rob's outfit – you sent us the photo – you told us he was wearing that . . . that . . . It was your fault, see? Everything I tried to do, you were right there . . .'

She blinked, her mouth open as she fought for the words.

'You drove that car at Gavin?' I said.

'Of course not, but he pushed Robbie out of the way, didn't he? And I drove Tom's car all the way into town, just for that. I didn't even hide it. No one sees me, do they? No one cares if I'm there or not. Who else could walk through the dark, could melt into a crowd?'

I looked down, craning my head. She wore big black boots. Men's boots.

'Please,' I said. 'Spare them. All of them. They don't deserve this. Whatever you think of me . . .'

Karen grinned. Her teeth, unlike Robyn's, were crooked at the front, the left slightly tucked in behind the right.

'Ah, you always could talk, Fi, but it doesn't matter now,' she said. 'Isn't that so beautiful? Unlike you, I'm always on time. If you sow the seed correctly, if you plan accurately, you don't even have to watch to know it'll be done.'

'I don't understand.'

Donna Summer went to Little Mix. I could see them in my mind, dancing, waving, still watching, no idea that the enemy was already with them.

'You've never understood.' Stamping her foot, Karen hissed into my face. 'It's always been so easy for you, hasn't it? Just you and your dad – no stupid brother, preening around the place, getting all the attention – no one to compare you to, every single day – even at the end of school dance, it was just you, wasn't it? I bet you didn't have to stay home to help with a difficult lambing while your brother – your own brother – wore your dress to the debs?'

A single, bitter tear fell from her eyes. Her body shook.

'All our lives,' she said. 'And he couldn't even let me have this. As a boy, he had everything. But that was never enough. He had to be a girl now too.'

'But he's not,' I said. The knife pricked my skin. 'No, please,' I said. 'You have to listen to me. He's not a girl. He doesn't want to be a girl at all. It's drag. It's dressing up, that's all. They lip sync. It's a show. It's like theatre, or like ballet, or like—'

'It's wrong,' she said. 'It's all wrong. None of them there – the others – they're no better. And Rob never cared. He never asked me how I felt about any of it. Never thought how it was for me to have a . . . a . . . a man like him as a brother, doing . . . THAT!'

She shook her head, each jolt of her chin more and more exaggerated. 'It should be me in a beautiful dress. It should be me with men looking up at me, with—'

'But they're gay men,' I said. 'It's just drag! It doesn't hurt anyone. Please, you can stop this. No one else has to be hurt, please, Karen. You can wear a dress. I'll buy you a dress. We can go out – we can go dancing . . .'

As quick as the anger had filled her, it stopped. Karen stepped back, keeping the knife on my neck.

'Yet again, you don't understand,' she said. She lifted the little black box. 'See? It's like farming. The hard work is already done. Either I press this now, or we wait together, and we listen, without having to lift a finger.' She giggled. 'Boom!'

It was like turning a light on and off, on and off.

'But you can still stop it?' I said. 'Please. I'll do anything.'

Behind her, I saw a movement. The gate creaked, a shadow passing behind the bushes.

'Stop? Why would I want to stop?' she said.

I saw a hand, gesturing me on. I had to keep talking.

'All those people,' I said quickly. 'Not just your ma and your grandpa, but so many other people there. Children . . . There are dogs—'

'It wasn't what I wanted,' she said. The manic strength slipped from her completely, and I saw the Karen I knew. Tears welled in her eyes. 'I never wanted to hurt anyone else,' she said. 'But that wasn't my fault! I never tried to hurt them. Only him. And I tried again and again, and you don't know what that's like . . . Every time, he's laughing at me. He's always there in everything I do but he's doing it better, being it better.'

'But Robyn never meant to hurt you,' I said. 'That was just banter, wasn't it? Just sibling stuff. Really. I'm sure if you just talk to him . . .'

She laughed, her eyes wide. I pressed my back against the pole, tugging on the binds. She pushed herself into my face.

'Talk?' She shook the black box in her hand.

I had to keep her from pressing the button.

'B-b-but no one else needs to get hurt,' I said, yet again. 'Really, Karen – we can go out, you and me. We can get the dresses and the make-up and—'

Her thumb moved to the button.

'There's no telling them. No telling any of them, with their fancy costumes and their ribbons and balloons. They're all the same,' she said. 'It's like pulling weeds so the crops can grow. Robyn's sly – he's tricky. He'll slither away. He knows I'm coming for him, but this way' – she grinned – 'I don't even need to try, see. He's such a hero, even if he finds my little gift there, he'll run straight for it, won't he? I bet you right now, he'll be standing on the bus with his arms in the air, waving to all the idiots who think he's something just because he's wearing that stupid dress – he'll be in the centre of the stage, just like he's always wanted.'

She was crazy. Stark, raving crazy.

The bushes behind her moved.

'But Ben?' I had to keep her looking at me. 'You killed Ben?' I said.

Karen's face hardened.

'I told you I wasn't aiming for him,' she said. 'Stop saying like I was aiming for him! I was never aiming for the others. They're nothing to do with me – they're someone else's problem. I was only ever aiming for Rob. And still – STILL – you got in my way!'

Something moved again in the hedge, closer. Slowly, so slowly . . .

Again, her thumb twitched.

'You had a gun?' I said. 'H-how . . . ?'

'Lots of farmers have guns,' she said, dismissing me. 'It's not exactly a big thing, Fi. Any idiot can point and shoot. Anyone who has to deal with foxes.'

'Or with murder,' I said.

'No!' Karen shouted. Spittle frothed on her lip.

Come on, I thought, glancing at the movement in the bushes. *Come on!*

'It's not murder if it's an accident,' she said. 'And, anyway, I—'

The fist came from nowhere. Mark burst through from behind a rhododendron plant, knocking straight into Karen. The knife fell. She stumbled back, started to lift her hand.

The second punch knocked her out cold.

'And that,' said Mark, 'was for taking Thora's wig.'

He took the knife, cut the cords, kicked the grey wig away from her reach.

'She says there's a bomb on the bus!' I said.

'Quick.' He started toward the gate. 'Hey!' He shouted at the nearest guard. 'Hey you!'

The TRASH bus had gone on ahead – it was too far away, I couldn't see it. I looked back at Karen, then to Mark.

'Go, Fi!' he said. 'Quick, get them off there!'

The guard was coming forward. Behind her, another. Karen stirred. There, on the ground, the little black box had fallen, the button up to the sky.

Mark stood square over Karen. His hand was swollen but his eyes blazed with rage. He pulled out his phone, started to tap.

He looked down to me.

'I thought it was you,' I said.

'And I thought it was you,' he told me. 'Otherwise, I would never have followed you. Now go!'

◆ ◆ ◆

How could I not find them? I tore through the crowd. By the second corner, I saw the first stages of panic. The guards on duty were no longer smiling and chatting but were starting to peel people away – someone was trying to stop the march but there were too many people already moving forward; it was too big a beast to disperse.

I pulled up at the corner. Why couldn't I see them?

Suddenly I heard it.

Robyn's high-pitched, terrified scream from the top of the bus. 'Fi!'

I started running. There, just before the big office blocks. They were there!

My heart was beating too fast. I hurtled down the hill. Someone shouted.

There were so many people. People at the windows, people in the streets. The shops spilled with families, with couples, with happy faces – so many happy faces.

A guard stepped out in front of me. I dodged, tearing around him. I could see them. The music was quiet, the crowd watching, looking at one another, questioning. There was Thora, on the top, ripping back a boa, ripping away the fabric; Merkin, running for the stairs.

I grabbed for the pole and pushed past them.

'Where's—'

Del came running down the stairs.

'Mark called,' he said. 'He said there's a bomb on the bus.'

Patrick turned back from the driver's seat. His face paled, his eyes filled with horror.

I nodded. 'I'll drive,' I told him. 'Go on! Go!'

He shook his head. 'You're sure it's a bomb?' he said.

Del nodded. 'The experts are on their way.' He stood frozen to the stairs, his phone in his hand, his mouth working.

Patrick looked past me, out of the window. Then he gripped the steering wheel with both hands and turned forward.

'Go on. This isn't your fight,' I told him.

He sucked in a breath. 'There are too many people around us,' he said quietly, his hands on the wheel. 'The streets are packed. They'll take too long to get here. I have to get this bus away from town. There's no room. In every direction, there's no room!'

I stared ahead at the road filled with people. But there, to the side, was a way out: a thin lane was free, a street that led not to the middle, but to the river.

'Take that street,' I said. 'Then at the end, turn left. Stick your hand on the horn and just go! Drive! Go through the barrier – if you can get us on the bridge, the road's clear.'

'How long?' I asked Del.

'I don't know. We can't find it,' he said. 'I don't . . .'

Crashing from seat to seat, I checked the lower level. Upstairs, I could hear Mae B moving, Thora crying.

'Go,' I said to Del. 'Get off the bus, and get everyone out of the way. Get out of here. Get the people out of the way!'

I pushed him and he staggered off the bus, Thora and Merkin thundering down the stairs behind him. The bus jerked ahead. Someone shouted – Del was gesturing wildly – Patrick put his foot to the floor and the bus shot forward, crashing through the metal barriers, racing down the thin street.

I held on and climbed up the steep stairs. Mae B stood, gripping the back of one of the seats. She pointed. There, on the side of the bus, screwed into the wooden panel, was a metal biscuit tin.

'Is that it?' she said.

'I don't know. I've never seen a bomb before.'

'Well neither have I!'

We turned again, the bus picking up speed. I fell sideways. I grabbed the handrail.

'Is the tin . . . ?' I fought to make sense of the inside of my head. 'Could it be something to do with the queens? Some make-up, or . . .'

'I'm fairly new at this,' she yelled, 'but as far as I'm aware, most drag queens don't screw their make-up tins to the side of a vehicle. And lipsticks don't bloody tick!'

I edged closer.

She was right. The further away from the music we were, the more clearly I could hear it.

'How long have we got?' I said.

'The tin doesn't have a number on it, Fi – ask the custard cream?'

I swore under my breath. The bus lurched again. We were still too close to the buildings. Patrick yelled at a man in the way, but the man wouldn't move. Ahead of us there was someone else, and a van was just reversing . . .

Suddenly, I heard them, yelling their war cries, the sound rising up over even the parade. I looked back – three bright coloured mopeds came haring down the thin street toward us, the women riders giving it everything they had, and on the back of each one, riding pillion, Thora Point, Miss Merkin and Del – their wigs streaming in the wind, their gowns bunched up around their middles. Like a valkyrie on a unicorn, Thora stood up, one hand on the shoulder of the woman driving, one stretched up into the air.

'Go!' she cried to the man in the road. 'Get out of the way! Get out of the way!'

The engines screeched, full throttle, as they veered around the bus. The man jumped clear from the road. Thora's ride wobbled, the woman struggling to keep on course, but Thora leaned forward again, lifting her sparkling train, shedding sequins in the air like a cloud of magic.

'Get out of the way!' Merkin screamed at the next pedestrian.

Del came up behind, raging forward, the woman driver leaning right over the handlebars, Del gripping her with both arms.

'Get out of the way!' Thora screamed at the next driver. 'Get your arse out of the road, you f—'

Patrick put his foot flat to the floor.

'Fi?' said Mae B. 'The bomb? A little help here?'

'What can we do?' I said. 'It's going to blow. It's going to kill us!'

'Help me.' Ripping off her wig, Mae B bent to the tin. She started to pull it, to wrench it from the wood.

'But what if—'

'Just help me!'

I grabbed the back corner and yanked. With each jolt, I was waiting to die, I was waiting for it to happen, but as we pulled together, the metal was moving, the screw was loosening.

'You're dressed like a mechanic, Fi,' Mae B hissed. 'Why couldn't you have packed a screwdriver?'

'Why couldn't you have a normal sister and not a homicidal maniac?'

'Pull!'

As Thora led the way up and over the bridge, the last screw gave way. We fell back. The tin opened in my hands.

Wires. Nails spilled over my lap. A black box. A light, flashing.

Mae B wrenched the bomb from my hold and threw it. It flew, high over the side of the bridge.

Thora shouted.

Merkin screamed.

The bomb fell into the Liffey with a splash. I scrambled up to the side of the bus.

We stood together as the explosion broke from the water like a wet fart.

Chapter Twenty-Nine

I don't remember how long we watched the ripples in the muddy river water, the waves spilling up on to the murky walls.

'Do you think I killed any fish?' said Mae B.

'If you were a fish, would you live in the Liffey?' I said.

Del staggered up the stairs.

It was over. My legs suddenly stopped working. Lurching away from the edge of the bus, I lowered myself into one of the seats. I could hear Thora directing the guards and Merkin thanking the moped drivers over and over again. Thanking them with kisses and hugs.

And Patrick was there somewhere – this kind, clever man I hadn't seen for years, who hadn't run away when he met my friends, and who hadn't run away from the bus.

Down in the road, someone shouted.

'Tommy? Tommy? You tell that Robyn—'

'Madam, if you'd just come this way?'

'Don't you tell me to move, Sonny Jim, that's my boy up there in the red dress, and—'

'Robyn?' Edna's voice was cored with sorrow.

I followed the others down the stairs. Edna was there with Marianne, Del's mother, and another older lady – a small, fragile woman with white hair and a delicate pixie face.

'Robbie!' Pushing the guard away, Edna came rushing forward. 'Mae B,' she corrected herself. Tears fell from her face. She pulled Mae into a fierce hold. 'Your friend found me. I can't . . .'

Next to the guards, Mark stood back, behind Grandpa Joe's wheelchair.

'It's OK, Mum.' Mae B smiled and straightened her wig and ran her thumb over her mother's cheek. 'We're all OK.'

'But Karen—'

'I know.'

'I should have seen. I should have noticed,' Edna cried. 'Your Ben,' she said, looking at Del. 'Your Eve,' she said to the other lady who could only have been Eve's mother.

'It's not your fault,' Marianne said to Edna. 'You do your best and, if you're lucky' – she touched Del's cheek – 'they do you proud.'

'You don't get to pick your family,' said Eve's mother.

'Yes, you do,' said Mae B. 'And I pick all of you.'

The flat was strangely quiet after the madness of the streets and then the intense hour with the guards. I moved around slowly, picking up Robyn's dresses, hanging them on the rail in his room. I should have been hungry. It seemed like a million years since I'd eaten breakfast but even the thought of cooking was beyond me. Frankly, the thought of anything much was beyond me.

I wondered where they'd taken Karen. She'd admitted to everything, to O'Hara's dismay. The last remnants of the old Karen slipped away as she described pushing Eve over in the rain and holding her face into the water until she stopped moving. Karen told them how she used her neighbour's car, driving at her brother faster and faster, until Gavin pushed him out of the way.

She told them how she took the neighbour's shotgun too. How she missed Robyn and killed Ben, then her face warmed with a rush of pride as she explained how she'd seen the homeless man sleeping and she'd tucked the gun in with his things, because sure, didn't he have nowhere to sleep anyway and couldn't he use a few nights in a cell. She told them that she'd been online for how to build a bomb, after she'd failed all her science at school, and then she'd broken into the bus and set the explosive in a tin, and how no one knew a thing until I ruined it all.

As Thora said, in the end, it's never those who shout the loudest who need to be heard the most. Or, as Merkin helpfully added, you can't help it if you're related to a bit of a nutter.

I brushed sequins from the top of the couch but I was fighting a losing battle. I opened the windows wide, letting the city air wash through the apartment. I wondered who would run Edna's farm now, and the land next door. Who would be there for the lambing and the cows? I scrunched up my eyes.

The doorbell rang. Before I could look out of the window, I heard footsteps on the stairs. Del came first, dressed in boy clothes, his face clean, his smile tired.

'Hey,' he said.

Also out of drag, Robyn held the arm of a young man on crutches. 'Fi, this is Gavin,' he said.

'Hi! You're very welcome,' I told him.

Mark was next and I reached up to hug him as Thora and Merkin trudged up the last steps.

'Why the hell would you live in here?' said Merkin.

'Because it's cheap and nasty,' said Robyn. 'Like us.'

I found myself pushed back against the wall. Following Merkin came Patrick, with Martha straining on the leash, delighted to see so many people in such a small space. Patrick smiled and I started toward him, but Thora caught the hem of my shirt and pulled me to the couch.

'Sit with me, our little Hagatha Christie,' she said.

'Oh, don't call me that,' I grumbled. 'Please, I know it's meant to be funny and all, but—'

'Never be afraid of who you are, darling girl,' said Thora. 'If you are yourself, then who can knock you down?'

'But I'm not,' I said. 'I'm not that person. I didn't do anything.'

'Pet,' said Thora, 'you're a smart young woman and you figured out what was happening – and when no others would listen, when we were too stubborn to hear you, you simply shouted louder. I can't think of a better name for my little straight girl—'

'Tea or coffee?' said Robyn, cutting in.

He met Thora's eyes with a hard glare.

'What?' she said.

'I hate that,' I told her. 'I've always hated the way you call me that. How about "Fi"? You could just call me my name?'

Thora shrugged. 'Fi will do, so,' she said. 'As will a shot of gin, while you're at it. Not too much tonic.'

'Oh,' said Robyn. 'Sorry. I don't think we have any gin. We have lemonade?'

'Are you trying to kill me?' said Thora.

On the other side of the room, Patrick had settled Martha on the rug, and Merkin was on her knees, cuddling the huge dog, kissing the top of her head. In the kitchen, Gavin and Robyn made the drinks, and as the sun dipped down toward the river, Mark went out for Mongolian takeaway, returning with more noodles than we'd ever seen in one place and Mrs Harper from downstairs. The others set on the food boxes like gannets, but even as Mrs Harper recognised Merkin and started telling her with delight how she'd known her mother, I still couldn't relax.

I sat on the floor at the back and pulled my knees to my chest. After a minute, Robyn sat beside me. I leaned against him with my head on his chest. Music drifted up from Temple Bar and the dust flickered and shone in the shafts of light that played through the window. Down in the road below, the little cobbled street was already filled with Dublin's weekend party people. I closed my eyes as I listened to Mrs Harper telling Merkin how much she looked like her mother.

'Was there really a bomb on the bus?' said Mrs Harper.

'Only a small one,' Robyn said.

'I nearly died!' said Merkin.

'Fi caught the one who set it.'

'Mark saved me,' I said. 'Then Robyn threw the bomb in the river—'

'And Patrick, here, saved half of Dublin,' said Thora. 'The amount of manmade fabric on that bus, we'd have shot into space like a screaming Catherine wheel!'

'Our Hagatha figured it out though,' said Del. 'Little Haggie, here.'

I started to protest again, but somehow the nickname didn't hurt so much as it had before. It didn't hurt at all. I grinned, and stuffed a small piece of mushroom into Del's open mouth.

Robyn reached up to the stereo, and soft Parisian jazz soothed my mind, slowing the edges. I closed my eyes and listened to Mark and Gavin talking about the singer, and to Merkin humming along to the song. In the background, I heard Patrick laugh and Thora tease him.

The thick band of anxiety that had gripped my chest for so long slowly began to ease.

We were safe. Karen was locked away, and no one was trying to kill us. But everything had changed. Our lives would never be the same. Del had lost his husband. Mark had lost his lover. The club had been battered and bruised, from Eve's murder to Karen's drive-by, to her horrific attempt on the TRASH bus at Pride.

TRASH was ruined. The money was gone. It would take weeks to recover the losses – months, even – if they ever could. Plenty of clubs had closed in Dublin for less.

Gavin winced; Robyn leaned to him and placed his hand gently over the cast on his leg. Gavin laced his fingers through Robyn's. A look ran between them, a question and an answer.

Thora talked with Merkin about TRASH, their words in harmony with the smooth jazz. Finding new acts and coming up with new club nights. Get people through the door again, they said – they had to keep going, to fight back. Thora's speech was determined but worry darkened her eyes under the thick lashes. She looked uncomfortable stuffed into our small couch. I wondered how bad the financial situation really was behind the bravado, and what would happen to the TRASH drag family if their home disappeared.

Still, there was no other way than to go on.

Soon enough, they'd all be heading off, Robyn back to Gavin's place, Thora to her elegant town house, Merkin to her costumes and fabric. Del would make some funny comment to everyone in the room and he'd keep smiling until the door was closed, and then he'd be home alone with the ghosts on the square.

And then there was me.

I looked up at Patrick.

Well, I thought. There was a fine thing for another day.

They were good people, my dad would have said. And they were my people.

Thora leaned forward. She squeezed my toes.

'Are you OK, pet?' she said.

I smiled. I wasn't OK, but then none of us were.

'Our Hagatha got the bitch in the end,' said Del proudly to someone. 'The guards came too, but Fi was there first.'

A thousand emotions filled my heart. I waited until the others were distracted and then I slipped away to my room. Pride was still going strong over the river. I settled into my chair, picked up my camera and opened the window. A man walked over the bridge. He turned his head to look at the water. His face was still and sad. I waited until he'd twisted just enough, and I took the picture.

Tears filled my eyes.

The TRASH family were arguing about the music, then suddenly Robyn's jazz was gone, and Kylie sang out through the building, the beat pounding through the walls.

I pulled my cardigan around my shoulders. Robyn made some kind of joke I couldn't hear and Del laughed. Thora called out, then Merkin cheered—

The door opened, just a crack. Robyn came over to the window. He touched his fingers to my face, wiping away my tears, and then bound his arms around me and I clung on, burying my face into his hair.

'We have a problem,' he said.

'Who's dead?'

'Del found your fleece kitten nightshirt and he threw it out of the kitchen window.'

I giggled.

'He owes me another,' I said.

'Make him buy it.'

'I will, so.'

We sat together, watching the Liffey.

'You want a coffee?' said Robyn.

'Always,' I told him.

ACKNOWLEDGEMENTS

My heartfelt thanks and admiration to all the drag artists who bring life and sparkle to Dublin's bars and clubs, especially the gorgeous, fabulous and extremely tall Victoria Secret who has been there for Fi and her friends from the beginning, answering my questions and kindly allowing me glimpses into her world. From live shows to podcasts to bingo to Pride, Dublin's drag queens and kings are the very best and they're in no way represented by my messy little troupe at TRASH.

Huge thanks to Ed Wilson at Johnson and Alcock, to Russel McClean, and to Hannah Bond, Leodora Darlington and everyone at Thomas & Mercer.

I'm extremely grateful to Jim Ryan, who let me shoot guns and play with knives; to my parents, who taught me to love books and to never give up on a dream; to Jane Flynn, Jane Warden, Anne Jewell, Susan Gerritsen, Jacqui Grima, Holly Murphy and Alice Summers for beta-reading; to everyone at The Rock Shop here in County Clare, Ireland, who never complained while I sat at my favourite table for hours, drinking coffee and hammering at my laptop. Thank you seems too small a word for Amanda Singh who has read everything, over and over again.

Lastly and always, my thanks and love go to my husband Roger Gale and to our dog, Rupert, who likes to have the last word.

ABOUT THE AUTHOR

Kitty lives with her husband, Roger, on the very westerly edge of Co. Clare, Ireland. She adores drag in all its forms and crime fiction in all its chilling splendour. Kitty is bi/queer. From a well-spent youth divided equally between the library and the LGBTQ+ scene, it was only a matter of time until both worlds collided in a flurry of fictional sequins.

Follow Kitty on Instagram @kitty_murphy_writes

Made in the USA
Monee, IL
19 July 2023

39322443R00173